LUX

Lakehouse Press, Inc.

This book is an original publication of Lakehouse Press, Inc.
All rights reserved.

Copyright © 2015, Courtney Cole
Cover Design by The Cover Lure (Matthew Phillips)

Library of Congress Cataloging-in-publication data

Cole, Courtney
LUX/Courtney Cole/Lakehouse Press Inc/Trade pbk ed

ISBN 13: 978-0692567906
ISNB 10: 0692567909

"But for Adam there was not found a helper fit for him. So the Lord God caused a deep sleep to fall upon the man, and while he slept took one of his ribs and closed up its place with flesh. And the rib that the Lord God had taken from the man he made into a woman and brought her to the man. Then the man said, 'This at last is bone of my bones and flesh of my flesh; she shall be called Woman, because she was taken out of Man.' Therefore a man shall leave his father and his mother and hold fast to his wife, and they shall become one flesh. And the man and his wife were both naked and were not ashamed."

Genesis 2:20-25

*THE END IS COMING IT'S COMING IT'S COMING IT'S
COMING. THE END IS COMING. THE END IS COMING
IT'S COMING IT'S COMING IT'S COMING IT'S COMING
THE END IS COMING IT'S COMING IT'S COMING IT'S
COMING THE END IS COMING*

*THE END IS COMING IT'S COMING IT'S COMING IT'S
COMING. THE END IS COMING. THE END IS COMING
IT'S COMING IT'S COMING IT'S COMING IT'S COMING
THE END IS COMING IT'S COMING IT'S COMING IT'S
COMING. THE END IS COMING. THE END IS COMING
IT'S COMING IT'S COMING IT'S COMING IT'S COMING
THE END IS COMING IT'S COMING IT'S COMING IT'S
COMING THE END IS COMING*

*THE END IS COMING IT'S COMING IT'S COMING IT'S
COMING. THE END IS COMING. THE END IS COMING
IT'S COMING IT'S COMING IT'S COMING IT'S COMING
THE END IS COMING IT'S COMING IT'S COMING IT'S
COMING. THE END IS COMING. THE END IS COMING
IT'S COMING IT'S COMING IT'S COMING IT'S COMING
THE END IS COMING IT'S COMING IT'S COMING IT'S
COMING THE END IS COMING*

*THE END IS COMING IT'S COMING IT'S COMING IT'S
COMING. THE END IS COMING. THE END IS COMING
IT'S COMING IT'S COMING IT'S COMING IT'S COMING
THE END IS COMING IT'S COMING IT'S COMING IT'S
COMING. THE END IS COMING. THE END IS COMING
IT'S COMING IT'S COMING IT'S COMING IT'S COMING
THE END IS COMING IT'S COMING IT'S COMING IT'S
COMING THE END IS COMING*

*THE END IS COMING IT'S COMING IT'S COMING IT'S
COMING. THE END IS COMING. THE END IS COMING
IT'S COMING IT'S COMING IT'S COMING IT'S COMING
THE END IS COMING IT'S COMING IT'S COMING IT'S
COMING. THE END IS COMING. THE END IS COMING
IT'S COMING IT'S COMING IT'S COMING IT'S COMING
THE END IS COMING IT'S COMING IT'S COMING IT'S
COMING THE END IS COMING*

*THE END IS COMING IT'S COMING IT'S COMING IT'S
COMING. THE END IS COMING. THE END IS COMING
IT'S COMING IT'S COMING IT'S COMING IT'S COMING
THE END IS COMING IT'S COMING IT'S COMING IT'S
COMING. THE END IS COMING. THE END IS COMING
IT'S COMING IT'S COMING IT'S COMING IT'S COMING
THE END IS COMING IT'S COMING IT'S COMING*

LUX

By Courtney Cole

Book three of the NOCTE Trilogy

LET THERE BE LIGHT.

Dedication

Resurgmus a cinis.

"We will rise from the ashes."

Because we always do, don't we?

This is for anyone who ever has,
And for everyone who ever will.

Foreword

My dearest readers,

The poet Dylan Thomas said,

"Do not go gentle into that good night...
Rage, rage against the dying of the light."

My characters are not gentle.
They raged,
And raged.

I haven't been gentle either,
Not with them,
And not with you.
My words have spun you around,
Tilted you until you didn't know which way was up.
Because we're all a little mad, aren't we?

You had to know Calla's head.
You had to be in her shoes.
You had to feel what she felt.
Because it all had to happen in order.

Now you're at the end.
You're faced with the darkness,
With the truth.
It looms ahead of you,
So close you can touch it.

Go ahead.
Reach out your finger.
Touch it.
Do it.
DoItDoItDoIt.

I dare you.

Prologue

There's a fork in the road and even though I see it, I can't avoid it.

One road goes left, one goes right, and neither of them ends well.

I feel it in my bones,

In my bones,

In my hollow reed bones.

He grabs my hand and we walk...through a tunnel...through a hall... through the dark.

"It'll be ok," he whispers.

Will it?

"We have to do this," he says. "But I'm with you. I won't leave you."

I nod because I believe him, because no matter what else, I know that much is true. He won't leave me.

The room is shrouded in shadows, in flame, in secrets. I step inside, and peer around, and the heat from the fire warms me, warms my blood, and the blood pumps through my heart.

I sing a song of nonsense, and it sings back. The notes echo and twist in the air, and I swallow them whole.

"Come out," I call behind me, because I know they're there.

I can't see them, but they're always watching.

The eyes appear, inky black, and glistening, and they blink once, twice, three times.

"I can see you," I announce and it growls and then I'm crushed beneath the dark, beneath the weight, beneath the oppression.

"You don't scare me," I lie.

Because it does scare me. It's followed me my whole life, and finally, finally, I'll find out what it is.

Why it's here.

Why it wants me.

Because above all, I know it's here for me.

I know it

I know it.

The walls around me pulse and hum and growl,

There's savagery here, there's grace.

But above all, there's oblivion and no matter what I do, I will be sucked into it.

I know it.

I feel it.

I'm crazy.

"Are you ready? she asks and we nod, because we aren't but it doesn't matter.

She nods and the flames lap, and the words start,

One for one for one.

I fall backwards from the precipice

into oblivion.

The endless

Endless oblivion.

Chapter One

The room swirls white and medicinal, filled with beeps and blank walls and cold skin. Goosebumps chase each other in confusion up my arm, and I gulp hard.

I'm in a hospital.

I'm cold.

I'm afraid.

My dead brother stares at me, his pale blue eyes evasive as he skirts my question. I ask it again.

"Finn, where's Dare?"

I ask him stiltedly, each word a sword that stabs my heart, because doom invades this room, in every inch, every breath, every moment.

Finn looks away, at the wall, at the floor, at anything but me.

"Dare is….you know where he is, Calla."

I don't, though, and that's the unbearable thing.

My eyes flutter closed and the last thing I see is the white hospital blanket that covers me. I close my eyes against reality, and Finn picks up my hand.

"Cal, you've twisted everything around in your head until you don't know what is real, and what is not. You know where Dare is. You know what is real. You've just got to *think*. You've got to face it."

This hurts, and I hate it.

15

"I…can't." My words are limp, falling onto the bed, tumbling to the floor.

Finn stares at me, into my eyes, into my heart. It pierces me, it grabs me with both hands and doesn't let go.

"Calla, you can. You're not me, you're you. And that's ok. That's who you need to be. Please, for the love of God, come back. Just come back."

My eyes open because his words are confusing.

"Come back from where?"

I'm clearly here in the hospital with him, with my dead brother. I'm already here. He's the one who's not, because he's dead. He's not making any sense.

He sighs, a soft sound in a silent room.

"Come back from where you are. You're needed here, Calla."

"But I *am* here," I say hesitantly, because Finn is already shaking his head.

"No," he says. "You're not, Calla."

Clouds surround me and lift me up and carry me away from logic, from reason, from reality. I fight to keep my feet down, to keep from being lifted away, into the sky, across the ocean.

"How do I come back?" I ask, and my voice is like a child's.

Finn stares at me, and his eyes are blue rocks, blank and shiny and bright.

"You *focus.* You do what you have to do. You think you have to be me, but you don't. I'm fine where I am, Calla."

"But you're dead," I almost whimper.

He grins, the crooked one that I love, the one I know like the back of my hand.

"Is that what I am? And if so, is that a bad thing? When you're dead, there's nothing to worry about. I'm ok, Cal. Come back. Just come back."

"I can't do it without you," I say firmly, because that's what I know in my heart.

Finn rolls his eyes. "Of course you can. You were always the strong one, Calla. You always were."

"But I don't know how to come back," I tell him. "Even if I wanted to, I don't know how. I'm too lost, Finn. I'm lost."

Finn is unsympathetic though, and his voice is firm.

"Do you know what I always did when I was lost?" Finn asks, and he's holding my hand again. I shake my head because I don't, and so he tells me. "I re-trace my steps."

"But…" my whisper trails off, and so I bolster myself. "But where do I start?"

Without Finn, I don't know if I want to start at all.

He stares at me because he knows me, because he knows what I'm thinking better than anyone else.

"You start at the beginning, Calla. Choose a point of reference that you know is true, and start there.

Don't let anything get in your way, and don't try to fool yourself, no matter how much pain you think the truth will cause. Do you understand?"

I do.

But I don't want to.

"Reality is real," he tells me sternly. "*I'm* not. You've been given a gift, Calla. Don't waste it. You have to find your new reality without me."

"But how can I do that when *you're* my point of reference, Finn?" my voice fractures. "How can I decide what is real when *you aren't*?"

My chest hurts and I can't breathe, because every breath I take is one more step that I take further away from my brother.

"You just have to find a way," he answers, and his words are cool and unflinching.

My tears are hot and I squeeze his hand because no matter what he says, I'm not letting go.

"I'm sorry, Calla." Finn's voice is small. His slim shoulders are hunched now and he's angled away from me.

"Sorry for what?"

"I'm sorry for everything."

The clouds clear for a minute, then surround me again.

"But it wasn't your fault."

"It wasn't?" Finn sighs. "Honestly, it doesn't matter anymore. Fault, cause, roots. None of that matters. All that matters is *you*. You have to face what is real."

His hand starts to fade and he seems to slip into the air, away from me. I grab at him, but my fingers come up empty.

"Finn!" I call. "Come back! Don't leave me!"

But he's gone, and I'm alone, and all that is left is Finn's soft voice, and it seems to come from nowhere, yet everywhere.

"If you have to live for both us, then do it," he whispers. "But *live.*"

"Finn?" I ask hesitantly, but there is no answer.

He's truly gone.

The room is empty and cold and stark.

My entire life, my brother has been my other half. He's loved me unconditionally, completely, with everything he has.

And now he's dead, and he's asking me to do something.

Something hard.

To exist without him.

To figure out, once and for all, what is true,

What is real.

I have to do it.

And to do that, I have to re-trace my steps.

If Finn is gone,

There's only one thing in my life that is true.

One true point of reference.

One important thing.

Dare.

With shaking hands, I close my eyes,

and try to think about Dare.

Because it's always been about Dare.

I try to focus on his dark eyes, and his bright smile, and his swaying shoulders...but thoughts of him won't form. They're stubborn and elusive, and all I can think of is the beginning.

The beginning

The beginning.

With a start, I remember scratched words from Finn's journal.

Mars solum initium est. Death is the beginning.

The beginning, the beginning.

I NEED TO START.

My breathing catches then quickens, because maybe once again, like always, Finn is telling me where to go.

Maybe the beginning is exactly where I need to be.

Chapter Two

The smell of the school gym permeates my nose. The dust motes float in the air, the floor scuffed and hot. Around me, the other kindergartners screech and run because Capture the Flag is our favorite game. Our skin smells like sweat, our breath is heavy and hot in our chests, and the sense of competition is so thick I can taste it.

I look up to find my brother Finn grabbing the other team's flag. He's as surprised by this turn of events as I am because one thing about my brother... he's not athletic. It's not his thing. His smile is beatific as he sprints toward our side, because if he can just manage this, he'll be the hero of the day. We'll win, and it will be because of him.

I wave my arms and motion for him to run harder, as if he weren't already. His skinny arms are pumping, his legs scrambling. But he needs to run faster because I want everyone else to know how amazing he is.

"Calla!" Finn shrieks, and for a second, I think it's from the excitement. "Calla!"

The tone of his voice is anxious or desperate and his hair is plastered to his forehead, and he's not excited. He's terrified. His eyes are wide and focused on something behind me, on the wall, on nothing.

I'm confused, but panicked, because something in me is triggered. The age-old innate instinct to protect my twin. Fight or Flight. Protect him.

I sprint to catch him, to try and shield him from the kids trying to bombard him for the scrap of material in his hand. I'm not sure what is wrong with him, but he's no longer trying to play the game. He's trying to escape it.

When I reach him, his eyes are sightless and he's screaming in terror. Around me, I hear other kids snickering and see them staring and I want to punch them all, but I don't have the chance.

Finn drops the flag and it flutters to the ground like an orange ribbon.

Before I can stop him, he shimmies up the old creaking rope, the one that goes to the ceiling. He hovers by the stained ceiling tiles, looking down at me, but not really seeing me.

"It's here, Calla!" he screams. "It's here. The demon. The demon. Its eyes are black." His eyes widen, and he shrieks again, shirking away as if something unseen is chasing him. He tries to climb higher, but there's nowhere else to go. He's at the top, next to the ceiling and something imaginary is chasing him and I can't breathe.

What is happening?

My heart pounds and I grab the rope, climbing it as quickly as I can to get to my brother.

One hand after the other, I push with my feet. The thick twine cuts into my hands, burning and hot, but it doesn't matter.

Only Finn matters.

But Finn isn't seeing me. He looks through me, and shrieks and shrieks and shrieks.

He scrambles away, and I'm terrified.

"Finn, it's me," I tell him softly, my voice as steady as I can make it. "It's me."

I have to help. I have to. What's wrong with him?

I touch his shoe, lightly, so very lightly, so lightly that I think he won't feel it.

But he does. His face twists and he turns because he thinks I'm a demon, and as he moves, his hands slip away from the rope.

Life is slow motion.

He falls away from the rope and he screams. He flails as he falls and the sound he makes as he hits the gym floor is startlingly soft, like a pillow. How can that be?

I'm stunned and detached as I stare down at my brother, at the blood pooling on the gym floor, at the teacher ushering the kids away from his body, at my brother, at my brother.

Finn's light blue eyes are open and staring at me, but he's not seeing me.

Not anymore.

Because he's dead.

My father is an undertaker, so I know what death looks like.

I don't remember how I get down from the rope, because my hands are numb, my heart is numb, my head is numb. I don't remember who picks me up from school. All I remember is lying in bed and staring at the ceiling and feeling lifeless, like the whole world could fall into pieces and float away and I wouldn't care. Because if Finn is gone, I don't want to be here either.

The sadness presses on me like a heavy, heavy weight, and I know I can't withstand it. It will crush me.

I close my eyes,

And it's dark, and I dream.

I'm in a darker place, and my brother is there. His eyes are dark and murky, without whites, and I realize that he's an embryo, and I'm an embryo and we haven't been born yet. I reach out my webbed fingers and touch his face through the liquid, through the fluid, and he's my brother. Although he doesn't have hair yet, I know it. I feel him, I feel his heart.

He looks at me through the dark, and just as if he were speaking, I hear a voice. It's him, it's my brother, it's Finn.

Save me and I'll save you.

He is loud, and quiet, and everywhere, and nowhere.

Something is troubling him, and I feel it in my bones, so I nestle closer to take it, to absorb it, because I can't let anything happen to him, not ever. I failed him once, and I'll never fail him again.

He brings me comfort and I bring him comfort and that's the way we'll always be.

I feel his skin. I feel his heart beating against me.

I feel our cells splitting as we grow, as we develop, as we become beings.

Save me, and I'll save you.

Yes, I will.

I will.

I awaken with a start, and the light is pouring into my bedroom window.

The bedding is pulled up to my chin and I untangle one hand, staring at it. My fingers are no longer webbed. My fingers are separate and long. I wiggle them in the light.

It was a dream.

It was a dream.

My thoughts are muddled though. It's hard to focus and something moves in the corner. Something with dark eyes. It stares at me for a moment, then it's gone, and I remember Finn's scream.

"The demon is here, Calla!"

My heart is frozen as I sit straight up in bed and stare at the empty corner, where I could swear a black-eyed being was standing just a scant moment ago.

That's impossible.

Impossible.

I feel so tired, so weak, so confused.

I shake my head, trying to clear it, but it refuses. The fog remains, mucking up my thought processes, interrupting everything.

From outside the door, I hear voices.

"Will she be ok?" my mother's voice is anxious.

"Her hold on reality is tenuous."

It's a murmur that cuts through my panic.

I pause, halting all movement, not even breathing. The whisper comes from the other side of the door.

"No, I don't want to do that. Not yet." The voice is hissing and firm, and it can't be real. There's no way. I'm frozen as it envelopes me, as reality slithers further away.

"We have to. She wouldn't want this."

Confused, I stare at the wooden planes of the door, at the grain.

Is this really happening?

Or is my mind playing tricks on me?

I gulp and draw in a shaky breath.

"Anything could send her back over the edge," the familiar voice cautions.

"That's why we have to handle her carefully."

Handle me?

The door opens and I look up to find three shadows looming over me.

My father.

My mother.

And someone I can't see, a faceless, nameless figure lurking in the shadows. I peer closely, trying to see if it's him, even while knowing in my heart that it can't be Finn.

It's impossible.

I scoot backward until my spine is against my brother's bed. I'm a skittish fawn, and they're my hunters. I'm prey because I'm in danger, and I don't know why.

But they do.

"Calla," my dad says, kindly and soothingly. "You're ok. *You're ok.* But I need you to trust me right now."

His face is grave and pale. The air in this room is charged now, dangerous, and I find that I can scarcely breathe.

I brace myself.

Because deep in the pit of my stomach I feel like I can't trust anyone.

When I open my eyes, the room is empty.

They'd given up.

Whatever they wanted to tell me, I'm safe from it now.

Because I'm alone.

With shaky steps, I climb to my feet and walk to Finn's nightstand. I pick up his St. Michael's medallion and fasten it around my neck. If he'd been wearing it at school, he'd be here right now. He'd be fine, he'd be safe.

Holding it in my fingers, I whisper the prayer, each word quick and stiff on my lips.

St. Michael the Archangel, defend us in battle. Be our defense against the wickedness and snares of the Devil. May God rebuke him, we humbly pray and do thou O Prince of the heavenly hosts, by the power of God thrust into hell Satan, and all the evil spirits, who prowl about the world seeking the ruin of souls. Amen.

I say the prayer three times in a row, just to make sure.

I'm protected.

I'm protected.

I'm protected.

I'm safe now. I'm wearing Finn's medallion. I'm safe.

I'm just drawing a shaky breath of relief when the door creaks open again and I'm faced once again with my insanity.

My startled eyes flash upward, finding the impossible.

Finn.

My dead brother.

Standing in the doorway of the bedroom.

He walks in just like normal, and there is no blood, no fear, no crazy look in his eye. His hair is brown, his eyes are blue, like always.

He sits next to my bed, his face pale as he takes my hand and his hand is real, and he's alive, and he's here. He's breathing and he's warm and he's here.

I exhale.

"The doctor says you're crazy, Cal," he tells me seriously. "You have to take your medicine, and everything will be ok."

I'm crazy, and everything will be ok.

Will it?

But I nod because *Finn is here,* and I'll agree to anything because he's not dead.

He's here.

And I'm here.

And I don't care if I'm crazy.

Finn squeezes my hand, and I breathe and breathe and breathe.

"Our cousin is here," he tells me finally. "He's going to stay for a while. He's nice and you'll like him."

I nod but I don't really care. All I care about is that Finn is here and I had a nightmare and it wasn't real.

My mom comes in and flutters about, and my dad speaks in a quiet voice, and they make me stay in bed. Later, my step-cousin comes in.

His voice is low as he introduces himself. He's three years older and his name is Dare.

"It's nice to meet you," I say politely, and I'm still tired. I look up at his face and I suck in my breath.

His eyes are black.

Chapter Three

Black like the night, like the dark, like onyx. Black like obsidian, like ink. I can't help but stare at Dare's eyes as Finn and I walk with him along the trails a few days later.

"Why do you keep looking at me?" he asks with impatience. His hands are grubby because we've been outside, on the beach and on the trails.

"Because your eyes are black," I tell him stoutly. Because honesty is the best policy.

He snorts. "They are not. They're brown."

With a flicker of hope, I study him again, watching the way the sunlight hits his eyes. He might be right. His eyes are very, very dark brown, like dark chocolate or the darkest of tree bark. Almost black.

But not quite.

I exhale in relief.

Finn watches me. He watches my relief, the way I can breathe now, and he sighs.

"Cal, it wasn't real. You know it wasn't."

His voice is soft because I'd told him everything. They way he captured the flag, the way he'd seen demons, the way *he'd died.*

He'd laughed at first, until he realized I was serious. And then he made me promise not to tell the

31

doctor, because the doctor and my parents already think I'm crazy and everyone is watching my every move. I have to rest, I have to stay in bed, I have to take my medicine. It's been exhausting.

"There is no black-eyed demon," Finn assures me quietly, so quiet. I stare at Dare's eyes from across the trail as he searches for pebbles to skip on the water. I'm not sure though, and Finn knows it.

"Trust me," he instructs firmly. "You have to."

"It felt so real," I tell him finally, limply. "At first it was you. You were crazy, and then you died. You died, Finn. But when I woke up, you were alive and I was crazy. I *am* crazy. I'm so confused, Finn. What is happening to me?"

My brother looks at me, then away, and he grabs my hand.

"I don't know. But I'm not dead and I won't let you be crazy, Calla. Never tell mom and dad the things you see. Only tell me, ok?"

I nod, because I can see the wisdom in that. They can never, never know.

"It's you and me, Cal," he says solemnly. And he's my brother, and I know he's right.

"You and me," I whisper.

He smiles.

"Let's take Dare to the beach before mom figures out that you're gone."

"Why do I have to stay in bed so much?" I grumble as we wind our way down the rocky trail to the sand that lies below. Finn shrugs.

"I don't know. They want you to rest. It'll help you get better."

I want to get better. That is something I know for a fact.

So when my mom finds us a little while later, agitated that I'm not in my bedroom, I go with her meekly back to the house. I climb the stairs to my room, and I watch Dare and Finn from my window.

They're building a fort out of the brush-pile, and they're laughing and running together, already oblivious that I'm gone, their faces flushed with play-time and fresh air.

That should be me.

I can't help but feel the resentment swell in me, from my feet to my hands to my heart. I should be running and playing. Not confined here, not in this bed. My new step-cousin shouldn't be playing with Finn in my place.

That should be me.

"Calla, my love," my mother murmurs as she comes back into the room, a cup of apple juice and a handful of pills in her hand. They're colorful like jewels, but they taste like dirt. "You have to listen to me. You have to rest, you have to recover. Do you trust me?"

I nod, because she's my mother, and of course I trust her. What an odd question. I turn to her and obediently reach my hands out for the pills.

One by one, I swallow them and they stick in my throat so I gulp at the juice. My pretty mother watches me sympathetically, stroking my red hair away from my face.

"Everything will be worth it," she assures me. "I promise you, Calla."

But there's something in her voice, something something something. Like she's trying to convince herself, not me. It's a fragile tone, an uncertainty.

But then she turns away and leaves me alone.

I turn onto my side and pull the covers up to my chin, staring out the window. A heavy fog descends upon me because of the pills, pulling my head under a current, a murky dark current, and I can't fight the sleepiness. It's here, it's heavy, it blurs my vision.

But before I stop seeing and the darkness covers everything, I see Finn and Dare on the lawns. They're playing and laughing and abruptly, Dare stops and tilts his head up, his dark dark eyes connecting with mine.

He stares at me, into me, through me.

My breath catches, because something feels off here, something feels odd.

Dare raises his hand and waves, and he runs off with my brother into the trees.

My brother.

Mine.

Resentment fills me again, because I'm in this bed and he's outside with my brother, playing the games I should be playing, with my brother,

Mine

Mine

Mine.

I can't stop the darkness though, and it arrives, covering up my resentment and my desire to play. It covers up everything, dulling it, deadening it. Sleep comes and I'm lost...in dreams, in nightmares, in reality.

Who can tell the difference?

Finn is there, and Dare is there and my brother reaches out his hand. Because I belong with Finn, not Dare. I should be playing, shrieking, laughing.

We run away, away from Dare, toward the cliffs, toward the sea.

When I look over my shoulder, Dare is watching us go,

with the saddest look on his face that I've ever seen.

He doesn't move to chase us, and I know that he's resigned.

He knows what I know.

He doesn't belong with Finn, I do.

Finn is mine.

***

When I wake, I hear voices reverberating through the halls of our home. I smell the carnations and the stargazers, the flowers of funerals, of death.

I pad across my bedroom and down the stairs.

The smell of hotcakes surrounds me and I inhale the maple syrup.

"Why is today special?" I ask my mom, because we only get hotcakes on special days. She looks up at me as she bustles through to the kitchen.

"Your cousin has to go back home early. His Latin tutor arrived ahead of schedule."

"Latin?"

My mother nods. "Your grandmother wants all of you to learn Latin. You and Finn will learn it too, probably starting next year."

"You can start right now, if you want," Dare interjects from the sofa. He's reclined there, with a blanket covering his lap. He looks paler than I remember from yesterday. "Iniquum. It means unfair."

I form the strange sound on my tongue, twisting it into submission. "Iniquum."

My mother hands Dare a plate filled with steaming breakfast food. He starts to get up, but she motions him to stay down.

"It's fine, sweetheart. Stay there and rest."

Rest.

With a start, I realize that no one has chastised me for getting out of bed.

"Your father would kill me if I let you wear yourself out," my mother adds, as if she doesn't recall that merely yesterday Dare was chasing Finn around the lawns.

"Did you hurt yourself?" I ask him curiously. He looks at me and rolls his eyes.

"No."

I'm confused, so so confused and I look at my brother, but Finn acts like this is normal, as though Dare is supposed to be in bed. Not me.

Not me.

"What is happening?" I whisper, so utterly lost. The room swirls and everyone moves like they're in fast-forward and I'm the only one standing still.

My mother glances at me. "I told you, honey. Dare has to return to England. Don't worry. We'll be joining him shortly, like we do every summer."

We do?

I look at Finn, and he looks excited, as though he's looking forward to going to England, as though we've done it every summer for all of our lives. The problem is... I don't have any memories of this *at all.*

"I really am crazy," I tell myself softly. "I'm as crazy as they say. I'm crazy."

Finn grabs a plate and hands it to me, stacked with steaming maple pecan pancakes, drizzled in syrup.

It's heaven on porcelain.

I know that.

I take bite after bite, but by the third one, I can't move my tongue.

For a second, I think it's my mind playing tricks on me again, making me think that I'm paused while everyone else is fast-forwarding, but then I watch my hand fall limply to the table, and my mom lunges to grab me and I can't breathe I can't breathe I can't breathe.

"Calla!" she says sharply, and she bangs on my back with her hand because she thinks I'm choking. I'm not choking. I just can't breathe.

I claw at my throat, claw at my face, claw at my tongue.

The air

The air

It won't travel down into my lungs.

The light

The light.

It surrounds me and I think I'm dying.

This is what it feels like, I realize.

To die.

It's warm and soft and inviting.

It's comforting, like home.

It doesn't smell like embalming fluid and stargazers, the way it does in the funeral home. It smells like rain, like grass, like clouds.

The light surrounds me, and my throat doesn't hurt anymore.

Nothing hurts.

I'm light as a feather.

I'm light as a cloud,

The light fills me up and makes me float.

I drift toward the ceiling, and I look down at myself, at my small body crumpled on the floor. My red hair spreads in a fan around me, like a pool of crimson blood and it fascinates me, the color. The endless color. The light distracts me though, shining as brightly as the sun from outside the house, glinting into my eyes. I suddenly realize that I'm ready to leave, I'm ready to let go, to drift away. I'm getting ready to glide through the window to touch it, when I see my brother's face.

He's as white as death,

He's terrified, and he's screaming my name, clutching at my hand, pulling at my body sprawled on the floor.

I falter, my feet on the windowsill, even as the light reaches my toes.

I can't

I can't

I can't leave him.

I can't leave him alone.

First he left me, but it turned out he really didn't. He would never leave me alone, and I can't leave him either.

With a sigh, I step down from the sill, and slip back into my body, and when I open my eyes again, I'm in the hospital.

"You're allergic to nuts," the nurse tells me solemnly, and my mom and my brother are sitting on the bed with me.

"You can never eat nuts again," my mother tells me, and her eyes are filled with terror.

"You died for a minute and a half," Finn announces, and he no longer looks afraid, instead, he looks intrigued. Because I'm safe now. Because I was dead, and now I'm not.

I should feel different, but I don't.

It intrigues me, too.

Chapter Four

Whitley Estate
Sussex, England

The flight is God-awful long.

We get to ride in First-Class, but I had to leave my dad and my room, and even though the flight attendants come to check on us frequently, and bring me apple juice and cookies and a blanket, it's not worth it. I know it's not worth it.

My legs cramp and I rub at them, glancing sideways at Finn.

"I don't want to go to England," I tell him. He shushes me with a finger to his lips, staring at our mom across the aisle. She sleeps heavily, thanks to a sleeping pill. I roll my eyes.

"She hasn't moved in three hours."

"So what? She could still hear you."

"She doesn't have bionic ears," I argue. But then I drop it, because what difference does it make?

"I just don't want to go," I continue, a little bit quieter. "Dad didn't want us to leave, I could tell. I don't see why we have to."

Finn glances over his shoulder at mom, then peers at me. "I heard them talking last night. Mom said that we have to go, so that her family can help you."

I yank my head back, startled. "Help me with what?"

My brother's blue eyes are guarded. "I don't know. Do you?"

I shake my head adamantly. "No. I have no idea. I don't need help."

I don't say anything else for the rest of the flight, and finally, finally, we arrive in London. My mother awakes easily, freshened from her nap. I'm exhausted, and it's on weary legs that I trudge through the busy airport.

A driver in a dark suit and cap is waiting for us and he leads us to a long sleek limousine.

"My name is Jones," he tells me seriously, and he has a giant nose. "I'll be helping with you while you are here at Whitley."

Helping with me?

Finn and I exchange looks as we pile into the fancy car.

My mother doesn't seem to notice. Instead, she seems nostalgic as she chats while we drive through town and into the countryside. She points out the window.

"See over there? I learned to swim in that pond."

I follow her finger and find a dismal little body of water, murky and black. Nothing like the Pacific

Ocean, the water that I learned to swim in. I feel sorry for her for that, but she doesn't seem sad.

Now that we're here, her accent is sharpened, cutting the air like a scalpel, like the British person she is. She says *bean* instead of *been*, and pronounces *schedule* like *shhedule*. Why haven't I ever noticed it before?

Finn reaches over and grabs my hand, squeezing it. "I think we're almost there," he says quietly, and I follow his gaze.

Towers erupt through the trees on the horizon, spires of stone, and a cobbled roof. I'm mesmerized as we pull through gates, gliding along a stone driveway and pulling to a stop in front of a giant house. A mansion, actually.

"Kids, this is Whitley," my mother says, already opening her door, her foot on the stones. I stare around her at the house that looms over her shoulder.

It's imposing and grand, ominous and beautiful, dark and bright.

All at once.

It's many things, but mostly, it's intimidating.

As is the tiny woman waiting to embrace my mother.

She stands in the front doorway, like a little bird. She's got dark skin and a bright scarf wrapped around her hair, and dark eyes that gleam, eyes that seem to see right through me. I shiver from her gaze, and she smiles crookedly, like she knows. Like she knows all about me, like she knows everything about everything.

She's introduced as Sabine, although my mother calls her Sabby. Like mom knows her oh-so-well, even though I've never heard her name before today. All of this makes no sense at all, and I wonder if Finn is as confused and overwhelmed as I am.

He doesn't seem to be as he shakes Sabine's hand. He smiles seriously at her, saying politely, "It's nice to meet you."

It's my turn next and Sabine stares through me, like she's reading my thoughts, her dark eyes drilling into mine.

"It's nice to meet you," I murmur obligatorily, like I've been taught.

Her mouth turns up at the corners, her wrinkled hand curled like a claw around my own. Her skin is cold, like ice, and I shiver again. She smiles in response and something puts me on edge, the hair standing up at my neck, and every vertebra in my spine straightens.

"The die has been cast, I see," she says quietly, almost to herself, and I'm the only one who can hear.

"What?" I ask in confusion, because her words make no sense. But she shakes her scarf-clad head.

"Don't trouble yourself, child," she tells me firmly. "It should be of no worry to you right now."

But it is, because her words stay with me.

She leads us to our bedrooms and on the way, she turns to me.

"You will listen to me while you are here," she tells me, and her voice is matter-of-fact, as though I'd never dream of arguing. I open my mouth, but her steely gaze closes it for me. "I will provide you with medicines and methods to control your…illness. I have your best interest at heart, always. And the best interest of this family. You will trust me."

It's a directive, not a question. She pauses at Finn's door and allows him to enter, before we continue on to mine.

Outside of the large wooden door, she turns to me. "If you need anything, let me know."

She leaves me alone and the room is cavernous.

"The die has been cast," I repeat to myself as I stare at my suitcase. It's waiting for me to unpack it, but my bedroom is too large to feel comfortable, and all I want to do is go home, away from this strange place with their strange words and ways.

"What did you say?" Finn asks from the doorway. He's staring at me, waiting for my answer as he comes in and looks around my room.

"I like mine better," he continues, without waiting for an answer.

I haven't seen his yet, so I can't argue, although I'm just happy that he didn't ask me again what I'd said. The words don't make any sense, and I don't need for him to tell me that.

The die has been cast.

What does that mean?

Finn bounces across the room and tumbles into the blue velvet chair by the window. He squeaks the springs in the cushion, and stares out the giant windows.

"This place is huge," he says, as if that isn't obvious. "And Sabine told me that we get to have a dog."

This perks my ears up. Because we can't have a dog back home. Dad is allergic.

"A dog?"

Finn nods, the happy bearer of good news.

This place is looking up.

A little.

My brother helps me unpack and put away my clothes, and I stare at the giant bed. "I'm going to be afraid to sleep here," I muse.

Finn shakes his head. "I'll come sleep with you. Then we won't be alone."

I'm never alone. That's the best thing about having a twin. I smile, and we find our way to the dining room together, because when we're together we're never alone, and because we aren't supposed to be late for dinner.

It is here, seated around the biggest table that I've ever seen, that we meet our grandmother.

Eleanor Savage is seated at the head of the table, her hair pulled back severely from her face. She's wearing pearls and a dress, and she doesn't seem happy, even though she says she's pleased to finally meet us. She emphasizes the *finally*, and glances at my mother as she says it.

My mother gulps but doesn't reply. This interests me. My mother is scared of my grandmother. But then again, as I look at the severe old woman, I'm guessing that everyone is scared of my grandmother.

Eleanor looks at me.

"We've always kept a pair of Newfoundlands here on the Whitley estate. We've recently had our old dogs put down. You and your brother will choose a new pair. The neighbor's bitch whelped."

I have no idea what *whelped* means, and I thought *bitch* was a bad word. But I nod because she wants me to, because she acts like she's bestowing an honor. She doesn't say *Welcome to Whitley, I'm your grandmother and I love you.* Instead she allows us to pick out the new estate dogs.

I don't say anything because I do want a dog, and I'm afraid if I ask questions she'll change her mind.

Instead, I focus on my dinner, which is an odd thing called Steak and Kidney pie. I shove the internal organs around on my plate, but my mom catches my eye and raises a stern eyebrow. I reluctantly put a bite in my mouth. It tastes meaty, but the texture is rubbery and turns my stomach. I swallow it without chewing.

"Where is our cousin?" Finn asks abruptly, and I realize that I had forgotten about him, the boy we met last year. The boy with the dark eyes, so dark they're almost black.

Dare.

My grandmother looks down her nose at us.

"Adair is eating in his father's wing, although you should know that children aren't allowed to ask questions here at Whitley."

I gulp because this stern atmosphere is scary, and because Whitley must be enormous. It's so big that we all have separate wings and rooms and suites. It's like an island floating in the middle of England.

I am on edge because I can see that my grandmother doesn't like Dare. It's in her voice, dripping with resentment and distaste. I briefly wonder why, but then put it out of my mind as I make my way back to my giant bedroom. It's not my business. He's a step-cousin who I don't even know. Like my father would say, *it's not my circus, not my monkeys.*

In the morning, Sabine wakes me from my sleep with a gentle rap on the door.

"Come with me, child," she says, her voice like a gnarled piece of driftwood. "We've got to go get the pups."

Excitement leaps in my chest and I charge from the bed, pulling on clothes as I go. *A dog.* Dogs don't judge you, they love you no matter what, and they never act like you're crazy. I can hardly wait to get one of my own.

Finn and I chatter as we ride with Sabine in an old truck, down the road to a neighbor's. A herd of fat fluffy black puppies surround us when we get out, and it isn't long before I pick one with big sad eyes, and Finn picks one with a wriggly body and wagging tail.

"They look small now," Sabine warns us. "But they'll be bigger than you someday. They'll have to be carefully trained to be obedient."

"What should we name them?" Finn wonders aloud as he holds his squirming puppy on the way back to Whitley.

Sabine glances at us. "Their names will be Castor and Pollux. It is fitting."

I find it interesting that she has already named them, but it doesn't really matter. Because I have a soft puppy sleeping on my lap and that's really all I ever wanted. I just didn't realize that until now.

It isn't until we're back at Whitley and in the kitchen feeding our new pets when I think of our cousin.

"Shouldn't Dare have gotten a puppy, too?" I ask, pausing with my hand on Castor's head. Sabine shakes her head and looks away.

"No."

Her answer is so immediate and firm that it puzzles me.

"But why?"

"Because, my child, he doesn't matter. Now remember what your grandmother said. Children don't ask questions here."

It's the first time that I truly see Dare's place in this home, and he plays the role of insignificance. I don't like it. Dare should have the same position as I have. He's Eleanor's grandchild, just like me. So why do they treat him like he's different, like he's disposable?

It leaves me with a sense of dread and a heavy feeling in the pit of my stomach.

Try as I might, that feeling won't go away.

Finn and I sleep with Castor and Pollux snuggled at our feet, and still, I somehow feel alone for the first time in my life because I'm in a place where a living breathing person has no importance whatsoever.

If it's Dare today, it might be me tomorrow.

Disposable.

Chapter Five

Whitley Estate
Sussex, England

I dream that I can't breathe, that something something something is strangling me. I struggle and struggle to take a breath, to move, and I simply can't. I startle awake to find Castor lying across me, with every ounce of his two-hundred pounds crushing me.

"Ugh, Castor, move," I mumble because his dog breath is rancid and his slobber is dripping down my neck. He pants harder, and doesn't budge.

I manage to roll out from under him and I fight hard to remember the little ball of fur that he used to be only one year ago.

"You're enormous," I tell him lovingly, patting his giant head. We'd only arrived yesterday and Castor and Pollux seemed to remember us, as though we'd never left. "I didn't even know a dog could get so big."

He seems as big as a small horse and his paws are bigger than my hands. I know that for a fact. I compared. He's as heavy as Finn and I put together, maybe more, and I love him. I love him as much as last year, as much as I ever did. Maybe even more. He's so big that I know he'd never let anything happen to me. Not ever. For some reason, that feels important.

"Let's go get some breakfast, boy." Castor pants at my heels as we wind our way through the halls, and his nails click on the stone. He sounds like a moose walking behind me. Nothing about him is subtle.

I pause at Finn's bedroom and peer in, and I smile when I see Finn and Pollux sprawled together in the sheets. Pollux is every bit as large as Castor, and he makes the giant bed seem small. He perks his ears when he sees me, but doesn't move.

"Shh, boy," I tell him. He closes his eyes as though he understands that I want my brother to sleep. We're jetlagged and down seems like up right now.

When I get to the kitchens, there is no one there. It's unusual, but it's far earlier than everyone else gets up on a normal day. Stupid jetlag. I grab a roll from the cabinet, pour some food for Castor, and eat my breakfast.

When I'm finished, I'm still alone in the kitchen.

So Castor and I head outside, stepping along the foggy paths as we explore.

I immediately wish I'd worn a sweater. It's chilly outside with the morning breeze and the sun only just now coming up. Goosebumps form everywhere on my body and scrape together on my legs as I walk, like prickly miniscule anthills.

The horizon is laced with purples and pinks and reds as the sun begins to tip over the edge. It seems abnormally huge, but it is because Whitley's grounds are so large, so vast. I'm marveling in the beauty of it when I hear a noise.

A rock tumbling along the path, maybe. A skidding sound, something that interrupts the stillness of morning.

I pause, but Castor bounds ahead without me, his giant body barreling down the path toward the stables, intent on finding the source of the noise.

"Castor!" I call, but he doesn't listen, and doesn't even look back.

"Castor!" A male voice barks through the stillness, and Castor skids to a stop at Dare's feet. "Sit!"

Castor sits obediently and immediately, poised in front of Dare.

I stare at him in awe.

"How did you do that?"

Dare looks up at me and I decide that he must be…. eleven? His hair is a bit shaggy, almost touching his shoulders even. But his eyes… his eyes haven't changed.

Dark

Dark

Dark as night.

"You have to be firm," he tells me, his voice clipped and British. "You have to be the boss. They've been trained this year, but they're still puppies. You have to control him."

I'm hesitant, because Castor is twice, maybe three times my size. Why would he listen to me?

"Call him," Dare tells me. "Do it firmly. Say, *Castor come*."

I do it, trying to mimic the sternness of Dare's voice."

Castor looks at me without moving, and Dare snickers.

"You've got to call him with authority, little mouse."

My head snaps up. "Don't call me that. I'm not a mouse."

He laughs. "Then don't act like one. Call him with purpose."

My lip curls and I snap, "Castor, come."

Castor gets to his feet and comes straight to me. He stands in front of me, waiting for my command. "Sit."

He sits.

Like magic.

Dare smiles, and his teeth are very white. "See? He's been trained. And I'm sure he remembers you. They were both trained with your scents."

"Our scents?"

Dare nods. "Yeah, yours and your brother's. Sabine kept a few of your shirts to use for them. It worked, didn't it? He knew you?"

I nod and I can't argue. He did know me. But it feels weird to know that my scent was being used without my knowledge this year, even though that's dumb. My scent doesn't belong to me. Not really. I put it out into the world, and once it's released, it never comes back.

Dare walks to me, a little bit skinny, a little bit gawky, but he seems so sophisticated to me, so worldly. He's three years older after all. The eleven-year olds at school won't even look twice at me. Well, unless it's to call me Funeral Home Girl. I cringe at the memory and Dare looks at me curiously.

"What?"

I swallow because I'll never tell him of that particular shame. "Nothing. What are you doing out so early?"

He's the one who seems to cringe now, but then he hides it. "It's the only time I can come," he shrugs, without explaining. "Don't tell Sabine, ok?"

That seems like a dumb thing to ask because we aren't doing anything wrong, but I agree. "Ok. What are you doing out here?"

Dare shrugs. "Nothing. Just walking around."

He's smart because he has a jacket on.

"Can I come with you? I don't know my way."

Dare hesitates, but finally nods. "Fine. But you have to be quiet. We don't want to wake anyone up."

"This place is so huge," I answer. "No one will hear us out here."

"There are eyes everywhere," he tells me. "Don't doubt it."

"Ok," I answer, because he wants me to agree. But I think he's being paranoid.

We walk along the path toward the grounds, far away from the house, and Castor stays a few feet in front of us. Every once in a while, he lifts his giant nose to the breeze, checking checking checking for something.

"What's he watching for?" I ask Dare curiously.

"Anything," Dare guesses. "Everything. Who knows? Newfoundlands are known for their hero instincts. He'd probably die to protect you."

"And you?" I ask quietly. Dare glances at me.

"Probably. But he's not mine. He's yours."

I'm dying to ask why Dare couldn't have a dog, because he so obviously loves Castor. But I don't. Because I have a strange sense that it would offend him, that it would hurt his feelings, and I don't want to do that. I have a strange fascination with this boy and his dark eyes.

Dare pauses on the path, and he seems to be trying to catch his breath. I suddenly notice that he's pale, paler than the last time I'd seen him. I touch his elbow.

"Are you ok?" I ask quickly, and he yanks away in annoyance.

"Of course," he snaps. "Why wouldn't I be?"

Because you can't breathe.

I don't say that though because obviously he doesn't want me to notice. So I wait quietly with him, patiently. Finally, after minutes and minutes, he continues on his way, although his steps are slower this time. Castor slows too, determined to stay near us.

A boy in my class at school has something called asthma. He has to carry an inhaler, and oftentimes during recess, he has to stop playing so that he can breathe. I decide that Dare must have that too, although it's stupid to me that he wants to hide it. Having asthma is nothing to be embarrassed about.

Dare points to a stone building in the distance.

"There's the mausoleum. Every Savage has been buried there. You will be too."

How depressing.

"And will you be?"

The question comes out before I can stop it.

Dare laughs, but there is no humor in it. "Doubtful, and I don't want to be. My father was French, and I'll be buried in France. They can't keep me here."

There is as much distaste in his voice now as there is in Eleanor's when she speaks of him. *Bad blood*, my father would say. But why?

"You don't like it here?" I ask, hopeful that he'll tell me something, anything, to help everything make sense.

Dare is silent though, his dark eyes trained on the horizon.

"Please tell me," I add. "I don't like it here, either."

"Why don't you?" Dare glances at me and he seems almost interested.

"Because I miss my dad. I miss my room. I live in a funeral home. Do you remember that?"

Dare nods.

"I don't like that part because the kids at school tease me, but I miss home. I miss the ocean. Whitley is too big. It's scary here because it's dark and everyone is quiet. It feels like everyone hides things from each other, but I don't know what."

"You don't know the half of it," Dare mutters and I look at him sharply. He looks away.

"Tell me about living in a funeral home," he says, redirecting my attention.

I smile because he doesn't sound mean or judgy. He just sounds interested.

"It's ok. It smells like flowers all of the time. The smell gets into my hair and my clothes."

"Do dead people look like they're sleeping?"

I snort. "No. They look dead."

Dare nods. "I figured."

We're quiet now, and we walk, and Castor pants. The tiny pebbles tumble under my shoes and I once again wish I were home, on the cliffs of Oregon. But then again, Dare isn't there, and he interests me.

The wind blows my hair and I raise my hand to shove it behind my ear, and as I do, something moves in the corner of my eye.

I turn, and what I see is the stuff of nightmares.

LUX

I see Castor and Pollux, broken and bloody, dragging themselves along the path, their legs broken, blood pouring from their eyes and their noses. Blood trails behind them, it fills the pads of their paws and leaves crimson prints on the ground. There is so much blood that I can smell it, I can taste it.

I scream and try to run to them, but my feet won't move. They feel like they've been glued to the ground and I'm frozen frozen frozen. My heart pounds and pounds, the blood racing through my veins and I can't move I can't move I can't move.

"Castor," I whimper.

Castor tries to pick his head up, he tries to come to me because he's obedient, he's been trained, but his bones his bones his bones are splintered. He can't walk and he falls to the ground with a loud boom, so loud and hard that it shakes the ground under my feet.

I scream

And scream,

My hands over my mouth.

Dare turns to me calmly, his eyes like lifeless pools, and it's him, but it's not him.

"You did this," he says, his voice dead like a corpse. I try to breathe but I can't

I can't

I can't.

I squeeze my eyes closed and fall to my heels, rocking on the path.

"Calla! Calla! Open your eyes! Shh! Everything is fine, it's fine. What's wrong?"

A voice is desperate and anxious and I focus on it, trying to come back to my body, trying to hear it.

"Calla!"

I focus on those two syllables, on the voice.

It's Dare's and it's full of life this time, not like before.

I open my eyes and his face is in mine, his dark eyes panicked.

"What's wrong?" he asks me, his hands closed around my arms. "Are you ok?"

I think he'd been shaking me, trying to get me to focus. But I don't know.

I shake my head. "What happened to the dogs? Oh my God. What happened?"

Dare cocks his head, quizzical. "What do you mean?"

From behind him, Castor whimpers and I startle, sitting up so I can see.

Castor is sitting a few feet away, staring at me with canine concern, whimpering because I've unnerved him, wagging his tail hopefully. His bones are fine. There is no blood.

He's fine

He's fine

He's fine.

I suck in a breath. It wasn't real. Was it real?

"I thought... Castor was..." my voice trails off, because this is exactly what happened when I thought my brother had died. It wasn't real.

It clearly wasn't real.

"I need Finn," I say finally.

Because Finn will help me understand. Finn is the only one who can know.

"Are you crazy?" Dare asks me as he helps me to my feet. "My step-father said you were."

"No!" I snap. But I'm not sure. I probably am. "That's a mean thing to say."

"My step-father is mean," Dare answers without apology.

From behind him, my mother rushes down the path, in a robe and her hair standing on end.

"What's wrong, what's happened?" she asks as she reaches me, pulling me into her arms. "I heard you scream."

Finn is behind her, and Sabine. They are all watching me, because they know what I won't admit.

I'm crazy.

"Nothing," I tell them all. "I thought I saw something and I didn't." Clearly I didn't. Pollux is with Finn and he's fine.

Sabine looks at Dare. "You know you aren't supposed to be out here," she tells him. "You know there will be consequences." He nods seriously and Sabine looks at me.

"You shouldn't be out here, either," she announces. "You shouldn't invite trouble, little one." She's stern and I feel like I'm in trouble and I don't know why. If anyone should be mad at me, it's my mother. But mom doesn't say a word, she just holds me in her arms.

"It's my fault," Dare interjects quickly before I can respond to Sabine. "She heard me and followed. It's my fault."

"It's no one's fault..." I start to say, but Sabine is already nodding.

"Don't misguide her, boy," she says. "Richard will hear about this, if he hasn't already."

Dare's face pales and he's silent, but it didn't stop him from trying to save me from trouble. He stood up for me. I grab his hand, but he pulls it away without looking at me.

"Let's go inside," Finn tells me, guiding my elbow with his hand. My mother rustles us to the house and back to our rooms, and I don't see Dare for the rest of the day.

Sabine comes to my room mid-morning and sets a tray down on my desk.

"Your mother sent me," she tells me, handing me a cup of steaming liquid. "Drink this and tell me what you saw this morning."

I take the tea and sip at it, and it's bitter and I hate it. I try to hand it back, but she shakes her head.

"Drink." Her voice is firm.

I drink, but I don't speak. I don't tell her that I saw the dogs broken and bloody. Because why would I have imagined such a thing? I must be a monster. Only a monster would do that.

She waits and I'm silent and finally she sighs.

"I know about you," she says, her hand on my thigh, her fingernails biting into my flesh. "You don't have to hide it. I told you to trust me."

I want to answer that you can't just tell someone to trust, that trust has to be earned. That's something my dad has always said and he's right. My dad is smart. But I keep my mouth shut about that.

"What do you know about me?" I ask instead.

"You know what," she answers. "I know what no one else does. I know all about you, child."

I shake my head though, because there's no way. I haven't told anyone what I saw. I sure won't be telling her.

She clucks and shakes her head. "I can't help you until you're honest," she tells me as she picks up the tray and starts for the door. She pauses though, and turns to me.

"You should stay away from Dare, though," she tells me. "Someday, he'll be your downfall."

"My downfall?" I can't help but ask. She smiles and it's grim as she nods.

"Your downfall. It will be one for one for one, Calla."

"What does that mean?" I'm confused but she's gone, the door closing behind her with a heavy creak.

Castor lies at my feet and I'm so happy that he's healthy that I hug his neck, breathing in his dog smell, and feeling his fluffy hair on my cheek. "I love you, Castor."

He pants in reply and lies with me as the room swirls around me, my vision foggy. I don't know what's happening, but I can't keep my eyes open. My eyelids are heavy

Heavy

Heavy.

My hands are hot, my legs are cold and everything is swirling into blackness. As I close my eyes, I see something on the edge of my periphery, in the shadows of my room.

A boy in a hood, a boy with black black eyes. He watches me, waits for me, and he seems so utterly familiar.

But it's not real. He can't be real. It's just like the bloody dogs.

I want to open my eyes to check, but my eyelids are so so so heavy.

So

Heavy.

Everything ceases to matter and I can't trust myself anymore.

I'm crazy.

As I drift into sleep, into oblivion, I think about Dare. The boy who risked trouble to keep me out of it. *"It's my fault,"* he'd said.

But it wasn't his fault.

He'd lied to try and keep me safe.

No one has ever done that before.

Chapter Six

Whitley Estate

"I love him."

My whisper is small in my large room, but it is heard by my brother. Because Finn has sneaked in like he does every night. Whitley is much too large for us to stay in our own rooms alone. There are far too many shadows, far too many things to fear. Our dogs lie at the foot of my bed, protecting us as we sleep. They are sentinels and it is comforting.

Finn pokes his head out of his covers, his light brown curls unruly.

"You're dumb," he announces. "You can't love Dare. He's our cousin. And I heard mom talking to Uncle Richard. Dare is a lost cause, Cal."

Rage almost blinds me, red and hot, billowing from the corners of my eyes like ink.

"Don't say that! It's not true. He's not lost. And Uncle Richard is a monster," I tell him. "You know that. Plus, Dare is only our step-cousin. We're not really related."

"Close enough," Finn answers. "You can't love him. It wouldn't be right."

"Why does it have to be right?" I sniff. "Who decides what is right and not right, anyway?"

Finn rolls his eyes before he covers his head back up with his covers. "Mom does. Besides, you have me. I'm all you need, Calla."

I can't argue with that.

So I drop it. Soon I hear Finn's even breaths, signaling me that he's asleep.

I lie still, watching the shadows move across the ceiling. I'm not scared when Finn is here, which probably really is dumb. I heard Jones telling Sabine that Finn couldn't beat his way out of a wet paper bag, but that's only because he hasn't hit a growth spurt yet. Regardless, I know he'd die trying to protect me. Somehow, that's comforting and morbid at the same time.

I close my eyes.

And when I do, all I can see is Dare's face.

Dark hair, dark eyes, stubborn glare.

I love him.

He's mine.

Or he'll be mine someday. I know it in my heart, as sure as I know my name is Calla Elizabeth Price.

I sleep to the sounds of the moors…the wind, the dark, the silence, the growls. The moors here at Whitley growl, although no one else seems to notice. At first I thought it was Castor, but it's not. He'd never growl at me. But the moors do.

After the morning sun wakes me up, I pull some clothes on and dash down to the kitchens, hoping to see him before breakfast.

COURTNEY COLE

"Is Dare here?" I ask as Castor and I skid around
the corner. Sabine eyes me from beneath her scarf as
she hands me a croissant.

"Shh, child. I think I saw him slip outdoors."

She's quiet so that no one will overhear her. I tell
her thank you over my shoulder and head for the
grounds, because that's where Dare likes to be. He
hates the house, and he hates most of the people inside.

But he doesn't hate me.

Even though I'm only eight and he's eleven. I
know this because he told me.

I race down the paths, over the cobbles and
between the gates of the secret garden with my dog on
my heels. I watch for Dare above the flowers, beneath
the massive angel statues, and I finally see him sitting
on the edge of a pond, his dark eyes thoughtful as he
skips a rock across the glassy surface.

"You're not supposed to be out here," I tell him
tentatively as I approach. He barely glances up.

"So go tell Eleanor."

His tone is sullen as he mentions my grandmother,
but I'm used to that.

My mother said his lot in life has left him grumpy,
that I'm to be patient.

I'm more than patient.

I live for every word out of his mouth.

I sit next to him, and even though I try, none of
my rocks skip. They just fall heavily into the water.

Wordlessly, Dare reaches over and adjusts my hand, making me flick my wrist as I toss the stone. I watch it skip once, twice, three times before it sinks.

I smile.

"What does 'lot in life' mean?" I ask him curiously.

His eyes narrow.

"Why do you ask?"

"Because my mom said you're grumpy because of your lot in life. But I don't know what that means."

Dare seems to turn pale, and he looks away and I think I've made him mad.

"It's not your business," he snaps. "You're supposed to be learning how to be a good Savage. And a good Savage doesn't pry."

I gulp, because Lord knows I've heard Grandmother Eleanor say that a million times.

"But what does it mean?" I ask after a few minutes, ever persistent.

Dare sighs heavily and gets to his feet. He stares into the distance for a minute before he answers.

"It means your place in the world," his words are heavy. "And mine sort of sucks."

"So change it," I tell him simply, because it seems simple enough to me.

Dare snorts. "You don't know anything," he tells me wisely. "You're just a kid."

"So are you."

"But I'm older."

I can't argue with that.

"Can I hold your hand?" I ask him as we make our way out of the gardens. "I forgot my shoes and I don't want to fall on the stones."

I'm lying. I just want to hold his hand.

He's hesitant and he seems a bit repelled, but he glances up toward the house, then reluctantly lets me cling to his fingers.

"You've got to be more responsible, Calla," he advises me with a sidelong look toward my bare feet. But he lets me hold his hand as we slowly make our way back to the house. He shakes off my fingers before we open the doors.

"See you at dinner."

I watch the house swallow him up before I follow him in.

As I walk down the hallway, I can't help but glance over my shoulder every once in a while because even the sunshine can't keep the shadows away at Whitley. Something always seems to be watching me, hovering around me.

Always.

When I find Finn in the library, I tell him that.

He shakes his head, annoyed, yet clearly concerned. Like always.

"Have you taken your pills today, Calla?"

"Yes." If I don't, I see monsters.

I see red-eyed demons and black-eyed serpents.

I see fire,

I see blood,
I see terrible
Terrible
Things.

Finn stares at me dubiously.

"Are you sure?"

I pause.

Then I grudgingly pull the two colorful pills out of my pocket.

He glares at me. "Take them. Right now or I'm telling mom."

When I don't rush to do it, he adds, "Or I'll tell Grandmother."

That threat bears weight, and he knows it. I hurry to get a drink of water, and I swallow the pills while he watches.

"You know better, Calla," he chides me, sounding more like a parent than a brother.

I nod. Because I do.

"They taste bad," I offer by way of explanation.

"That's no excuse."

"What isn't?"

Our mother breezes into the library, red-headed and beautiful, slim and glamorous. If I'm lucky, I'll look just like her some day.

"Nothing," I hurry and tell her.

She seems suspicious, but she's in too much of a hurry to ask again.

"Have you seen Adair?" she asks us both. "Your uncle is looking for him."

We both shake our heads, but Finn is the only one telling the truth. I'd rather die than tell that monster where Dare is.

"What does uncle Dickie want with Dare?" I ask her as she turns to leave.

She pauses, her face drawn and tight. "It's grown-up stuff, Calla Lily. Don't fret about it."

But of course I do.

Because every time Uncle Richard finds Dare, I hear screaming.

And even though you'd think that was the worst part, it's not.

The worst part is when the screaming stops.

Because silence hides an abundance of sins.

That's what my mom says.

And she's always right.

At least, that's what my dad says.

At dinner, I mention my dad.

"I miss him," I tell my mom. "Why doesn't he ever come with us in the summers?"

She sighs and pats my hand before picking up her shrimp fork.

"He does, Calla. You know that. He'll be here for the last couple of weeks, just like he always is."

"But why do we come here every year?" I ask again, and I feel stupid, but it's a good question. Every summer, year after year. Dad has to stay home in

Oregon to work, but we get to come here because mom's family is rich.

"Because Whitley is also our home, and we have to," my mom says tiredly. "And because of the Savage name, you have opportunities. The best doctors, the best of everything. But we have to spend summers here to get that. You already know all of this, Calla. I have to make sacrifices for you, Calla. Just appreciate that."

I do.

I do appreciate that. I don't understand it, but I appreciate it.

What I don't want to tell her is that sometimes, what I *know* blends with what I *don't*. It twists and turns and bends, turning into shapes that I can't recognize. Facts blend with dreams, and dreams blend with memories, and then reality isn't real.

I always feel too silly to ask anyone but Finn what is real and what is not.

They'd think I'm crazy.

I'm not.

Dare kicks me lightly beneath the table and I glance at him quickly.

He grins, his familiar, ornery grin and I love it. Because it always seems like he's daring me when he smiles.

Daring me to…what?

He leans over.

"I'm going to the garden tonight after dark. Wanna come?"

I hesitate.

It's dark out there. And the moors. And at night, they growl.

Dare notices my hesitation.

"Are you scared?" he whispers mockingly.

No, of course not. I shake my head. Accusing someone of being scared is the worst insult possible, I think.

He smiles again.

"Then sneak out and meet me at midnight. You know Finn will be surrounding himself with his Latin books. I know you won't want to join that."

No, of course I don't. Latin annoys me, but Finn has developed a fascination for it, and spends every free second studying it.

"You know you want to," Dare adds.

"Fine," I agree, trying to sound grudging, but chills run up and down my arms in anticipation, because what does he want to do out there in the dark?

He's so... rebellious. It's hard to say.

True to my word, I sneak out of my bedroom and slip out of the house at midnight. I run as fast as I can down the paths because I swear there's something chasing me.

Something dark,

Something scary.

But when I glance over my shoulder,

There's never anything there.

I burst through the garden gates, and Dare is already here.

He smiles, and his teeth are pearls in the night.

"Hey," he greets me casually, like it's not midnight and we're not breaking rules.

"You're not supposed to leave the house," I remind him.

He shrugs. Because he's Dare and he's a rule-breaker. "So?"

It's a challenge and I don't address it. Mainly because I don't have a good answer.

I don't know why he's not supposed to leave the house. It's never made any sense to me. It's not fair. But then again, Uncle Richard has never been *fair* to Dare.

"You and I are alike, Calla," Dare tells me, and the night is quiet and his voice is soft. "I'm in prison here, and you're in prison in your mind."

"No, I'm not," I protest stoutly. "I'm medicated. I'm fine."

Dare shakes his head and looks away. "But you know what it feels like."

I do. I have to admit that I do.

"No one knows what it's like to be me," I whisper. "Not even Finn. It's lonely."

"*I* know what it's like," Dare finally answers. "You'll never have to explain it to me. You're not alone."

While we sit and examine the stars, our shoulders bump into each other and absorb each other's warmth, and I think that might actually be true.

Dare and I are the same. When I'm with him, I'm not alone.

"Why are you a prisoner?" I ask after a few minutes, broaching a forbidden topic, hesitant and afraid that he'll snap at me. But he doesn't.

His shoulders slump and he closes his eyes and he lifts his face to the moon.

"It's not anything you should worry about," he says with tired words. "They don't want you to know."

"But why?"

"Because."

"Because isn't an answer."

"It is right now," Dare tells me. "Someday, you'll probably know. But for now? All that matters is this. We're breathing, and there are stars, and we had chocolate cake for dinner."

He's right. It was a good dinner.

And it's a good night.

I'm alone with Dare in the garden.

We're breaking rules,

And that feels good.

***

Water creeps up around me, over me, drowning me. I twist and turn, fighting to break the liquid bonds encircling my hands and feet. I can't move, I can't breathe, and there are black eyes staring at me from the surface.

I see them, peer into them, fear them, as they blur then disappear.

Down,

Down,

Down I go.

Away from him.

My savior.

My anti-Christ.

"It's your fault," I whisper, and the words are swallowed by the water, stuck in my throat. Am I talking to him or to me? It doesn't matter. My lungs fill and fill and fill, and there isn't any air. There is only a void where my heart should be.

"This isn't real, Calla." I hear Finn's voice, but I know he's not here. No one is, I'm submerged and the water is murky and dark. My fingers clutch at something, at nothing, at everything.

Focus.

I narrow my eyes and I breathe, a deep breath like they taught me. I fill my body with air like I'm filling a chalice, starting at my belly, then my diaphragm, then my throat, then my mouth. I exhale slowly, like I'm blowing through a straw, I push it at out, expelling it until there's nothing left, just me and my withered empty lungs.

I do it again.

And again.

And when I'm done, I can see again. I'm in the hospital, and I'm not a little girl anymore. I'm Calla Price, and Finn is gone, Dare is gone and I'm alone.

I close my eyes because this is not a reality I want.

The darkness behind my eyelids flickers and wavers and moves, and I know that I'm not in a hospital at all. I'm in a box, a casket. I'm alone and there is a satin sheet pulled up to my waist and there are calla lilies in my hands. White ones. They smell like they're wilted because they are. Dying flowers smell the sweetest.

I release them and push my lifeless hands against the pleated silk lid, pushing with all of my strength. It doesn't budge. I hit it, over and over and over, but to no avail. I'm locked in. I'm stuck, I'm stuck, I'm stuck.

I'm buried alive, I'm alone, I'm cold, I'm dead.

Images flash around me, in front of my eyes, in my eyes, behind my eyes.

Tires squealing in the rain, screaming, metal.

Water.

Drowning.

Me.

Finn.

Dare.

Everyone.

Are we all dead?

My eyes startle open and I *am* in the hospital.

The walls are white, my hands are warm, I'm alone,

And I must be

Crazy

Crazy

Crazy.

Chapter Seven

Dare stares at me from across the library and I have to physically stop my feet from twitching.

His mouth turns up. He's thirteen and I'm ten and he thinks he's so much bigger.

"Calla, are you paying attention?"

My mother draws my attention away from Dare, and I try to focus on her words. What had she been saying? She sighs because she knows I have no clue. What she doesn't know is that even now I feel Dare's stare on me, it's on my skin, it's warming me, it's warning me, it's...

"Calla, you have to listen to Sabine more. She's here for your benefit. She knows what is best for you. She's been telling me that you hide your pills, that you don't want to take them."

I gag from the mere memory of how my pills get stuck in my throat, their waxy coating sticking on my tongue.

"They taste awful," I say defensively.

My mother looks sympathetic, but she is still firm.

"Calla, do you know that if you'd been born even a hundred years ago, you'd be the village lunatic? You'd run raving your madness down the streets and no one would be able to help you. But since we have the benefits of modern medicine now, you're going to be able to live a completely normal life. Don't piss that away, my darling."

Her voice is kind, which softens the sharpness of her words, words in which I can hear the striking influence of my grandmother Eleanor. Mom bends to hug my shoulders, and I inhale Chanel and cashmere. I want to cling to her, to linger in her thin arms, but I know that's impossible. She's got a lot to do. She always does when we're at Whitley.

She pulls away and pushes her shoulders back, looking at my brother.

"Finn, I want you to come to town with me today. Father Thomas wants to speak with you about being an altar boy."

I giggle at the look on Finn's face because we hate mass.

Absolutely without any kind of equivocation.

Hate.

It's so gloom-filled and harsh, so repetitive and boring.

I know Finn wants to be an altar boy about as much as I want to take my meds every day, but he obediently disappears with my mother and Dare and I are left alone. He looks away from me almost pointedly, and I feel cold because of it.

"What do you want to do today?" I ask him, shivering, my fingers tracing out the design of the elaborate oriental rug beneath me.

Dare looks away. "Nothing."

He's stretched out in a window seat, his head resting against the glass. He stares aimlessly at the grounds he's been forbidden from.

I refuse to take no for an answer, because I'm bored, because I know he's bored, and because if we don't get out of this stuffy house, I might die.

"Wanna go out to the garden?" I ask hopefully. "Sabine put new koi in one of the ponds. We can go feed them."

"You know I'm not supposed to," Dare tells me roughly, without even looking in my direction.

"Since when do you care about that?" I ask him in confusion, and I see that his hands are curled into fists at his sides. What in the world? We'd only arrived here two weeks ago for the summer, but Dare has been acting like a completely different person than he was last summer, more subdued, quieter. I don't like it.

"I care about it today," he snaps, and I'm hurt by his tone. He's so abrupt, so…mean.

"What's wrong with you?" I whisper, almost afraid to know because he seems like he's angry with me, like he doesn't like me anymore.

His fist seems to shake as it rests against his leg, his face pale as he so adamantly avoids looking at me.

Finally, he sighs and turns his face, his dark eyes meeting my own.

"Look, Calla," he says tiredly. "You're just a kid, so you don't get it. I'm not the same as you. If I mess up, I pay for it. It's not worth it to do what I want anymore. It's easier to just do what they say. It doesn't matter anyway. None of it will matter."

The complete look of resignation on Dare's face startles me, because that's never been him. He's always been rebellious his whole life. He's always given me hope, he's always made me believe that my opinion matters, that my dreams matter, that anything is possible.

But now?

He looks so sad and alone and hopeless.

"Don't say that," I tell him. "Of course it matters. You can do what you want to do. You don't have to listen to them."

"Don't I?" His question is soft. "Did anyone ask me to be an altar boy like Finn? No. Because I don't matter, because my last name is DuBray and not Savage. I only matter that I have a purpose, and that purpose isn't going to be good for me. I'm a lost cause, Calla, and they know it."

He's right about that.

I've heard them whispering. Just last night, I heard Grandmother Eleanor and my mother whispering in the shadows.

Should we bring in another tutor?

I don't see the point.

It's all for nothing. Richard is right.

I'd wanted to spring out of bed and confront them, because they weren't being fair.

Yes, Dare bucks the rules. But why shouldn't he? Richard is horrible to him for no reason. His rules are too strict, too impossible, and any other kid Dare's age would rebel. It doesn't make him a lost cause.

It's too unfair for words.

And now Dare's new despondent attitude?

It's too much.

"Get up," I announce, walking toward him and grabbing his hand. I yank him until he has to get up, and then I pull him toward the door.

"Let's ride into town."

That's against all the rules and we both know it. If we got caught, we'd be in serious trouble, both of us. Dare's not supposed to leave the house, but I'm not supposed to leave the grounds. It's forbidden.

Dare starts to shake his head automatically, but I hold up my hand.

"Are you scared of them?"

He pauses and I'm delighted to see an old familiar gleam in his eyes.

There it is.

The *Dare Me* stare.

My heart flutters because the real Dare is back, even if only for a minute. He's not afraid of anything. He can't be.

"Okay," he agrees. "Scooters though, not bicycles. I don't want you to wear yourself out."

It's annoying because everyone is always saying things like that.... like I'm an invalid instead of crazy. But when Dare says it, I don't argue.

"Fine," is all I say.

We sneak out the back doors and down to the garages, where we grab the motorized scooters.

As we ride into town with the wind in our faces, I turn to Dare.

"Why don't you talk like the rest of them? Only every once in a while do you say things in the English way. It's weird."

Dare stares at me drolly. "My father was French. I refuse to speak like Richard."

"But you're English now," I point out. "And sometimes, you do sound like it."

"That's the meanest thing you've said to me all day."

I haven't said much to him today yet, but I don't point that out. Instead, I pay attention to the road so that I don't hit a pot-hole and bend a wheel like last time. We have to be like Ninjas, in and out of the village without our family knowing.

Or there will be hell to pay, especially for Dare.

"Why is my uncle Richard so mean to you?" I ask him as we stow our scooters on the village sidewalk. He shrugs.

"Lots of reasons, I guess," he answers, pointing at the ice cream parlor. "Want some?"

Always. He knows that.

He buys me a dish of chocolate and he gets vanilla, and we sit in the shadows of the alleyway, nursing our ice cream. I watch mine begin to melt, as condensation forms on the cup in my hand.

"Your uncle doesn't like me because I make him think of things he doesn't want to," Dare finally says.

"What things?"

Dare shakes his head. "Grown-up things, Calla. Nothing you need to worry about."

But I do. I worry about it. I can't stop worrying about it, about him. I'm so tired of things being kept from me, tired of being treated like a little girl.

"Who screams at night?" I ask tentatively, and Dare turns his head and I know that he knows. But he shakes his head.

"I don't know what you're talking about."

"It's ok," I whisper, because I know he's lying. "You can tell me. I won't tell anyone."

For a second, for one second, I think he's going to. He looks at me like he's speculating, like he's pondering and I think he's going to confide in me, but then...he doesn't. He just takes a bite of ice cream and moves further away from me, edging down the pavement.

"There's nothing to tell," he says blankly, and I know the matter is closed. He doesn't trust me. Not yet.

"Fine."

I eat my ice cream until it's gone and when it is, I turn to him.

"I don't want to go back," I say.

"We have to," he replies, taking my cup and throwing them both in the trash.

"Because we're both prisoners?" I ask, remembering his words from long ago.

He stares at me for a long time, his dark eyes hardening, hiding his pain.

"Yes."

"You could leave, you know," I suggest hesitantly. "You could run away. If you hate it so much here, I mean."

Dare stares into the distance, his eyes so very dark. "And where would I go? There's nowhere I could go that the Savages wouldn't find me."

He's so bleak as he climbs to his feet and reaches down to help me up. Our ride back to Whitley is silent.

When we roll back through the gates, Richard is waiting.

His car is parked halfway down the driveway, and he's leaning against it, waiting for us like a tall, coiled snake....a snake poised to strike. My heart pounds and leaps into my throat and I'm frozen.

"Go to the house, Calla," my uncle tells me, his eyes hard and focused on Dare, and they contain a strange gleam, something that turns my stomach to ice.

"But...it was my idea!" I tell him quickly. "Dare didn't want me to go alone."

Richard turns to me, his face oh-so-cold, and Dare nudges me.

"Just go, Calla," he says quietly.

Richard is satisfied by that, because Dare is being submissive and my uncle shoves him into the car. "You know you're not to leave the house, boy," he snaps, a vein pulsing beside his eye. He slams the car door far harder than necessary.

I watch them drive up the driveway, I watch Richard yanking Dare into the house, and I can't stand to follow them and hear what I know I'll hear. I dash into the back doors, into the kitchen, and I throw myself in Sabine's arms.

She listens to me cry and when I'm done, she calmly looks at me.

"We'd better go get those scooters, child."

She walks up the drive with me, and we push them back, and I ask her a million questions.

"Why does Richard hate Dare? Why is he so mean? Why isn't Dare supposed to leave Whitley?"

Sabine listens but she doesn't answer until long after we've put the scooters away and returned to the kitchen.

"Things aren't what they seem, little Calla Lily," she tells me. "It's time that you wrap your young mind around that."

No amount of prodding will get her to say more, and when I go to bed that night, all I can think about is Dare and his dark eyes staring at me as that car disappeared down the driveway.

When the screaming starts, I close my eyes against it, trying to tune it out, because when I hear it, all I can do is imagine those beautiful dark eyes filled with pain. It crushes me, and I sleep to escape it.

Chapter Eight

Price Funeral Home and Crematorium

The Oregon sky hangs misty and cloudy and dark. I watch the lightning stretch from one end of the horizon to the other, illuminating the darkness, exposing the night. It casts a purple light upon everything, and the world seems mystic.

I hold Dare's letter in my lap because it's precious. He seldom writes to me and when he does, I save them.

Dear Calla,

This one says.

How are the dead people? Whitley is the same. I'm practically living with dead people too, you know. Eleanor is close to 200, or at least she looks like it. And Sabine, God. Who knows how old she is?

I'm sending a picture of Castor and Pollux. They were swimming in the ocean and Pollux caught a fish. Someone on the beach thought he was a bear and started screaming. It was the funniest thing ever. Castor hunts for you when you're gone, and he sleeps next to your bedroom door, until I make him come with me.

See you this summer,
Dare

His words are etched on the paper, scrawled with a nonchalance that is typical of Dare. Somehow, he makes me miss Whitley, even though the estate is huge and scary and everything there feels wrong. But Dare is there, and my dogs are there. I miss Dare during the winters, although I'd never have the guts to tell him.

I pin the picture of the dogs on my bulletin board, and do my math homework, and then when I go to sleep, I dream about Dare.

I dream and dream and dream. My dream turns my stomach to warm sunlight, and a weird sensation travels through my thighs and belly, a hot feeling like fire.

I dream that sunlight filters in through the Carriage House windows, and that I'm seated on the couch, lounging on my side. I'm completely naked but for high heels and my cheeks are flushed, and I'm older. Maybe seventeen? My hair is long and red and curls around my shoulders, flowing down my back .

Dare sits in front of me and he's got a pencil in his mouth, chewing on it as he studies me, then he draws on the paper. He's drawing me, and he's beautiful and he's beautiful and he's beautiful.

"You're so beautiful, Calla-Lily," he murmurs. "You're so much better than I deserve."

The light shines into his eyes and they seem like gold instead of black, and his teeth are ever white. A silver ring gleams on his finger and it spins in my mind,

Spinning

Spinning,

And I startle awake,

And when I gather myself,

I realize my cheeks are flushed, just like in my dream.

It's hours before I finally go back to sleep, and even the next day in school, I find myself thinking about that dream. It's a situation that I would be unlikely to be in... exposed like that in the sunlight. It's so out of my character.

I manage to focus my attention for long enough to take my math test, and then Finn and I are out for the day, and on our way home in the brisk cold Oregon air.

As we hike up the road lugging our heavy backpacks, our Chucks squeak on the rocky road, the light sheen of rain making it slippery. I curl my hands inside my mittens while I inhale deeply. Breathing in the salty smells of the ocean, I absently stare over the side of the cliffs toward the beach below.

Something bright blue catches my eye in the rocks below. The blue is out of place against the drab winter background of the beach. I pause, interested, dropping my backpack as I inch closer to the edge to get a better look.

Someone stares back at me, and the eyes aren't friendly.

They're dead.

I gasp, loud and long and Finn's hands yank me away from the edge.

"What's wrong with you, Calla?" he demands in agitation. "You could've fallen over the side. You know not to mess around with these cliffs."

I can't answer. I'm so completely shocked and appalled as I point with a shaky mitten-clad finger.

That couldn't be what I thought it was. *Who* I thought it was.

But it is. I lean forward and look again and I see that I wasn't wrong.

I also see that no matter how much death a person is exposed to, nothing prepares you for the dead and unexpected face of someone you know.

Finn peers around my shoulder, and I feel him startle as he recognizes the body on the rocks below.

"Is that Mr. Elliott?" he asks in shock. I nod dumbly, unable to make my lips move.

Mr. Elliott is one of the few teachers who has ever been nice to me, although he never really liked Finn. Apparently, skinny underdeveloped boys don't impress him much, and so he never stepped in when the football guys stuffed Finn into trashcans in the locker room.

I hated that. But I can't deny that I still liked him…for how he treated *me*.

Specifically, he never made me participate in dodge ball.

He knew I'd be pummeled into a bloody pulp, so he always let me sit it out. And he never acknowledged that he knew why. He never said the humiliating words, *I know everyone hates you so I won't make you a target.* I always appreciated that.

But now, he's dressed in jogging clothes and lying in a broken heap at the bottom of the cliffs. One of his knees is bent, and his foot is cocked at an unnatural angle, pointed up at the sky.

As Finn pulls out his phone and calls the police, all I can focus on are Mr. Elliot's socks. They're the old-school kind, the gym socks that you pull up to the knee…the ones with the stripes. His stripes are bright blue.

A man is dead, and all I can think about are his socks.

Maybe everyone is right and there really is something wrong with me.

Two hours later, my mother rushes to assure me that there isn't.

"It was shock, honey," she tells me, stroking my hair slowly away from my face. "Most people don't get upset right away. It's a delayed reaction."

She wipes my face with a cloth, and makes chocolate chip cookies, and everything is fine until two days later, when it's my turn to help my father.

I stare at my father's perfectly manicured hands, the fingernails that are cut into perfect squares, as he pulls the crisp sheet back up over Mr. Elliott's body.

"I wonder if he had a heart attack and fell from the cliffs?" My dad muses calmly. "Or if he slipped? Poor guy."

My dad is unflappable, his voice matter-of-fact and speculative.

He doesn't ask me if I'm okay, because it doesn't occur to him that I might not be. Death is his business and he deals with it on a daily basis. Nothing bothers him anymore, and he forgets that it might be unnerving for someone else.

I swallow.

"Is the M.E. coming?" I ask, and my voice sounds tremulous in this large sterile room. It's cold in here because it has to be, and I rub the goose-bumps off my arms. My dad glances at me as he wheels the metal gurney into a cooler.

"Of course," he nods. "The medical examiner always has to come and sign the death certificate. You know that."

I do. But somehow, staring at the familiar and dead face of my gym teacher causes the things I know to fly right out of my head.

I nod back.

"Are you hungry?" I ask him, wanting an excuse to leave this room. "I can make you a sandwich."

My dad glances up at me again, and smiles. "I could eat," he answers. "I'll come down to the kitchen in a minute."

I slip from the prep room and close the door behind me in relief, leaning against it for a second with my eyes closed as I try to un-see Mr. Elliott's blank face. The last time I'd seen it, it'd been red and taut as he yelled at us during gym. Seeing it so empty and devoid of life is just flat-out jarring.

"You okay?"

My mother is concerned about me still. Always. I nod, because I don't want to worry her. She's always worried about me, it seems.

"Yeah. It's just...he was nice to me."

That night, after dinner, I have ear-buds in while I do Chemistry homework, but I still hear my parents bickering in the next room.

"I don't like it," my mother says. "We're surrounded by too much death here. It's not good for her."

"She needs to prepare for it," my father says, and his words make me pause, my fingers icy as they hold my pencil.

"Perhaps," my mother answers, and she sounds so sad. "But not yet. She doesn't need to face it yet."

There is silence and I wonder if my father is comforting her, as I so often see him doing. He holds her close and murmurs into her red hair, and his voice is low. It always works.

In a minute, though, they continue.

"As much as I hate it, I think we should spend more time at Whitley. The atmosphere is quiet there.

It's good for Calla's mind." My mom is quiet, her voice thin.

My father doesn't like the idea, I can tell. "And you'll have to spend more time with Richard? Laura, please. The reason we came here was to get away. We have to participate, but we don't have to be with them every day of our lives."

Participate in what? I don't even realize I'd whispered out loud, until I receive an answer.

"I know," a voice says, and my head snaps up.

In the corner of my room, a boy stands, his hood pulled up and shadows covering his face. He's tall, he's slender, he's familiar.

I don't feel afraid, although I probably should.

"Who are you?" I ask.

He shrugs. "Does it matter?"

"Yes," I answer firmly, and I think he smiles. I can barely make out the curve of a lip.

"It doesn't matter because I know what they're talking about, and you don't."

"I've seen you before," I say slowly. "But where?"

He doesn't answer and instead shakes his head.

"Your teacher," he says, and his words are soft and enunciated. "You can change it."

"Change what?"

"*It,*" the boy says impatiently. "You can change it. If you try."

"I'm crazy, aren't I?" I whisper, and I'm surprised when he shakes he hooded head.

"No, they just want you to think so."

This perplexes me, and I want to ask more, but I blink and he's gone and of course I'm crazy.

I fall asleep thinking about the boy and his dark shadowy face and Mr. Elliott.

I dream about Mr. Elliott, and how he was simply dead and it was so startling.

The surprise of it was the worst part, the shock when I saw him broken on the rocks. But even more surprising is how in my dream, he drags himself off of the rocks, and his legs is crumpled, but he still pulls himself on his elbows, and then he blows his whistle and shouts for everyone to line up on the basketball court.

I'm frozen, because he was dead and then he wasn't.

I'm unsettled enough to not go back to sleep for the rest of the night.

I'm still unsettled by it when I get ready for school in the morning, and I'm expecting the school to still be somber, to be in mourning, but they're not.

That annoys me. It's like the world should acknowledge that someone important died, but it doesn't. It just keeps chugging on like normal.

I dread going to gym class because...just because. It will be weird, it will be creepy, it will unsettle me.

But I never guess how much.

Because when I dress out and line up on the base-line with everyone else, Mr. Elliott limps from his office on crutches to stand in front of us, his whistle around his neck and his blue-striped socks pulled to his knees.

Then behind him, the hooded boy is in the corner, and he whispers, and I hear his whisper as clearly as if he's right in my ear, even though he's across the room.

"I told you."

That's when I break down.

I can't help it. I hyperventilate, and then I fall onto my hands and knees, and I can't breathe, and they have to call the nurse.

The other girls snicker and laugh and stare at me, and it doesn't matter because I have bigger problems than them.

I'm insane, and getting crazier by the day.

My mom picks me up, and I try to tell her that I'd had a dream that Mr. Elliott was dead, but she doesn't believe me. She makes a call, and my medicine is changed, and the pills taste worse than before.

Finn holds my hand because he'll never leave me, and I know that, and I'm grateful. I'm also grateful that I'm the one afflicted with whatever this is.

My brother is too kind, too good, too sweet.

I'm the one who deserves it.

I kill gym teachers in my mind.

I'm clearly a monster.

Then I dream them back to life, so I'm clearly crazy.

Chapter Nine

I drink the tea.

I have to. My mother makes me, because I'm so upset. Every day I grow more upset, because every day, I feel more unstable.

One night, my parents are on the lawn beneath my window, long after they think I fell asleep and I peer at them through my open window. My mom tells dad that we're going to Whitley. I want to run down and argue, because I want to stay here, but at the same time, Dare is at Whitley. I'm not disappointed when my father finally caves in.

"Fine. But use care, Laura. You know I can't come with you. Not yet."

"I will," my mom says tiredly. "Richard won't touch me again. Not anymore. They got what they wanted."

"You know it was necessary," my father says, and he sounds just as tired.

"I'm so tired of what is necessary," my mother snaps, and her voice is so venomous that it takes me aback. "I have free will. We all do. That's why we're here."

"Free will is an illusion," my father answers and his words his words his words are so dark.

"I hate to say that I'm starting to think you're right," mom replies. "My mother always gets what she wants. She and Sabine…"

Sabine?

I'm clouded by confusion, and I'm paying so much attention to them that I don't pay attention to what I'm doing, and my hand slips from the window, and my head thumps the sill.

My dad's head snaps up, quicker than lightning, and for a minute for just a minute for just a minute, his eyes flash black in the moonlight.

I gasp, and I shirk away, because my dad is supposed to have blue eyes, blue like Finn's.

But for a long second right now, they gleam and glimmer black, like a pool, like onyx, like the demons that I've been seeing for my whole life.

They're as black as sin.

I scream and I faint, and when I come to, I'm back in my bed, and the hooded boy is next to me. He holds my hand and his fingers are pale.

"There's a ring," he tells me. "And if you give it to me, your brother will always be safe."

"What do you mean?" I ask, and I'm paralyzed with fear, at the mere thought that Finn might someday be in danger.

"You aren't crazy," the boy says. "What you dream is real. What you see is real. There is more to your family then you know."

But the moonlight, the moonlight, it shines into my room and it illuminates his eyes and they're black black black as night, and I scream so loud my room shakes and my parents come running.

When they burst through the door, the boy is gone.

"There was a demon here," I cry, but there isn't anything here now, and they can see that. "His eyes were black," I insist, and I swear I swear I swear my father looks away, almost like he feels guilty.

I swallow hard, I swallow my fear and it tastes almost like poison.

"I saw you outside," I tell them. "I heard what you said. Why does grandmother always get her way? And Sabine?"

But my mother looks at me blankly and my father kisses my forehead.

"Honey, that didn't happen," she says, and my father nods in agreement.

"You must've been dreaming," my father adds, and while that should comfort me, it doesn't.

Because the hooded boy, the boy with the black eyes, told me that my dreams are real, and if they are, if that is true, then my parents are lying and the world is a scary scary place.

Chapter Ten

The conifers, the ferns, the never-ending moss...all of it is wet, all of it is suffocating. I run down the path toward the cliffs, and I feel like I can't breathe, like my chest is constricted, like there's a rock on my ribs, crushing my bones.

"That's what Dare feels like," a voice calls from behind me. I turn, and it's the boy, and he's whispering, but in my ears it echoes like a scream. "His heart hurts, Calla, and it's your fault."

I spin around and face him, and my hair whips in the wind, my pink Converses slip slip slipping in the rain.

"What do you mean?" I ask, and I'm panicked, because when he speaks to me, it always feels true. "What's wrong with Dare?"

"His heart is weak," the boy says and his eyes penetrate me, seeing into my soul, reaching in and twisting it, twisting it, twisting it. "You gave him your heart condition. It was supposed to be yours, but you gave it to him. Iniquum, Calla."

Unfair.

I'm confused because that's not right. I would never. I would never. I would never hurt Dare.

The hooded boy nods. "No, you didn't do it on purpose, but Fate is Fate, Calla. It must be paid. But you can change it."

I stop, and the rain runs down my face, soaking my shirt and I shiver in the cold.

"How?" and my voice comes out like a whimper.

"You just can," the boy says, and for one minute, I see his cheek and it is silver in the moonlight. "By night you are free."

"By night I am free." The words the words the words seem familiar and I don't know why. "I've heard that before."

"Yes, you have," the boy nods. "Think about it, dream about it, because your dreams are real."

My dreams are real.

I'm dreaming now.

I thrash in my bed and Finn wakes me up and his pale blue eyes are so worried.

"Cal, are you ok?"

His skinny hands grip my arms, and I'm shaking in the sheets. Finn curls up with me and holds me, his cheek against my hair. "I've got you. It's fine, Cal. It's fine."

His breath is warm and familiar, and his heart beats against mine, in perfect rhythm, because we are the same, he is mine and I am his, and we're twins. We're closer than closer than close.

"I had a bad dream," I whisper, and my face sinks into the pillow. I can't stop thinking about it, and the words swirl in my mind.

By night I am free.

By night I am free.

Finn eventually falls asleep in my bed, holding on to me for dear life, so afraid that I'll slip away into something bad, into something panicky or manic. I won't. Because I'm restless and I feel I feel I feel like the answer is here, it's here somewhere, it's close.

I cautiously crawl from the bed, careful not to wake my brother. I drift through the house, moving from room to room, and I feel like I'm pulled to something to something to something .

I float through the visitation rooms, past the caskets and the corpses and the flowers. I drift through the chapel by the piano past the altar. I stroll into the Salon, and I stop in front of the window seat and Finn's journal is there, on the cushions.

The Journal of Finn Price. It's embossed on the leather and it was a gift from my parents. He hasn't had time to write much yet, but it's his and it pulls me and I open it.

It's blank, the pages are white, but something something something makes me run my fingers over the linen pages, and there are indentions, like someone pressed hard into the paper.

I turn on the lamp and I hold the paper under the light and there are words there, words scratched into the pages, like someone pressed hard on a pen and the pressure bled through.

Nocte Liber Sum.

Nocte Liber Sum.

By night I am free.

I am stunned, and I drop the journal because the words the words the words are the same. I curl up on the seat and I soak in the moonlight and I'm overwhelmed.

What is happening to me?

What is real?

I don't know anymore.

I don't know.

I don't know.

I fall asleep, curled up into a ball, and when I sleep I dream.

I dream of Dare, and I dream of Whitley. I dream that Dare is not at the whim of my uncle. I dream that he is free, he is free

He is free.

Chapter Eleven

The plane ride seems ridiculously long this year and my gawky adolescent legs are cramping when we finally de-plane. I walk stiffly through the cluttered halls of Heathrow.

I immediately find Jones waiting for us and we pile into the dark car that will take us to Whitley. The entire drive, through all of the rolling English hills, there's only one person I can think of.

Dare.

I'm fidgety and my brother notices. He puts one pale hand out to still my bouncing knee.

"What is your problem, Cal?" he asks, his thin eyebrow raised. There's concern in his eyes though. I see it before he hides it.

Like always, the concern I see there is for me.

He's afraid I'm fidgety because I'm manic. He thinks I'm flying high, unable to come down. There'd only been one episode like that this year, and it was months ago, after Mr. Elliott died. I'm better now, so there's no reason to worry today. Sometimes, I resent their concern. I resent seeing it in their eyes. I resent that their concern is necessary.

I shake my head, though, pushing my annoyance down. It's not their fault I'm crazy. "I'm fine. Just tired of traveling."

He nods and he's not convinced, but he never is. He always, always errs on the side of caution when it comes to me.

He reaches over and grabs my hand and holds it for the rest of the drive.

I can hear his thoughts in the silent car.

If I hold her down, she can't fly away.

I want to laugh at that.

But I don't. It makes them nervous when I laugh at unspoken things.

Sabine waits for us as we climb from the car, and she doesn't look a bit different from last year. She's still small, still wiry, still has her hair twisted into a scarf. And she still has a thousand lifetimes in her old eyes.

She wraps me into a hug and I inhale her, the smell of cinnamon and sage and unidentifiable herbs from her garden.

"You've grown, girl," her dark eyes appraise me. I have. Several inches.

"You haven't," I answer seriously, and she laughs.

"Come. We'll get you some tea."

I don't want her 'tea'. It's infused with herbs, and she ships it to my mother for me to drink throughout the year. It's gypsy treatment, and it makes me sleepy.

"I don't need it yet," I protest as she pulls me to the big kitchen.

She doesn't bother to answer. She simply pushes me into a chair at the kitchen table and she sets about boiling a kettle.

She sits across from me while we wait.

Her fingers drum on the table, twisted and old.

I don't want to be here.

I want to find Dare.

He's sixteen now and I bet he's grown this year. I can't wait to see how he's changed. He's only written me a couple of letters, and he never included any pictures. But then again, he never does.

"Tell me about the demons," Sabine murmurs. Her fingers stop moving and the only sound is the steam escaping the kettle as it heats. It screams a bit, an eerie sound that hangs in ears.

I imagine that I'm the steam. I'm screaming and I'm twirling up and around, dancing on the ceiling upside down. My long red hair dangles against the marble countertops.

"They're gone," I lie.

"They're not," Sabine shakes her head. Because she can see into my head with her old eyes. She can see into my soul, and she can reach amid the lies and pull out the tiny kernels of truth. She knows what is true even when I don't.

"I *want* them gone," I amend. She shakes her head now.

"I know you do, child," she says sympathetically. "Tell me about them."

She prepares the cups and I tell her about my monsters. Because she's right. They're with me always.

"They have black eyes," I tell her. "They follow me. At school, at home, when I'm walking, when I'm sleeping. Sometimes, they chase me. There's one boy in particular. He follows me, he wears a hood."

"This happens even with your medication?" Sabine asks, her voice very level. "Even with the tea?"

I hesitate to answer. But she'll know if I lie.

I nod.

She nods too, and she stirs her tea and looks out the window.

"Can you tell them apart?" she asks. "From real people?"

I nod again. "Yes." Because their eyes are black.

"It'll be ok, Calla," she finally says.

Will it?

"Are you sleeping?" she asks, her wrinkled hands twisted into her small lap.

I shrug. "Sometimes." Sometimes there are too many nightmares.

She stares at me. "You know you're worse when you don't get enough rest."

I know.

I push away from the table after only taking two sips of tea. "I'm gonna go find Dare," I announce.

111

Sabine startles.

"No one told you?" she asks in surprise, her tiny body stiff.

I freeze.

"Told me what?"

Her dark eyes hold mine. "There was an incident. Dare is in the hospital."

I suck in my breath, but she's quick to reassure me. "He's fine, child. He'll be home in a few days."

"An incident?" my voice is shaky. "Was the 'incident' named Richard?"

Sabine shakes her head. "Calla, calm yourself. You don't know what happened. You need to…"

But I'm already running out the door and her voice fades to nothing as I sprint through the halls toward the front door. My weariness from travel has been forgotten.

"Jones!" I call as I near the foyer. "I need a ride."

He appears from nowhere, as he always does. "Miss?"

"I need a ride to the hospital."

He stares at me. "Does your mother know?"

I nod, a lie.

"Yes."

He can't check with her, because he knows full well she's taking a nap to rest up from the trip. He's apprehensive, but he can't say no because I might be a child, but I'm a Savage child.

"Very well. I'll pull the car around."

We're heading toward town within a minute.

The country turns into the city and the streets all lead to one place.

To Dare.

I'm out of the car before the wheels have even stopped turning, racing into the hospital, through the people, only stopping to ask directions to Dare's room.

Then I'm off again, running through white halls and sterility, and I don't stop until I burst through the door of a room on the fifth floor, until I see Dare resting in a bed.

He's alone, and the room is quiet.

I pause, hesitating now.

He's asleep, his dark lashes inky against his cheek.

I marvel at how big he is, how much he's grown over the last nine months, at how beautiful he is even in slumber. He's long, he's slender, he's strong. He's a man. I gulp and the wave of warmth that gushes through me is confusing at the same time that it's familiar. I've always felt it when I looked at him, but it's more pronounced now.

It's unarguable.

Dare opens his eyes.

"Cal?" he asks in confusion, groggily, and he searches the doorway behind me.

"I'm alone," I tell him quickly, striding into the room and sinking into the chair next to him. "What happened? Why are you here?"

I itch to reach over and grab his hand, to offer him comfort, to touch him.

But I can't. Because he probably wouldn't want that. He'd reject me and that would be devastating. I'd never recover.

"I'm fine," he assures me. "It's no big deal. Just a minor hiccup."

"Did my uncle do this?" I ask, the words cold on my lips, the thought even colder in my head.

Dare shakes his head. "No."

"Where is he?"

"Not here," his answer is blatantly obvious. "I'm alone."

"Not anymore," I tell him stoutly.

You'll never be alone again. I swear it.

"Why are you here?"

I meet his gaze and in his, I find the thread of rebelliousness that I was so afraid had been smashed by the Savages. He grins.

Dare me.

"I got myself a tattoo for my sixteenth birthday. And I had a reaction to the ink, apparently."

"A tattoo?" I can't even keep the joy out of my voice. Because this is so Dare. And this is something Richard and Eleanor will hate. That, in itself, gives me joy. "Is it something cute?"

He stares down his nose at me. "Cute? Like a puppy?"

"Maybe. Or a kitten."

He shakes his head. "I don't do cute."

I snicker. "Well, what is it?"

"Writing. On my back."

I wait. He sighs.

"It says Live Free."

My heart picks up because that's so utterly perfect. I tell him that, and he grins again. "I know. But who knew I'd have a fracking reaction?"

"Can I see it?"

He shakes his head. "Nah. Not right now. It's covered up with bandages and it doesn't look good. But you can see it after the swelling goes away."

He's casual and friendly, but the notion, *the mere thought,* of looking at Dare's bare back gives me a thrill. I've changed a lot since last summer. He just doesn't know it yet. I started my period, I have to wear a bra... I'm completely different. On the outside, and on the inside. Unfortunately, they tell me that the monthly spike in hormones will contribute to my craziness, but I'm not going to dwell on that. I'll just take what they tell me to take, and everything will be fine. It has to be.

Dare looks at me now, his dark eyes serious. "You'd better get back to the house. They're going to know you're gone. Jones is probably on the phone right now with Eleanor."

I lift my nose in the air.

"I'm not afraid of her."

He laughs, unconvinced. "Really?"

He knows better than that. Everyone is afraid of her. People say my grandfather died because he wanted to… to get away from her.

"I'm not going to leave you alone," I tell him quietly, resolute.

His eyes waver for a minute, because I know that I'm one of only two people in the entire world who would risk Eleanor's wrath for him. And I'm the only person in the world who risked it to be here with him today.

"It's ok. I'm fine here," he tells me, and his tone is strong, and his heart is brave. This is why I love him.

I love him.

I love him.

I love him because he's strong, because he's rebellious, because he's so serious and sweet and because he lives free now. He lives free even if no one knows it yet but me.

"When will they let you come home?" I ask hesitantly, because even now, I know that I have to go. Finn's probably beside himself. They're probably combing the estate for me, and once Jones calls them… all is lost. They won't let me out of their sight again for a month.

"Probably tomorrow," he promises, and for a split second, there's warmth there, in his tone, in his eyes. He looks at me and *he sees me.* No one else does… no one but Finn.

Everyone else sees who I could be.

Who I might be.

Who I should be.

They don't see who *I am*.

But Finn does. And Dare does.

It makes me feel closer to them than anyone else in the world.

"Go," Dare urges me. His phone is ringing and I know who it is. I know it before he even answers it.

"She was here," he confirms into the mouthpiece. "But she's on her way home now. I wanted her to come. It was my fault." His eyes burn into mine, and I shake my head because why is he taking the blame? He's protecting me yet again.

He nods to me, toward the door, his attention still with Eleanor who I know is on the other end of that call.

Go, he mouths to me. *I'll see you tomorrow.*

Reluctantly, I make my feet move away from him.

I don't want to leave him alone, because I know what alone feels like.

But I have no choice. If I don't, they'll come get me, because we're all prisoners. Prisoners of expectations, prisoners of responsibility, prisoners of life.

But someday… I'll live free, just like Dare.

I don't even glance at Jones when he opens my car door.

"I know you called them," I grumble.

"You lied to me," he says quietly as he climbs into the front. I don't have an answer to that. Because it's true. I did lie.

When I get back to Whitley, everyone is so relieved, everyone but Finn. After dinner, he glares at me when we're in the privacy of the empty library.

"You could've told me," he says stiffly. "I would've gone with you. I care about him, too."

Not like me, you don't. But obviously I don't say that. Finn made his opinion known long ago and he's said it many times since. *You can't love Dare.* But he's wrong. I can, and I do.

"I didn't want you to get in trouble," I tell him, which is only partially true. I wanted to see Dare alone.

Finn doesn't believe me because he knows me. He knows me better than anyone. When he walks me back to my room, he touches my elbow at my door.

"You've got to behave. Eleanor will talk mom into leaving you here with Sabine all year long. Or worse. Is that what you want?"

"No, of course not," I say quickly, because the idea of being separated from Finn makes my heart constrict and pound in terror. But at the same time, the idea of being here with Dare makes it soar.

I'm a contradiction, an endless, endless contradiction.

Finn is pacified and we say goodnight and he sleeps in his own room tonight, because he doesn't know how unsettled I am, and how I don't know why.

I can't settle in, and I can't settle down.

My blood is rush, rush, rushing through my veins, through my heart, pounding through my temples, and my feet itch to run, run, run away... down the halls, out the doors and away from this house.

But of course I don't.

I stay glued to my bed like I'm tied down, like the invisible manacles are real. I ignore my racing thoughts and twitching fingers.

It's a few minutes later when the screaming starts, echoing down the hallways and through the night, and I get goose-bumps because I have a startling realization.

Dare is in the hospital, not here.

The screaming has never been his.

I'm confused, shocked, unsettled.

I focus on the wailing, on the shrieks, and I ponder life here at Whitley. Nothing is what it seems, I guess. I'm not sure who I can trust, who I can't.

The screams finally dwindle, then die out, and I'm able to relax, my muscles sinking into my sheets.

Nothing is what it seems, and I know nothing.

All I know for sure is that Dare is an outcast, frowned upon by everyone, and I hate that. It's unfair. If I could change that, I would. Because Dare deserves the moon and the stars and everything in between.

Maybe I will. Maybe I'll somehow figure out a way to change it.

I fall asleep with my teeth gritted together. I relax my body, and focus on Dare. I focus on what the family would be like if he hadn't been born into it, if he was safe somewhere else.

I love him enough to want that for him, even if it means he'd be gone from me.

The thought of being apart from him breaks my heart into jagged shards, but the thought of him laughing and running through a loving home, a home where he is appreciated, puts the shards back together.

He deserves that.

He does.

***

When I wake in the morning, I eye everyone with suspicion at breakfast.

I've always thought Dare was screaming, that Richard was hurting him in the night, that everyone was closing their eyes to it, turning their backs on what was happening.

But if that's not the case, *and thank God*, then what is happening here?

My mother quietly picks at her breakfast and I shove my food around my plate, ignoring Finn's concerned stares and my grandmother's coldness.

My grandmother's fingers are like spiders, long and thin, as they curl around her water glass. Her eyes are steel as she looks at me over the rim. I look away. At the wall, at the table, at my own arm. At anything but her cold eyes.

I trace the outline of the vein on my wrist as it throbs against my skin, my life's blood pulse, pulse, pulsing through me. The blood is blue, the blood is red, the blood is mine. I stare at the skin, at the bump, at the vein. It bends with my arm, it caves when I move, it--

"Calla?"

My mother interrupts my thoughts and I yank my attention from my arm to my mother.

"Yes?"

"Don't stray too far today," she instructs, and something is troubled on her face. Something disturbs her perfect features.

Something.

Something.

What is it?

"Will Jones pick up Dare today?" I ask her as she sets her glass on the table. My mother clears her throat a little and Eleanor is still.

My grandmother stares pointedly at me and my heart speeds up. Why aren't they answering?

"You should rest today, Calla," Eleanor finally answers, without acknowledging my question. My mother clears her throat again, a small and strange sound. It causes the hackles to rise on my neck, because something is

wrong

wrong

wrong.

"Is Dare coming home today?" I ask again, more firmly this time, and this time directed at my mother. She stares at her eggs for a long time before meeting my gaze.

"You need to rest today, my love. You've been wearing yourself out."

Her face is expressionless and odd, and panic starts to rise in me like a wave, a wave that threatens to overtake me and pull me under.

"I'm fine," I manage to utter. "I'm fine."

My mother nods and Finn reaches for my hand beneath the table. He squeezes my fingers lightly, then harder. Our silent signal to let things drop. He wants me to let it…Dare?…drop.

No.

Never.

I turn to my grandmother. "Will Dare be here for dinner?"

Finn is squeezing my fingers hard enough to cut off circulation, but I ignore it. I focus on the faces in this room, the treacherous, treacherous faces.

I can hear shoes scraping on the floor, silver scratching porcelain plates, light breathing. I count my breaths.

One

Two

Three

Four

Five

Just before my sixth, Eleanor abruptly pushes her chair away from the table and walks for the door.

"You're disturbed, child," she quietly says as she passes. "Go to your room and I'll send Sabine."

My mother looks away and Finn squeezes and I have a terrible dark feeling sitting on my chest.

"But why?" I call out after her because clearly she is the only one who will answer.

She doesn't. Silence follows her and descends upon the dining room and everyone seals their lips and I'm terrified.

Where is Dare?

I rise from my chair, but my chest constricts. Tight, tighter, tightest. I can't breatheIcan'tbreatheIcan'tbreathe. I tumble to the floor and the anchor the albatross the stone .... They all sit on my chest and break it, and crush it and hold me down. I'm crushed to the floor, my heart hurts and I can't breathe.

I can't breathe.

Finn's face swirls in front of mine.

"Calla, breathe," he instructs, his hand on mine, his blue eyes filled with worry. "Breathe."

I can't. I can't. I can't.

"Finn," I whisper. But that's all I can do, all I can say, all I can plead.

Something is wrong here.

Something.

Something.

Something.

Everything.

I can feel it.

Then I feel nothing because everything fades away.

When I wake, I'm in my room alone. It's dark outside, early morning. I've been sleeping all day and all night, probably a product of Sabine's herbs. I stir, rub my bleary eyes and finally sit.

I'm alone.

Dare.

Dare.

My memories of this morning erupt like a volcano in my head and I lurch for the phone. I call the operator and ask to be connected to the hospital because I obviously don't know the number.

When someone answers, I stumble with my words.

"Yes, can you connect me to Dare DuBray's room, please?"

"Just a moment." The woman's voice is perfunctory, but I feel relieved. *Just a moment.* I'll hear his voice in a moment. Thank God. They can't keep me from him. No one can.

I wait.

And wait.

And then the perfunctory woman is back.

"What was the name again, miss?"

"Adair DuBray," I tell her tightly.

There is a pause and clicking on a computer.

"We don't have a patient by that name," she tells me.

"Was he discharged?" I ask hopefully. "He was there yesterday for an infection. He got a tattoo and..."

"Miss, we haven't had a patient by that name. Not yesterday, not ever. He's not in our system. He wasn't here."

"That's a mistake," I whisper, but she's resolute.

"There's no mistake, miss."

Numbness descends like a fog and I replace the phone on the table.

He *was* there. I saw him. I stood by him, I yearned to hold his hand, and his back says LIVE FREE. I know that.

Confusion jumbles in my head, which is nothing unusual. I'm always confused, but I've never been confused about Dare.

Where is he?

What is real?

"What is wrong with you?" Finn hisses at breakfast, his fingers pressing into my knee to get my attention. I shake my head.

"Nothing."

"You're lying," he accuses, and as usual, he's right about me.

He always is.

I know what he's thinking.

I can't take care of myself. I'm an invalid. I'm crazy.

I nod to reassure him. "I'm okay."

He nods back, but he's unconvinced.

It doesn't matter though.

"I'm going to sketch today," I tell him. "The grounds, the garden. Wherever the wind takes me."

"I'll come with you," Finn says quickly, his hand already on mine because he doesn't trust the wind, or anything else with me. But I shake my head.

"No. I'd like some quiet time."

I want to fill my lungs up with the breeze, I want to be a hollow reed, absorbing the world, sucking it down, figuring it out.

I level a gaze at Finn and he stares back, and finally, he acquiesces.

"Ok. If you need me, just shout."

I nod, knowing full well that he can't hear me from across the grounds.

I grab a notebook and a pencil, then I make my way quietly outside, feeling Finn's gaze between my shoulder blades with every step.

I walk away from the Savage house, from the Savage lawns, from the Savages. I walk to the gardens, where it is serene and quiet, where I feel Dare's presence, even when he isn't here.

I sit beside the bubbling brook, dipping my feet in the cool water as I watch it pass over the stones, polishing them.

My mind floats away, carried on the breeze.

Dare's absence consumes me. How can someone simply be gone?

Eleanor is so stern, so rigid. She can make anyone disappear. I believe that. She has power and money and hatred.

A lot of hatred.

"See? You can change things." The boy in the hood is suddenly next to me, and his presence makes me jump. "But you're not the only one."

I stare at him, at the black void where his face should be. I reach out to pull his hood down, to reveal his face, but he stops me with his hand.

"You're going to have to focus."

"Focus?"

He nods, and his hands are on mine, and his fingers somehow make me so very very tired, like he's leeching my energy away with his mere touch. I want to put my head down and sleep, I want to close my eyes, close my eyes, close my eyes… my eyelids flutter closed, and he yanks his hand away and the darkness the darkness the darkness overtakes me and the sleep coming in waves.

But

Then

A

Voice

pulls me from the dark.

"Calla."

The voice is thin, transparent.

It's also familiar.

Dare.

I snap to attention, opening my eyes, scanning the area, but I don't see him.

"Dare," I call out hopefully.

Am I hearing things?

"I'm here," he says, and he sounds so far away.

I spin around and he's behind me, but something seems off and I can't put my finger on it, and I peer into the air and I'm crazy.

"You're not crazy," he tells me quickly, reading my expression. "I'm here."

"I don't understand," I whisper, and he strides to me. When he reaches me, he drops to his knees. I reach out a finger and touch him, and he's real. His shoulder is sinewy and warm.

"You've grown up," he says, and that's not what I expected to hear, because he saw me yesterday and didn't mention it.

"You've disappeared," I tell him, and he smirks.

"I haven't."

"Then why aren't you in the house? Why are you out here? Why is everyone acting like you don't exist?"

My questions are nonsense, just like this situation.

He smiles and he's sad. I can see it in his eyes,

His

Dark

Dark

Eyes.

"Are you real?" I ask calmly, as calm as I can.

"As real as you are," he answers.

"Am *I* real?"

He stares at me, his gaze level.

"If you aren't, then we're both crazy."

I can't rule that out, because Whitley has secrets, and I don't understand any of it. And when I'm confused, I babble.

"I never know what is real," I tell him, and then I launch into my life story. I tell him everything, how Finn died but it turns out he didn't, how my gym teacher died, but didn't, how I see demons and black-eyed beings, how the moors growl at me, and how I'm always afraid to ask about reality. I tell him all the things that I've always been afraid to tell anyone but Finn, and I even tell him about the hooded boy.

"So basically, I'm always scared," I finish, and Dare actually takes my hand. He reaches over, encloses my fingers within his own, and my heart threatens to pound right out of my chest.

His hand is warm and his eyes are soft.

"Don't be afraid," he tells me. "We'll get this sorted."

What a British thing to say. I tell him so, and he smiles.

"That's the meanest thing you've said to me all day."

He looks around me, still smiling, and whistles to the wind, beckoning it. He waits, then whistles again.

"Where are the dogs?" he asks me, confused. "Castor never leaves your side."

Now I'm the confused one.

"What dogs? Who is Castor?"

He stares at me, his dark head cocked. "You're not being serious. Right?"

I stare back, every bit as confused as he is.

"I'm being dead serious. What dogs?"

"Castor and Pollux. They're your dogs. Yours and Finn's."

I shake my head. "We don't have dogs. My dad is allergic."

"You don't have them in Oregon," Dare answers impatiently. "You have them here."

"You're on drugs," I announce. "That's what this is all about. Or maybe I'm on drugs. One of us is definitely on drugs."

"We're not on drugs," Dare answers. "If you don't believe me, ask Sabine. She can tell you about the dogs."

130

I stare at him doubtfully, but I trot indoors to find Sabine.

"Why isn't anyone talking about Dare?" I ask her bluntly. She stares at me with her knowing eyes, and she doesn't flinch.

"I don't know what you mean," she says throatily.

You do. But I don't say that.

Instead, I ask her about Castor and Pollux, and she looks at me as though I've lost my mind, but at the same time, there is somethingsomethingsomething in her eyes. Something strange, something that gleams as she looks at me, something dark

Dark

Dark.

"I don't know what you're talking about," she answers.

"You don't know about Castor and Pollux?" I ask to clarify. "We didn't have dogs?"

She shakes her head and I decline her tea and I feel her gaze upon my skin long after I've left the room.

That night, I find a long dark hair in my bed among my sheets.

A dog hair.

It terrifies me as I hold it in my hand, it's long and thick and coarse, and I run from my room, running for Dare, and I can't find him anywhere.

I search the house, I search the grounds, I search the stables, I search the garages, and when I've finally given up, when I'm finally trudging back up to the house in the dark, there's a shadow on the path. I catch a glimpse of the boy, and he's staring at me, and his face is hidden. He points up and I follow his finger, and there's a room with a light on.

I chase the light, up the stairs, and when I finally see light underneath the door-crack of a lone door, I burst through it and come skidding to a halt.

I'm in an abandoned nursery.

It's got two bassinets and a creepy rocking horse. Its wooden eye watches me lifelessly as I idly stare around the room.

The walls are pale yellow and old, the floor is gleaming hardwood, the ceilings are high. There are chandeliers even in here, in a place where children were supposed to flourish.

But the toys are scarce and the formality is abundant.

The silence is unnerving.

There are no children here but something something something pulls me.

The silence roars in my ears and my feet move on their own accord, toward one of the bassinets. It's still, it's quiet, it's eerie, and when I get to the edge, I pull on it with my fingers and it rocks toward me.

A hoodie is lying inside.

It's a simple jacket, but it's the one the boy was wearing and it fills me with dread, and I sink sink sink with it to the floor, and the floor seems to swallow me, seems to grab at me with barbed fingers.

"This was your mother's nursery," Sabine says from the door. "And Richard's."

Two bassinettes, which indicates that they were babies at the same time.

My heart pounds.

"Are they...I didn't know... are they twins?" My words are limp, and Sabine doesn't truly answer.

"Twins run in your family, girl."

She trails her twisted fingers along the walls as she paces paces paces toward me, and with each step, her face seems to get more grotesque under the twisted scarf of her turban.

She drops something into my hand and it's a locket and it's inscribed with a calla lily. "Go ahead," she urges me, and it comes open in my hands.

There are pictures inside.

One of Eleanor, when she was very young, and one of another woman.

They both look young, and dark-haired and dark eyed and

Oh

My

God.

"You," I breathe. "It's you. Are you and Eleanor... sisters?"

"Twins run in your family," she says simply.

She sinks to her heels next to me, and she pulls me to her and hums, rocking rocking rocking me, and I think she's singing a gypsy song and I'm confounded and stunned and still.

"Did you know that sons must pay for the sins of their fathers?" she asks, and then she hums again, and again and again. "Roma believe that, and it is true. Roma beliefs are different from yours, but we know. We know."

"What do you know?" I ask her the question as I slightly pull away, trying to look at her face.

"We know what you don't want to see," she replies. "We know the things that aren't explainable, the things that don't seem possible. We know things happen that are bigger than us, more powerful than us. And sometimes, a sacrifice must be made for that."

"What do you mean?" I ask and I'm afraid, so so afraid, so afraid that I want to break free and run.

"A sacrifice is something you give," she looks at me, her dark eyes so cold and flat. "You give it willingly, to save something important."

"I know what a sacrifice is," I tell her. "But what does that have to do with me?"

"Everything, my girl. Everything."

I break free from her grasp and I run, and she doesn't follow.

Chapter Twelve

I summon all of my courage and I open the doors to Eleanor's office.

She sits at her desk, sharp and stern in her tightly buttoned sweater and she stares over her reading glasses at me as I approach.

"Grandmother," I say hesitantly, and she waits like a serpent on a rock.

"Yes?" her eyebrow arches.

"Will you tell me the story of our family?"

She is silent as she puts her book down and stares at me, examining me.

"You've been speaking to Sabine?"

I nod. "Is she your sister?"

Eleanor looks out the window and for a moment just a moment, I see the young girl in her face, the one that was in the locket. She looks softer for a second, then she hardens as she looks at me once more.

"Yes."

"So we're all related?"

"All?" She raises her eyebrow again.

"Me, Dare, Olivia, Finn...."

There's something in her eyes something something something, but then it's gone and she shakes her head and she denies everything.

"You're still troubled, child. Olivia died when she was young. I don't know who 'Dare' is."

"He's her son," I cry out, and my fingers shake. "I know him. I knew him. I was raised with him."

"You're so troubled, girl," Eleanor says, and her voice is softer now, softer.

"How can we all be related?" I ask and I feel weak now, like my knees will collapse.

She sighs and she breathes. "Because our bloodline is pure," she says and I think briefly of the royal bloodlines of Egypt. They married amongst themselves to keep their bloodlines pure.

"Like that," she says and I don't know if she read my mind, or if I said it out loud. I never know these days.

"We're from the oldest bloodline in the world," she adds proudly. "We have powerful blood, Calla. Ancient blood. You have no idea."

"No, I don't," I agree. "Does my mother?"

My grandmother seems amused. "Your mother has always known," she tells me. "Since she was a child. She's known her place, she knew her purpose. She was strong. Unlike you. Your mind is weak and we must handle you."

"Handle me?" my words are a whisper and she smiles again.

136

"A sacrifice must be made," Eleanor says bluntly. "And you must make it. We'll shelter you and strengthen you until then, but when the time comes, *you will be strong,* girl."

It's a directive, not a question.

I will be strong.

I'm not strong now as I fumble out the door and trip down the long halls to my bedroom. When I arrive, when I tumble through the door, Dare is sitting in my window seat and he's pale and he's troubled.

"Something isn't right," he says, and his British accent is clipped. "Something is very wrong."

"I know," I agree, and I collapse next to him and he rubs my back and we stare out the window together at the moors and the moors growl.

"We're all related," I tell him, and he stares at me in surprise.

"That's not possible," he replies, but I can hear the doubt in his words.

I nod. "Eleanor just told me. Only she said that your mother died young and that you don't exist."

"I'm as real as you are," he says firmly, and his hand is on my back and he does feel real.

"She says we're like the Egyptian pharaohs," I explain. "Our bloodline is pure."

"What does that mean?" Dare asks, and he's dubious now.

"I don't know."

And I don't.

Chapter Thirteen

Days turn into weeks, and with every week, things get stranger. All traces of Dare have been eradicated from Whitley. Not a picture, not a mention. I'm so convinced that I'm crazier than ever that I even stop confiding in Finn.

It's not something my brother appreciates.

"You're not yourself," he announces one day in the library. "Something's wrong and you're not hiding it very well."

He's so worried that it twinges at my heart. I want to tell him, I wanttowanttowantto. But I can't. Can I?

"Have you ever imagined someone into existence?" I ask him carefully, grabbing his hand and squeezing it ever so softly.

"No," he answers slowly. "Have you?"

"I don't know," I answer honestly. "I thought we had a cousin. A step-cousin. But everyone is acting like he doesn't exist, like he never did. And I'm starting to wonder if I made him up in my head."

Finn takes a breath, then another, and he squeezes my hand, and squeezes it hard. "Delusions are common with your condition, Cal," he finally answers.

"It wouldn't surprise me a bit if you dreamed him. You're fine. I promise, you're fine."

"But you don't know who I'm talking about?" I ask softly.

Finn shakes his head slowly.

No.

But Dare is so real.

Dare is real now as he sits across the library and stares at me, listening to our words and smirking.

He's real when he follows me back to my room, and he's real as he leans against the door.

"Come with me back to Astoria," I suggest. "We'll get this sorted."

"What a British thing to say," he grins.

"That's the meanest thing you've said to me all day."

He laughs, completely unoffended.

On the night before I leave for home, Eleanor comes to my room, creeping in the dark, moving in the shadows. Her skinny arms are like limbs, the shadows scraping the walls like dead leaves.

"Calla, I have something for you," she tells me. I sit up in my bed, startled because I'd never even heard her come in and she's never been in my room before.

She holds her hand out, and a ring glistens in her palm.

It's silver and shiny, a plain band, thick and heavy.

I look at her questioningly.

"It was your grandfather's," she says simply by way of explanation. I take it immediately, curiously examining it by moonlight. It feels cool in my hand, significant somehow.

"Did my grandfather die because he wanted to?" I ask. "To get away from you?" *Because that's what people say.*

Eleanor actually laughs, a husky noise in the night.

"Child, your grandfather never did anything he didn't want to do. And that included dying. He was like you, you know."

This grabs my attention with both hands and holds it.

"What do you mean?" I ask sharply. "How was he like me? He was crazy, too?"

She sits next to my bed. "Don't say you're crazy, Calla. It's demeaning and you're a Savage. You aren't understood, and I can't explain it. That doesn't mean you're crazy. Your grandfather was a good man, and he was just like you, only he wasn't strong enough to sustain. He couldn't keep going on. But I know that you are. Keep his ring. It will hold you to the ground, and help you to always remember where you are. When the time comes, you'll do what is right."

This is confusing and I tell her that. She smiles again.

"Give me your hand."

I obey and she strokes the palm, her brow knitted together as she examines me.

"Your heart line is broken, child," she murmurs, tracing it with her fingers. "It forks into two, then three. It's as I've always said. One for one for one."

"What does that mean?" I ask. I'm sure it's a valid question because *how confusing.*

She ignores me. "Your life line is long and deep," she announces. "It indicates you are stronger than you know, that you are cautious."

"I don't feel strong," I tell her.

"I know," she answers. "But you are. Your life line breaks into many branches, which means you have to choose. You have to choose, child. Never let anyone tell you otherwise."

"I have to choose what? Choose what? To live?"

What a silly thing.

Eleanor stares at me, unflinching. "Take your grandfather's ring. It belongs to you more than anyone else."

It will hold you to the ground and make you remember where you are.

"Who am I?" I ask, and my question is desperate and my words are hot.

Eleanor shakes her head. "You'll figure it out, and it will all be as it should."

Her words swirl and twirl, and an image comes into my head, something I've never seen, but I have. Somehow.

Files, in a drawer, in Eleanor's desk. My name, and Finn's name and Dare's name.

My eyes meet her and I'm defiant.

"If Dare isn't real, why do you have a file in your desk with his name on it?"

She looks at me and her gaze is hard, and it's like rocks, like pebbles, like stone.

"You don't know what you're speaking of."

"I do," I insist, and I think harder, and they're like memories, and I don't know where they came from. "Finn and I inherit your fortune, but Dare doesn't. Only if we die."

It's proof it's proof it's proof.

"Calla," she sighs. "You don't understand."

She pulls me up and I go with her to her office and she opens her drawer and there *are* files in there. Two. One with my name and one with Finn's. We inherit the fortune, but Dare

But Dare

But Dare.

I'm confused and my grandmother's lip twitches as she stares as me in the dim light from the lamp.

"Your riches don't come from money anyway," she assures me. "So don't fret. Your riches come from your blood."

I go back to bed and I pray for Dare, I pray that he'll come to me, but he doesn't. I fall asleep in confusion, but that's nothing new it's nothing new, I'm used to it.

The night passes slowly, and Dare doesn't come until the next morning.

"I'll miss you," he murmurs as I climb into the car and my head snaps up and he's gone.

His brilliant smile is the last memory I think of before I board the plane for America. It's the last thing I see before I fall asleep that night, and it's what I dream about as I sleep in the familiarity of my room in the funeral home.

Dare. I need him.

I need him here.

I can't be without him.

He can't be gone.

He knowsme knowsme knowsme.

I wake to find Dare seated on the edge of my bed, calmly watching me sleep.

"How did you..." I breathe, and I'm confused and startled and afraid. He smiles again and his black eyes glint in the morning light.

"I don't know."

"You're here."

He arcs an eyebrow. "It seems so."

Happiness bubbles up in me, through my belly and into my chest.

"I'm glad," I murmur.

"Me too."

Dare finds the funeral home fascinating, and I take him on a tour. Through the embalming rooms, the Viewing Rooms, the chapel. I show him where we keep the caskets when they come in, where my father keeps the hearse and the family cars. The things that other people find so creepy, and that I find just a normal part of life.

"It smells like flowers here," Dare observes, his large slender body filling the doorway.

"It does," I agree. "It gets into your clothes and then you smell like a funeral home all day."

"Nope," he answers. "Just flowers."

I let it go because I'd rather smell like lilies than death any day of the week.

I show him the beaches and the ocean and our sailboat. I show him the Carriage House and the forest and the cliffs. "Watch your step here," I tell him seriously. "The ledge is thin."

"Will do, mate," he answers.

Mate?

I don't want to be his mate. I want to be...

I don't know what I want to be.

But when I show Dare the old abandoned amusement park the next day, Joyland, I take a minute to scratch our initials into the wood.

DD and CP.

It's Valentine's Day so it feels appropriate.

Dare smiles, and rolls his eyes.

"You're 13. I'm 16."

I lift my chin. "So? In a couple of years, we'll be 16 and 19. And I'm the only one who knows you exist."

That feels so strange to say, and I briefly think that he's my imaginary friend. Don't most children have them?

But staring at him makes warmth gush to my girl parts, and I don't think imaginary friends do that.

Dare chuckles and we leave the park. "So talk to me about it when you're 16," he suggests. But his voice is filled with somethingsomethingsomething.

Interest?

Promise?

Darkness.

I don't know.

All I know is that when he is with me, I feel invincible. I feel strong. I feel like me, but a better version.

So I do the only thing I can think of to do. I slide my grandfather's ring off of my thumb and give it to him.

"I can't take this," he protests softly, but he's so so touched, I can see it.

"It will remind you of where you are," I tell him. "And *who* you are. I want you to have it. You're a Savage, too. As important as anyone else."

He slides it onto his middle finger and the movement is mesmerizing, and the sheen of the ring the sheen of the ring the sheen of the ring shines in the light and the world swirls.

It swirls

It swirls

It bends

It breaks.

The pieces drift around me and form pictures and I feel I feel I feel like I've been here before.

I stare at Dare, and he's different, he's older. My hand is older, too. Long and slender and strong, as I reach out to touch Dare's face.

"Do you want to turn back, Dare?" I ask, and my voice is flirty, and we're here in Joyland but it's older and dirtier.

"Not on your life." Moonlight shines upon his face, and drenches us, illuminating the dark stubble outlining his jaw.

"Let's do it then." I smile, and my heart is full and we disappear into Nocte.

The darkness swallows us, then blends together, then falls away, and then I'm once again standing in the sun, and Dare is staring at me, confused, bewildered.

"Calla?" There's concern in his voice, and there is no stubble on his clean-shaven face.

I shake my head, shaking all of the confusion away, because it's notrealnotrealnotreal.

"I'm ok," I whisper, but I'm not really. Because sometimes I'm here, and sometimes I'm not.

Keep his ring. It will hold you to the ground, and make you always remember where you are. Eleanor's words echo through my head and I focusfocusfocus on them.

I'm here.

Dare's here.

Yet a minute ago, as real as anything, I wasn't here. I was somewheresomewheresomewhere else.

We go home, back to the funeral home, and the days inch, fly, swirl past. They turn into weeks, and the weeks turn into months, confusing wonderful beautiful months.

Dare spends my birthday with me, then two. He spends Christmas. He spends every day in between. Every day, he becomes more and more unsettled.

Because he's not real.

Because I don't know *what* he is.

"If I could fix everything, I would," I tell him one day as we stand on the cliffs. The wind whips at my hair and I shove it away. Dare stares at me and there's sadness in his eyes.

"I know, Calla Lily."

He's so vulnerable, and sad, and he's seventeen now and I'm fourteen.

I lean up, because I need to kiss him more than anything in the world.

"Kiss me," I whisper, looking hungrily into his eyes. He looks away and the warmth the warmth the warmth. It warms my belly and floods my heart.

"I shouldn't," he answers, low and husky, and he's unsure because he might be a figment of my imagination, or we might be related, and he shouldn't he shouldn't he shouldn't.

148

But he wants to. I can see it see it see it. His eyes are cloudy and tormented.

"Do it anyway," I reply, hoping, praying, holding my breath.

So he does,

He lowers his dark head and his lips press into mine, hard, warm, firm, real.

My first kiss.

Kissing him is like taking a fresh wintry breath. It gives me life, it fills me up, filling all of my darkest, most emptiest places.

"I shouldn't have done that," Dare mutters, yanking away, and I don't want him to leave, but he does it anyway.

He stalks away and I trail behind, my fingers on my lips, still in too much wonder to care that he's regretful. I know why... because I'm fourteen and he's seventeen and he's my cousin and he thinks that creates a chasm.

But it doesn't.

It's not a chasm,

It draws us closer together.

He's mine. He just doesn't know it yet.

After dinner, I find him down at the woodshed, punching at it like a machine.

"Dare, stop!" I plead, holding onto his hands, trying to prevent him from injuring himself further. There is blood on his shirt, blood gushing from his knuckles. His face is so tormented, so pained.

"Do you know what it's like not to be able to change something?" he asks, and his voice is so ragged, so painful to hear that it tears my heart into ripped pieces.

"Of course," I tell him. And I lead him to the Carriage House where I clean up his wounds.

He strips his shirt off and muscle ripples from the top of his back to the bottom, and LIVE FREE is bold and strong. I can't breathe because he's beautiful and warm and vibrant, and he's right here.

So close.

So close

So far away.

He studies me, my face, my eyes. And when he sighs, it's such a lonely sound. "You don't know what it's like," he says and he's resigned. "Not like I do. Because you don't remember everything, but I do."

I open my mouth to reply, but he doesn't allow it.

"I'll be sleeping here in the Carriage House," he tells me. "Instead of in the funeral home. It's for the best. Maybe things aren't going to change after all, this time. Maybe this will always be how it is, and if that's the case, then I just want to let go, Cal."

"Let go?"

He nods and I'm dying dying dying inside, because he can't do that. I need him.

He won't let me argue because he thinks it's the right thing. My soul is crushed, but I leave anyway, because that's what he wants. For now.

But my room is empty and I'm empty and I want nothing more than for him to come back and sleep on my floor where I can wake up in the night and make sure he's safe.

I curl onto my side in my cold sheets, and again, I press my fingers to my lips where his glorious mouth had been just hours ago.

I'd give anything for him to be back. In my room, in this world. Just here.

I fall asleep and my slumber is restless and dark.

The dreams

The dreams

The dreams.

The boy is back, in his hood, and he stands in the middle of the road.

"You weren't supposed to give the ring to him," he tells me. "You were supposed to give it to me. I could've saved them, Calla."

"Saved who?" I demand, but then I know.

"You know who," he nods. "You must change it. You must change it. You must change it so I can have the ring."

Because if I don't, there is water and burning rubber and fire. There is screaming and it's my mother, I think. There's sand, there's a white sheet, there's sobbing, wailing, dying.

My mother's eyes are lifeless

And Finn

Finn

Finn.

A voice is whispering, chanting.

St. Michael the archangel, defend us in battle.

Be our defense against the wickedness and snares of the devil.

May God rebuke him, we humbly pray, and do thou O prince of heavenly hosts,

By the power of God,

Thrust into hell Satan,

And all the evil spirits prowling the world

Seeking the ruin of souls.

Amen.

The wordsthewordsthewords.

Protect me St Michael, Protect me St Michael, Protect me St Michael.

Over and over and over, and I wake, sitting straight up in bed, a sense of loss so profound that I can't stand it. I feel crushed under the weight of it and there's nothing I can do, nothing I can do,

But run to Dare.

I run through the dark house,

Out the door, through the night,

And into the Carriage House.

I leap onto the couch next to him, wrapping the sheet around us both.

He stirs, but he doesn't push me away.

"The nightmares, Dare," I whimper. "Make them stop."

"Shh, little mouse," he says quietly and his arms wrap around my waist, pulling me close. "You're safe now."

But I don't think I am.

I don't think I am.

"I don't want to be alone," I tell him, turning into his chest. He lets me.

"You aren't," he promises. "Not ever."

This can't be my life. It has to change. It has to be normal.

I'm determined to fix it

Fix it

Fix it.

I fall asleep finally, since Dare is so near, and I fall asleep twisting his ring round and round and round, because it is somehow a key, and the boy in the hood wants it, and because of that, because of that...

I know he probably shoudn't have it.

I sleep uneasily,

Restlessly.

And when I wake,

Finn is in the window.

His face is startled,

And he clutches a St. Michael's medallion in his hand.

Protect me, St. Michael.

The voices, the words.... They swirl around me so loudly that I can hardly focus on Finn's horrified face, but I do. I concentrate and look and see him.

Finn looks from me to Dare.

Wait.

To Dare.

To Dare.

Does he see Dare?

I race after my brother, my sheet trailing behind me.

I reach him only when we get to the porch of the house, and my mother is coming out the door.

Finn opens his mouth to say something, but my mother looks at me, at my sheet and at something behind me.

Before I turn, I already know what it is.

Who it is.

Dare.

I'm stunned, floored, because she can see him and Finn can see him and he's real. This is real.

This is real.

The tension snaps around me like a whip and I don't mind because he's real.

"Adair DuBray," my mother snaps, taking the scene in for what it looks like. "How could you have done this? You've ruined everything to seduce my daughter?"

I don't know what to be... appalled, defensive, or grateful that the universe has righted itself and everyone can see Dare.

He's real.

He's real.

I'm not crazy.

But he's *ruined everything?*

"You can see him?" I ask stupidly, and everyone looks at me like I'm insane because I am.

"It's not what you think," he mutters to them, and he doesn't seem confused. He doesn't seem surprised that they can see him at all, and he doesn't seem to be happy with me.

"Then get in here and tell me what it is," my mother snaps. "And I'm calling your father."

"Step-father," Dare corrects, but no one is listening by this point. My mother has already spun around and stalked into the house, presumably to call Richard.

"What is going on?" I ask Dare bewilderedly as we follow my mom and brother.

He glares at me, disgruntled.

"You got drunk last night," he tells me. "That's what. I took care of you, cleaned you up, and now your family thinks I'm some sort of freak who seduced you."

I'm shocked now, completely still.

"I didn't get drunk last night," I say stiltedly. "I've never been drunk. I had a nightmare and didn't want to be alone."

"No," Dare raises an eyebrow. "You were drunk and puking everywhere. Now they all think I'm a sex-crazed guy who has sex with children. Brilliant."

He's pissed and I'm becoming that way because this doesn't make sense and that didn't happen.

"I'm not a child," I snap. "And I wasn't puking last night."

But he's no longer listening.

He follows my mother and takes his proverbial medicine as she hands him the phone. He nods and I can hear the yelling voice from halfway across the room, through the phone. He takes the phone and he paces outside, and I wait wait wait to figure this out.

There will be hell to pay and I know it's my fault, and I don't know why.

What the hell is going on?

Nothing makes sense.

The rest of the day is awful, as my father looks at me in disappointment, and my mother glares at Dare.

"You're going to be on the next flight to London," she tells him. "It leaves in the morning."

He nods and doesn't argue. I do, but no one listens.

"Mom, we can't be separated," I tell her earnestly, as I watch Dare from the window. He disappears into the Carriage House without even turning around. I know he probably feels me watching, but he doesn't check to see. He's on his phone and I don't know who he's talking to, and everything scares me.

The idea of being separated makes my heart pound.

"He understands me," I tell my mother.

"Calla Elizabeth," she turns to me, her face stern. "You are sixteen-years old. I'm your mother. *I* understand you. Dare is going home to Sussex."

Sixteen? I'm fourteen. Aren't I?

I open my mouth.

"But…"

"This is for the best," she interrupts firmly.

I don't want this.

But no one cares, and I seem to have lost a large chunk of time.

After dinner, Finn approaches me. He's dressed in a button-up shirt and his hair is freshly washed.

"What were you thinking?" he asks, and he honestly can't tell. He knows me better than anyone and he believes this nonsense too.

"I didn't sleep with Dare," I tell him. "I wasn't drunk. I don't know what's going on, but it's not what it looks like."

He doesn't believe me, but he doesn't argue.

"I'm going to a concert," he tells me. "I still have your ticket. You're coming right?"

His words.

He says them tiredly, like he's said them a hundred times before.

My memory is murkymurkymurky, but I remember Quid Pro Quo. A concert. I was supposed to go, and I *am* sixteen because we have driver's licenses. But this will be Dare's last night here, and I have to see him. I have to talk to him. I have to fix this.

I shake my head and turn toward the wall. "I'm sorry. I can't."

"Fine," Finn sighs. "I'll go alone. I just don't know what's going on with you, Cal."

"That makes two of us," I snap.

Finn leaves and I'm alone.

Alone is my least favorite thing to be.

"Calla," my mom calls. I find her in the salon downstairs. I approach her carefully and she's stern when she speaks to me.

"I'm going to book club. You will stay here and out of trouble."

My eyes fill with tears and hers soften for a minute and she grasps my hand.

"You'll be fine," she tells me. "There are just things you don't understand."

"I'm so tired of being told that," I answer. "So tired. Just tell me already. Make me understand."

"You can't be with Dare," she says helplessly. "You can't. It could only end in heartbreak for all of us. He'll be your undoing."

"My undoing?"

She looks away, at the floor, out the windows. "The undoing of us all. There is so much about our family that you don't understand, that I don't want you to understand. It's ugly and complex and even tragic. All I need you to know is that I would rather die than let you be with him. That's how important this is. You have to choose your brother, or else all of this will be for nothing."

Her words whirl around me, round and round and round.

I would rather die. Choose my brother?

"But why?" I ask her and I'm limp, and I'm breathless. "Choose Finn how?"

I can't breathe, and I'm scared and my mom sees that.

"Are you all right, Calla?" she asks quickly, and she sits me in a chair and leans me back, rubbing my temples and of course I'm not all right.

"Breathe, my love," she tells me. "Breathe."

She takes a pill from her pocket and gives it to me and I swallow it, and I'm so inexplicably sad.

She stares at me, just stares and stares and stares, and then she holds my hand.

"He's going to die for you, Calla," she finally says and her words are so soft, her voice so thin. "One of them will die for you. You have to choose Finn."

"What?" my voice is a screech and I don't understand. "What do you mean?"

"You'll be given a choice, and you can't fail."

This

Doesn't

Make

Sense.

But I remember Sabine saying the same thing… *you'll have to choose, and don't let anyone tell you otherwise.*

"I don't understand," I tell her. "Why do I have to choose between Finn and Dare?"

"Because I didn't make the right choice," she says weakly. "I chose wrong, and you'll have to pay for my sins, or this will go on and on and on."

"Did Sabine tell you this?" I ask her, "Because Sabine is crazy. That old gypsy stuff isn't real. It can't be."

"I used to believe that," she says, and her face is so sad. "When I was a little girl. But time tells everything, Cal. Time is everything. Once upon a time, in the very beginning, there were two brothers. They were both supposed to offer a sacrifice to God, but only one brother's was accepted. Then, in a jealous fit of rage, his brother killed him. They are our family, Calla. Our blood. We have to make everything right, we have to sacrifice, or this will go on forever."

"This is crazy," I tell her. And I know crazy. "I'm dreaming."

"You're not," she answers simply. "Stay here and rest. I have to take Dare to the airport. You will be fine. I've sacrificed everything to make sure of it."

I feel sick and she leaves, and I sink to the floor and rock, my tears streaming down my face and staining my shirt.

This can't be happening.

"But it is," the voice is back, and before I look, I know who it is.

The hooded boy.

"What is your name?" I demand, and my fingers are shaking.

"I don't have one. I was sacrificed without one."

"Sacrificed by who?"

My breath is coming in pants.

"By my mother. I was sacrificed for my brother, and you shouldn't have given him the ring. I could've prevented all of this."

The world stops and spins and stops again.

"Your brother? You're Dare's brother?"

He nods and he's sad, and he pulls down the hood and he's Dare's identical image.

"It should be Dare," he tells me. "It needs to be Dare. Do not choose your brother."

He tries to pull me to him, to kiss him, but his lips are cold and they feel dead and I yank away in a panic, because touching him takes my energy. It makes my eyes want to close and stay closed.

"You're as cold as death," I manage to say, and he smiles and it chills me.

"I am death," he answers and he's calm. "I'm descended from the Daughter of Death, and it will always be. I'm a son of Salome."

This isn't happening.

His eyes flash black, and I reach for the phone, and I call Dare's number.

"Hello," he says quietly, and he knows that I know.

"Your brother is here," I tell him, and my words are stilted and stiff.

"Run away, Calla," Dare tells me and he is urgent. "Run away."

"I can't," I blurt, and the hooded boy is grabbing me, and I hear my mother shrieking at Dare.

"Good bye, Calla," Dare says, and his voice is soft and it's gentle and it's firm. "Run. Tell him to come get me." Then he's gone, and my phone is dead and I'm desperate so I call my mother, and I know she's in the car with Dare.

"Yes," she sighs into the phone, already knowing that it's me.

"Mom, we have to talk about this," I tell her urgently. "It doesn't make sense. This isn't real."

"Calla, I will do anything for you, and I have. This is a Savage matter, and we don't need to speak of it. What has been put into place will be put into motion and you will be safe."

"But..." my voice is limp and she interrupts me.

"No buts. We've said everything we need to say. I need to go. The rain is bad, and the time is right..." She interrupts her own sentence with a scream.

A shrill, loud, high-pitched shriek. It almost punctures my ear-drums with its intensity and before I can make heads or tails of it, it breaks off mid-way through. And I realize that I heard something else in the background.

The sound of metal and glass being crunched and broken.

Then nothing.

"Mom?"

There's no answer, only loaded pregnant silence.

My hands shake as I wait for what seems like an eternity, but is actually only a second.

"Mom?" I demand, scared now.

Still nothing.

Then

A

Whisper.

"Oh, God. *Finn.*"

It's my mother.

Her voice is hoarse and cracked and terrified and weak.

"My baby. What have I done?" Before the phone goes dead, before I can ask, she screams a haunting, shrieking wail, the torment of a mother.

"Finnnnnnnnnnnnnnn!"

The line goes dead

And my heart goes dead

Because

FINN.

FINN.

FINN.

Chills run up and down my back, and goose-bumps form on my arms because somethingsomethingsomething terrible has happened to my brother.

My other half.

My heart.

I feel it.

Chapter Fourteen

I know it in my heart as I race out to the porch, as I stare at the smoke winding its way into the night sky, just a little ways down the mountain.

Finn is down there. I know it.

I know it

I know it.

I know it as I sink to a heap on the steps, gripping the phone.

I know it as I try to breathe and can't.

I know it as Dare limps across the lawn, his forehead bloody.

I know it as he stands in front of me, battered and raw.

"Calla?" he whispers, his hand on my shoulder.

There's blood on his fingers.

"Calla?"

I somehow manage to move my head, to look up at the boy I love, the man I hate, the man I'm afraid of now. I don't know why, I just know I do. All of these emotions swirl in me and I don't know where they're coming from and it doesn't matter right now. Only one thing matters.

"Where's Finn?" my lips move.

Dare stares at me, his dark eyes guarded and urgent.

"We've got to call an ambulance."

I'm frozen, so Dare grabs my phone and punches at the numbers, crimson blood staining the keys.

His voice blends into the night as he speaks to the dispatcher, but one phrase penetrates the fog of my consciousness.

"There's been an accident."

I wait for him to finish, I wait as he calls my father, I wait until he hangs up and stares down at me before I finally speak.

"Was it?" I ask him, my voice shaking and frail and thin. "Was it an accident?"

He closes his eyes.

I close mine too.

Because I know it wasn't.

I know my mother killed my brother.

And it wasn't an accident.

Dare sees it in my eyes, he knows that I know, and I hear his phone drop to the porch, and I hear it shatter.

Just

Like

My

Heart.

Chapter Fifteen

The world is black
   The world is punishing
   The world is mine
   The world is black
   The world is punishing
   The world is mine
   It's mine
   It's mine
   It's mine.
   Forgive me, St. Michael
   Protect me, St. Michael.
   Forgive me forgive me forgive me.
   The world is a dark dark tunnel.
   It's swirling and falling and crushing and
   Forgive me, St. Michael.
   I'll do anything to save my brother.
   Words from somewhere, words I've seen before,
float into my head, in Finn's scrawling writing.
   Serva me, servabo te.
   Save me, and I'll save you.
   Save me, Calla.
   Save me.

Chapter Sixteen

"He's gone, honey."

I open my eyes and I'm staring at the wall, my phone in my hand. The darkness is gone, and I can see, and Dare's arms are wrapped around my shoulder, holding me up. He's not bloody now. His shirt is clean as new.

My dad stares at me, and he's shocked, and how did he get here?

"Calla?"

I turn my face to look at him, but looking at him makes it feel too real, so I close my eyes instead.

I can't do this.

"Calla, they found Finn's car. It's in the bay. He drove off the edge... your mom was in the ravine, but Finn's car plunged the opposite way. Down the rocks, into the water."

No, it didn't.

He couldn't have.

"No," I say clearly, staring at my father dazed. "He was wearing his medallion. He was protected."

My father, the strongest man I know, turns away and his shoulders shake. After minutes, he turns back.

"I want to see," I tell him emptily. "If it's true, I need to see."

Because he's died before in my dreams, and then he was alive. I never know never know never know when I'm crazy.

My father is already shaking his head, his hand on my arm. "No. Your mother is on her way to the hospital. We have to go. You can't see Finn like this, sweetie. No."

"Yes."

I don't wait for him to agree, I just bolt from the house, down the steps, down the paths, to the beach. I hear Dare behind me, but I don't stop. There are firemen and police and police tape and EMTs congregated about, and one of them tries to stop me.

"Miss, no," he says, his voice serious, his face aghast. "You can't go over there."

But I yank away because I see Finn.

I see his red smashed car that they've already pulled from the water.

I see someone laid out on the sand, someone covered by a sheet.

I walk toward that someone calmly, because even though it's Finn's car, it can't be Finn. It can't be because he's my twin, and because I didn't feel it happen. I would've known, wouldn't I?

Dare calls to me, through thick fog, but I don't answer.

I take a step.

Then another.

Then another.

Then I'm kneeling in the sand, next to a sheet.

My fingers shake.

My heart trembles.

And I pull the white fabric away.

He's dressed in jeans and a button-up, clothing for a concert. He's pale, he's skinny, he's long. He's frail, he's cold, he's dead.

He's Finn.

I can't breathe as I hold his wet hand, as I hunch over him and cry and try to breathe and try to speak.

He doesn't look like he was in a crash. There's a bruise on his forehead and that's it. He's just so white, so very very white.

"Please," I beg him. "No. Not today. No."

I'm rocking and I feel hands on me, but I shake them away, because this is Finn. And we're Calla and Finn. He's part of me and I'm part of him and this can't be happening.

I cry so hard that my chest hurts with it, my throat grows raw and I gulp to breathe.

"I love you," I tell him when I can breathe again. "I'm sorry I wasn't with you. I'm sorry I couldn't save you. I'm sorry. I'm sorry."

I'm still crying when large hands cup my shoulders and lift me from the ground, and I'm pulled into strong arms.

"Shhh, Calla," my dad murmurs. "It'll be okay. He knew you loved him."

"Did he?" I ask harshly, pulling away to look at my father. "Because he wanted me to go with him, and I made him go alone. And now he's dead. I called mom and they're both dead."

Dad pulls me back into his arms and pats my back, showing a tenderness that I didn't know he possessed. "It's not your fault," he tells me between wracking sobs. "He chose this. He knew you loved him, honey. Everyone knew."

I choke back another gasping sob, because how could he have chosen this? My mother killed him on purpose. I feel it in my bones in my bones in my bones.

This can't be happening.

This can't be happening.

This isn't my life.

I shake off my father's arms and walk woodenly back up the trails, past the paramedics, past the police, past everyone who is staring at me. I walk straight up to Finn's room and collapse onto his bed.

Out of the corner of my eye, I see his journal.

I pick it up, reading the familiar handwriting written by the hands that I love so much.

Serva me, servabo te.

Save me, and I will save you.

Ok.

Ok, Finn.

I close my eyes because when I wake up tomorrow, I'll find that this was all a dream. This is a nightmare. It has to be.

Sleep comes quickly and when I wake up, I'll save Finn.

Because really, he's all that matters.

If he's dead, I want to be dead.

He can't be dead.

I'll give anything for him.

I'd give my life.

"You could," the hooded boy says, and he's here on the edge of my bed. "You could give your life. You could jump, you could sacrifice yourself, and then it would all be over. Or… you could offer your mother instead."

"What?" I ask stiffly.

"You heard me. You've heard me all along. You have the power to change it. You always have, and you always do. Change it to the way it should be. Do it."

I'm appalled, I'm frozen, I'm filled with dread, because I would rather. I would rather give anything than my brother.

I fall asleep with the sheets wrapped like a rope around my hands, and I dream the dreams of the tormented.

Chapter Seventeen

I dream.

I dream of Sabine and her raspy voice, and of words that she said to me.

"You must choose," she'd said, and she says it now in my dream and I don't know what she wants me to do.

So I ask her.

"You know," she nods.

But I don't.

She nods again, and all I know is that if I could choose anythinganythinganything in the world, it would be for my brother to be with me, to be alive. I'd give anything.

"Anything?" Sabine asks, and I nod.

"Anything." My answer is firm.

Sabine nods once more, and light streams in my window, and into my eyes as I open them.

I'm fine for a minute, until I remember.

Finn.

I close my eyes again, and the heavyheavyweight presses on my lungs again, and I can't breathe, and I don't want to.

I trudge down the hall to my brother's room and I stand in front of the door.

I stare at the wood, at the grain, at the indention, at the handle. I don't want to open it because I know what I'll find.

But I have to. I have to see it.

Reaching down, I turn the knob.

The door creaks open, revealing what my heart knew I'd find.

An empty room.

The bed is still there, neatly made. Finn's posters are still on the wall, of Quid Quo Pro and the Cure. His black Converses sit next to the door, like he's going to wear them again, but he's not. His dirty laundry is still in his hamper. His books line the shelves. His favorite pillow waits for him, his CDs, his phone. All of it.

But he's not coming back.

I grab his shoes, his smelly boy shoes and I clutch them to my chest and I sink into his smelly boy bed and I'm numb. I stare at the wall without seeing it, at the posters without registering the faces. I'm wood, I'm stone, I'm brick. I don't feel. I don't feel. Nothing can hurt me.

I'm like this for a while, until

Little

By

Little,

Sounds begin to filter into my consciousness, and there's water. Running water, and I feel dew-like condensation on my skin, and for a second, I'm annoyed because Finn knows to turn on the exhaust fan when he showers, but he always forgets.

Wait.

My head yanks up as Finn's bathroom door opens and he sticks his wet head out.

"Calla! What are you doing in here? And why do you have my shoes?"

I faint.

Or I think I faint.

When I open my eyes again, Finn is holding my hand.

"Are you ok?" he asks, and his blue eyes are worried.

"Yeah," I manage to say, once I'm over the shock of being seated next to my dead but now alive brother. "I think so."

Mybrotherisalive

Mybrotherisalive

He's alive.

He's holding my hand.

I shake my head and try to drive the nonsense out, and suddenly, everything is clear for the first time in a long long time. I can think without murk, without voices.

What the hell?

Sabine's words come back to me *You have to choose, You have to choose.*

Last night before bed, I'd chosen Finn, over anything, over my own life.

Did I do this?

It's not possible.

Did I do this?

Finn looks at me. "Why aren't you dressed? You've got to go get ready."

"For?" I arch an eyebrow.

He's quiet and still, I remember the accident, and a heavy sense of foreboding slams into me right before he answers.

"For mom's funeral."

Oh.

God.

My mother is dead and my memory has holes.

I somehow trip down to my room and put on a black dress, and I somehow trip down the stairs with my brother and sit in the family section of the chapel, and my dad holds my hand.

The casket is white and there are star-gazers on it, and the lid is closed.

Someone reads a poem, then another.

Someone else speaks about angels and Heaven.

My dad cries silently.

Finn is stoic, and grips my arm.

I'm numb.

Because I thought mom was in the hospital and Finn was dead.

Only Finn is here and mom is dead.

You

Have

To

Choose.

Reality isn't real.

Like always.

The music plays as they roll the casket out, down the long aisle, as if my mother is on parade, her last parade.

We stand and the funeral-goers file past us, one by one by one.

I'm sorry for your loss.

Heaven has gained another angel.

If you need anything, just call.

All trite words from people who don't know what else to say.

And then someone new stands in front of me. His eyes are dark, his hair is dark, his body is lean. He's wearing a black suit just like all of them, but he's wearing a silver ring, and it gleams in the sunlight, and something something something ripples through me, but I don't know what it is.

"I'm so sorry," he tells me, and he's got a British accent.

I feel the strangest feeling in the pit of my stomach as he shakes my hand, as he touches me and there's electricity, but I brush it away because I don't know him and he doesn't matter. Only Finn matters. And mourning my poor mother.

The stranger passes through the line and I turn to the next visitor, and the next and the next and the next.

The day is exhausting.

The day is never-ending.

I lean my head on the family car window as we drive home from the cemetery. We're surrounded by all things green and alive, by pine trees and bracken and lush forest greenery. The vibrant green stretches across the vast lawns, through the flowered gardens, and lasts right up until you get to the cliffs, where it finally and abruptly turns reddish and clay.

I guess that's pretty good symbolism, actually. Green means alive and red means dangerous. Red is jagged cliffs, warning lights, splattered blood. But green... green is trees and apples and clover.

"How do you say green in Latin?" I ask Finn absently.

"Viridem," he answers.

And then something else occurs to me, something out of the blue.

"What does Quid Pro Quo mean?"

Finn stares at me. "It means *something for something*. Why?"

"No reason," I answer, but my heart is pound, pound, pounding. Over and over. Because something for something. Did I give something to get something?

ThumpThump,ThumpThump.

I trudge up to my room and drop into bed without even showering.

I feel a thousand pounds of guilt on my chest because I only have one thought, one thought that makes my chest tighten and constrict and pound.

I love my mom,

I love my mom

I love my mom.

But thank God it wasn't Finn.

Quid pro quo.

Chapter Eighteen

I wait at the hospital for Finn to get out of Group, for him to converse and compare with the other patients who have SAD. Because for whatever reason, his thoughts are muddled now, not mine.

It's nothing I can explain,

It's nothing I can understand.

Ever since I thought he died, ever since we buried my mom, Finn's mind has deteriorated, and mine has strengthened.

I don't know why.

I'm just thankful that he's alive.

So while I wait for him, because I'd drive him here every day for the rest of my life in gratitude that he's alive, I read my book, I listen to my music, I close my eyes.

It's how I can ignore the shrill, multi-pitched yells that drift down the hallways. Because honestly, I don't want to know what they're yelling about.

I stay suspended in my pretend world for God knows how long, until I feel someone staring at me.

When I say feel, I *literally feel it,* just like someone is reaching out and touching my face with their fingers.

Glancing up, I suck my breath in when I find dark eyes connected to mine, eyes so dark they're almost black, and the energy in them is enough to freeze me in place.

A boy is attached to the dark gaze.

A man.

He's probably no more than twenty or twenty-one, but everything about him screams *man*. There's no *boy* in him. That part of him is very clearly gone. I see it in his eyes, in the way he holds himself, in the perceptive way he takes in his surroundings, then stares at me with singular focus, like we're somehow connected by a tether. He's got a million contradictions in his eyes…aloofness, warmth, mystery, charm, and something else I can't define.

He's muscular, tall, and wearing a tattered black sweatshirt that says *Irony is lost on you* in orange letters. His dark jeans are belted with black leather, and a silver band encircles his middle finger.

Dark hair tumbles into his face and a hand with long fingers impatiently brushes it back, all the while his eyes are still connected with mine. His jaw is strong and masculine, with the barest hint of stubble.

His gaze is still connected to mine, like a livewire, or a lightning bolt. I can feel the charge of it racing along my skin, like a million tiny fingers, flushing my cheeks. My lungs flutter and I swallow hard.

And then, he smiles at me.

At me.

Because I don't know him and he doesn't know better.

"Cal? You ready?"

Finn's voice breaks my concentration, and with it, the moment. I glance up at my brother, almost in confusion, to find that he's waiting for me. The hour has already passed and I didn't even realize it. I scramble to get up, feeling for all the world like I'm rattled, but don't know why.

Although I do know.

As I walk away with Finn, I glance over my shoulder.

The sexy stranger with the dark, dark gaze is gone.

I fight the feeling, the very strange feeling, that I've seen him before. There's no way that's possible.

There's no way I could forget someone like him.

But still.

There's something

Something

Something.

***

A week later, I take my brother to Group again. When we're inside, Finn turns to me before he slips into his room.

"There *is* a grief group. You should check it out."

"Now you sound like dad," I tell him impatiently. "I don't need to talk to them. I have you. No one understands like you."

He nods, *because no one understands like him.* And then he disappears into the place where he draws his strength, around people who suffer just like him.

I try not to feel inadequate that they can help him in ways that I can't.

Instead, I curl up on my bench beneath the abstract bird. I pop earbuds in my ears and close my eyes. I forgot my book today, so disappearing into music will have to do.

I concentrate on feeling the music rather than hearing it. I feel the vibration, I feel the words. I feel the beat. I feel the voices. I feel the emotion.

Someone else's emotion other than my own is always a good thing.

The minutes pass, one after the other.

And then after twenty of them, *he* approaches.

Him.

The sexy stranger with eyes as black as night.

I feel him approach while my eyes are still closed. Don't ask me how I know it's him, because I just know. Don't ask me what he's doing here again, because I don't care about that.

All I care about is the fact that he *is* here.

My eyes pop open to find him watching me, his eyes still as intense now as they were the other day. Still as dark, still as bottomless.

His gaze finds mine, connects with it, and holds.

We're connected.

With each step, he doesn't look away.

He's dressed in the same sweatshirt as the other day. *Irony is lost on you.* He's wearing dark jeans, black boots and his middle finger is still encircled by a silver band. He's a rocker. Or an artist. Or a writer. He's something hopelessly in style, timelessly romantic.

He's twenty feet away.

Fifteen.

Ten.

Five.

The corner of his mouth tilts up as he passes, as he continues to watch me from the side. His shoulders sway, his hips are slim. Then he's gone, walking away from me.

Five feet.

Ten.

Twenty.

Gone.

I feel a sense of loss because he didn't stop. Because I wanted him to. Because there's something about him that I want to know.

There's something about him that I feel like I *do* know.

I take a deep breath and close my eyes, listening once again to my music.

The dark haired stranger doesn't come back.

***

The rain might make Oregon beautiful, but at times, it's gray and dismal. The sound of it hitting the windows makes me sleepy, and I itch to wrap up in a sweater and curl up with a book by the window. At night, when it storms, I dream. I don't know why. It might be the electricity of the lightning in the air, or the boom of the thunder, but it never fails to trigger my mind to create.

Tonight, after finally falling asleep, I dream of *him.*

The dark-eyed stranger.

He sits by the ocean, the breeze ruffling his hair. He lifts his hand to brush his hair out of his eyes, his silver ring glinting in the sun.

His eyes meet mine, and electricity stronger than a million lightning bolts connects us, holding us together.

His eyes crinkle a bit at the corners as he smiles at me.

His grin is for me, familiar and sexy. He reaches for me, his fingers knowing and familiar, and he knows just where to touch me, just where to set my skin on fire.

I wake with a start, sitting straight up in bed, my sheets clutched to my chest.

185

The moonlight pouring onto my bed looks blue, and I glance at the clock.

Three a.m.

Just a dream.

I curl back up, thinking of the stranger, and then curse myself for my ridiculousness. He's a stranger, for God's sake. It's stupid to be so fixated on him.

But that doesn't stop me from dreaming about him again. He does different things in my dreams. He sails, he swims, he drinks coffee. His silver ring glints in the sun each time, his dark eyes pierce into my soul like he knows me. *Like he knows all about me.* I wake up breathless each time.

It's a bit unnerving.

And a bit exciting.

After two such nights of fitful sleep, rain and strange dreams, Finn and I kneel in front of plastic storage boxes, sorting through stuff from my closet. Piles of folded clothes surround us, like mountains on the floor. Rain pelts the window, the morning sky dark and gray.

I hold up a white cardigan. "I don't think I'll need many sweaters in California, will I?"

Finn shakes his head. "Doubtful. But take a couple, just to be safe."

I toss it into the Keep pile. As I do, I notice that Finn's fingers are shaking.

"Why are your hands shaking?" I stare at him. He shrugs.

186

"I don't know. Do you feel like we've been here before? In this same time and exact place? Is your heart ok? Have you had chest pains?"

I'm alarmed because what new craziness is this?

"My heart is fine," I tell him firmly. "I'm fine, Finn."

He eyes me doubtfully and then presses his ear to my chest and listens and my heart beats and beats and finally he's satisfied. I'm so used to odd behavior from him, but this is very strange.

"Finn, are you ok?"

He nods. "Quite positive. It's just déjà vu, I guess."

I let it go, even though it makes me uneasy. If I don't shield Finn from distress, he could have an episode. Obviously, I couldn't shield him from losing mom, but I do my best to protect him from everything else. It's a heavy thing to shoulder, but if Finn can carry his cross, I can certainly carry mine. I unfold another sweater, then toss it in the Goodwill pile.

"After mine, we'll have to do yours," I point out. He nods.

"Yeah. And then maybe we should do mom's."

I suck in a breath. While I would like nothing more, just in the name of moving forward, there's no way.

"Dad would kill us," I dismiss the idea.

"True," Finn acknowledges, handing me a long sleeve t-shirt for the Keep pile. "But maybe he needs a nudge. It's been two months. She doesn't need her shoes by the backdoor anymore."

He's right. She doesn't need them. Just like she doesn't need her make-up laid out by her sink the way she left it, or her last book sitting face down to mark its page beside her reading chair. She'll never finish that book. But to be fair to my dad, I don't think I could throw her things out yet, either.

"Still," I answer. "It's his place to decide when it's time. Not ours. We're going away. He's the one who will be here with the memories. Not us."

"That's why I'm worried," Finn tells me. "He's going to be here in this huge house alone. Well, not alone. Surrounded by dead bodies and mom's memory. That's even worse."

Knowing how I hate to be alone, and how I especially hate to be alone in our big house, I shudder.

"Maybe that's why he wants to rent out the Carriage House," I offer. "So he's not so alone up here."

"Maybe."

Finn reaches over and flips on some music, and I let the thumping bass fill the silence while we sort through my clothes. Usually, our silence is comfortable and we don't need to fill it. But today, I feel unsettled. Tense. Anxious.

"Have you been writing lately?" I ask to make small-talk. He's always scribbling in his journal. And even though I'm the one who'd gotten it for him for

Christmas a couple of years ago, he won't let me read it. Not since he showed it to me one time and I'd freaked out.

"Of course."

Of course. It's pretty much all he does. Poems, Latin, nonsense... you name it, he writes it.

"Can I read any of it yet?"

"No."

His answer is definite and firm.

"Ok." I don't argue with that tone of voice, because, honestly, I'm a bit nervous to see what's in there anyway. But he does pause and turn to me.

"I don't think I ever said thank you for not running to mom and dad. When you read it that one time, I mean. It's just my outlet, Cal. It doesn't mean anything."

His blue eyes pierce me, straight into my soul. Because I know I probably *should've* gone to them. And I probably would've, if mom hadn't died. But I didn't, and everything has been fine since then.

Fine. If I think hard enough on that word, then it will be true.

"You're welcome," I say softly, trying not to think of the gibberish I'd read, the scary words, the scary thoughts, scribbled and crossed out, and scrawled again. Over and over. Out of all of it, though, one thing stood out as most troubling. One phrase. It wasn't the odd sketches of people with their eyes and faces and mouths scratched out, it wasn't the odd and dark poems, it was one phrase.

Put me out of my misery.

Scrawled over and over, filling up two complete pages. I've watched him like a hawk ever since. He smiles now, encouraging me to forget it, like it's just his outlet. He's fine now. *He's fine.* If I had a journal, I'd scrawl *that* on the pages, over and over, to make it true.

"Hey, I'm going to go to Group again today. Do you want to come with? If not, I can go myself."

This startles me. He normally only goes twice a week. Have I missed something? Is he worse? Is he slipping? I fight to keep my voice casual.

"Again? Why?"

He shrugs, like it's no big deal, but his hands are still shaking.

"I dunno. I think it's all the change. It makes me feel antsy."

And shaky? I don't ask that though. Instead, I just nod, like I'm not at all freaked out. "Of course I'll go."

Of course, because he needs me.

An hour later, we've walked down the hallways filled with our mother's pictures, past her bedroom filled with her clothes, and are driving to town in the car she bought us. We both pointedly avoid looking at the place where she plunged over the side of the mountain. We don't need to see it again.

Our mother is still all around us. Everywhere. Yet nowhere. Not really.

It's enough to drive the sanest person mad. No wonder Finn wants extra therapy.

I leave him in front of his Group room, and watch him disappear inside.

I take my book to the café today for a cup of coffee. I've grown accustomed to the rain making me sleepy since I've lived in Astoria all my life. But I've also learned that caffeine is an effective Band-Aid.

I grab my cup and head to the back, slumping into a booth, prepared to bury my nose in my book.

I'm just opening the cover when I feel him.

I *feel* him.

Again.

Before I even look up, I know it's *him*. I recognize the feel in the air, the very palpable energy. I felt the same thing in my dreams, this impossible pull. What the hell? Why do I keep bumping into him?

When I look up, I find that he's seen me, too.

His eyes are frozen on me as he waits in line, so dark, so fathomless. This energy between us... I don't know what it is. Attraction? Chemistry? All I know is, it steals my breath and speeds up my heart. The fact that he's invading my dreams makes me crave this feeling even more. It brings me out of my reality and into something new and exciting, into something that has hope and life.

I watch as he pays for his coffee and sweet roll, and as his every step leads him to my back booth. There are ten other tables, all vacant, but he chooses mine.

His black boots stop next to me, and I skim up his denim-clad legs, over his hips, up to his startlingly handsome face. He still hasn't shaved, so his stubble is more pronounced today. It makes him seem even more mature, even more of a man. As if he needs the help.

I can't help but notice the way his soft blue shirt hugs his solid chest, the way his waist narrows as it slips into his jeans, the way he seems lean and lithe and powerful. Gah. I yank my eyes up to meet his. I find amusement there.

"Is this seat taken?"

Sweet Lord. He's got a British accent. There's nothing sexier in the entire world, which makes that old tired pick-up line forgivable. I smile up at him, my heart racing.

"No."

He doesn't move. "Can I take it, then? I'll share my breakfast with you."

He slightly gestures with his gooey, pecan-crusted roll.

"Sure," I answer casually, expertly hiding the fact that my heart is racing fast enough to explode. "But I'll pass on the breakfast. I'm allergic to nuts."

"More for me, then," he grins, as he slides into the booth across from me, ever so casually, as though he sits with strange girls in hospitals all of the time. I can't help but notice that his eyes are so dark they're almost black.

"Come here often?" he quips, as he sprawls out in the booth. I have to chuckle, because now he's just going down the list of cliché lines, and they all sound amazing coming from his British lips.

"Fairly," I nod. "You?"

"They have the best coffee around," he answers, if that even *is* an answer. "But let's not tell anyone, or they'll start naming the coffee things we can't pronounce, and the lines will get unbearable."

I shake my head, and I can't help but smile. "Fine. It'll be our secret."

He stares at me, his dark eyes shining. "Good. I like secrets. Everyone's got 'em."

I almost suck in my breath, because something is so overtly fascinating about him. The way he pronounces everything, and the way his dark eyes gleam, the way he seems so familiar because he's been in the intimacy of my dreams.

"What are yours?" I ask, without thinking. "Your secrets, I mean."

He grins. "Wouldn't *you* like to know?"

Yes.

"My name's Calla," I offer quickly. He smiles at that.

"Calla like the funeral lily?"

The very same." I sigh. "And I live in a funeral home. So see? The irony isn't lost on me."

He looks confused for a second, then I see the realization dawn on him.

"You noticed my shirt yesterday," he points out softly, his arm stretched across the back of the cracked booth. He doesn't even dwell on the fact that I'd just told him I live in a house with dead people. Usually people instantly clam up when they find out, because they instantly assume that I must be weird, or morbid. But he doesn't.

I nod curtly. "I don't know why. It just stood out." *Because* you *stood out.*

The corner of his mouth twitches, like he's going to smile, but then he doesn't.

"I'm Adair DuBray," he tells me, like he's bestowing a gift or an honor. "But everyone calls me Dare."

I've never seen a name so fitting. So French, so sophisticated, yet his accent is British. He's an enigma. An enigma whose eyes gleam like they're constantly saying *Dare me.* I swallow.

"It's nice to meet you, Dare," I tell him, and that's the truth. His name rolls off my tongue like I've said it a thousand times before. "Why are you here in the hospital? Surely it's not for the coffee."

"You know what game I like to play?" Dare asks, completely changing the subject. I feel my mouth drop open a bit, but I manage to answer.

"No, what?"

"Twenty Questions. That way, I know that at the end of the game, there won't be any more. Questions, that is."

I have to smile, even though his answer should've annoyed me. "So you don't like talking about yourself."

He grins. "It's my least favorite subject."

But it must be such an interesting one.

"So, you're telling me I can ask you twenty things, and twenty things only?"

Dare nods. "Now you're getting it."

"Fine. I'll use my first question to ask what you're doing here." I lift my chin and stare him in the eye.

His mouth twitches again. "Probably the same thing as you. Isn't that what normal people do in hospitals?"

I flush. I can't help it. Obviously. And obviously, I'm out of my league here. This guy could have me for breakfast if he wanted, and from the gleam in his eye, I'm not so sure he doesn't.

I take a sip of my coffee, careful not to slosh it on my shirt. With the way my heart is racing, anything is possible.

"Was I right? Why *are* you here?" Dare asks.

195

"Is that your first question? Because turn-about is fair play."

Dare smiles broadly, genuinely amused.

"Sure. I'll use a question."

"I brought my brother. He's here for... group therapy."

I suddenly feel weird saying that aloud, because it makes my brother sound *less than* somehow. And he's not. He's *more than*. Better than most people, more gentle, more pure of heart. But a stranger wouldn't know that. A stranger would just slap him with a *crazy* label and let it be. I fight the urge to explain, and somehow manage not to. It's not a stranger's business.

Dare doesn't question me, though. He just nods like it's the most normal thing in the world.

He takes a drink of his coffee. "I think it's probably kismet, anyway. That you and I are here at the same time, I mean."

"Kismet?" I raise an eyebrow.

"That's fate, Calla," he tells me. I roll my eyes.

"I know that. I may be going to a state school, but I'm not stupid."

He grins, a grin so white and charming that my panties almost fall off.

"Good to know. So you're a college girl, Calla?"

I don't want to talk about that. I want to talk about why you think this is kismet. But I nod.

"Yeah. I'm leaving for Berkeley in the fall."

"Good choice," he takes another sip. "But maybe kismet got it wrong, after all. If you're leaving and all. Because apparently, I'll be staying for a while. That is, after I find an apartment. A good one is hard to find around here."

He's so confident, so open. It doesn't even feel odd that a total stranger is telling me these things, out of the blue, so randomly. I feel like I know him already, actually.

I stare at him. "An apartment?"

He stares back. "Yeah. The thing you rent, it has a shower and a bedroom, usually?"

I flush. "I know that. It's just that this might be kismet after all. I might know of something. I mean, my father is going to rent out our carriage house. I think."

And if *I* can't have it, it should definitely go to someone like Dare. The mere thought gives me a heart spasm.

"Hmm. Now that *is* interesting," Dare tells me. "Kismet prevails, it seems. And a carriage house next to a funeral home, at that. It must take balls of steel to live there."

I quickly pull out a little piece of paper and scribble my dad's cell phone on it. "Yeah. If you're interested, I mean, if you've got the balls, you can call and talk to him about it."

I push the paper across the table, staring him in the eye, framing it up as a challenge. Dare can't possibly know how I'm trying to will my heart to slow down before it explodes, but maybe he does, because a smile stretches slowly and knowingly across his lips.

"Oh, I've got balls," he confirms, his eyes gleaming again.

Dare me.

I swallow hard.

"I'm ready to ask my second question," I tell him. He raises an eyebrow.

"Already? Is it about my balls?"

I flush and shake my head.

"What did you mean before?" I ask him slowly, not lowering my gaze. "Why exactly do you think this is kismet?"

His eyes crinkle up a little bit as he smiles yet again. And yet again, his grin is thoroughly amused. A real smile, not a fake one like I'm accustomed to around my house.

"It's kismet because you seem like someone I might like to know. Is that odd?"

No, because I want to know you, too.

"Maybe," I say instead. "Is it odd that I feel like I already know you somehow?"

Because I do. There's something so familiar about his eyes, so dark, so bottomless. But then again, I *have* been dreaming about them for days.

Dare raises an eyebrow. "Maybe I have that kind of face."

I choke back a snort. *Hardly.*

He stares at me. "Regardless, kismet always prevails."

I shake my head and smile. A r*eal* smile. "The jury is still out on that one."

Dare takes a last drink of coffee, his gaze still frozen to mine, before he thunks his cup down on the table and stands up.

"Well, let me know what the jury decides."

And then he walks away.

I'm so dazed by his abrupt departure that it takes me a second to realize something because *kismet always prevails* and I'm *someone he might like to know.*

He took my dad's phone number with him.

Chapter Nineteen

Time swirls and twirls and twists as it goes.

It's tenuous, it's sharp, it's complex.

Adair DuBray does rent the Carriage House, and he's elusive, and he's mysterious and every day, I want to know him more.

Every day, I feel more like I know him already.

Every night, I dream about him, growing closer and closer to him.

A month passes, and one night, we stand at my favorite place, the blue tidal pools, and stare at the stars.

Dare points upward.

"That's Orion's belt. And that over there.... That's Andromeda. I don't think we can see Perseus tonight." He pauses and stares down at me. "Do you know their myth?"

His voice is calm and soothing and as I listen to him, I let myself drift away from my current problems and toward him, toward his dark eyes and full lips and long hands.

I nod, remembering what I'd learned about Andromeda last year in Astrology. "Yes.

Andromeda's mother insulted Poseidon, and she was condemned to die by a sea monster, but Perseus saved her and then married her."

He nods, pleased by my answer. "Yes. And now they linger in the skies to remind young lovers everywhere of the merits of undying love."

I snort. "Yeah. And then they had a corny movie made for them that managed to butcher several different Greek myths at once."

Dare's lip twitches. "Perhaps. But maybe we can overlook that due to the underlying message of eternal love." His expression is droll and I can't decide if he's being serious or just trying to be ironic or something, because *the irony is lost on you.*

"That's bullshit, you know," I tell him, rolling the metaphorical dice. "Undying love, I mean. Nothing is undying. People fall out of love or their chemistry dies or maybe they even die themselves. Any way you look at it, love always dies eventually."

I should know. I'm Funeral Home Girl. I see it all the time.

Dare looks down at me incredulously. "If you truly believe that, then you believe that death controls us, or maybe even circumstance. That's depressing, Calla. We control ourselves."

He seems truly bothered and I stare at him, at once nervous that I've disappointed him and certain that I'm right.

I *am* the one surrounded by it all the time, after all…by death and bad circumstances. I *am* the one whose mother just died and I know that the world continues to turn like nothing ever happened.

"I don't necessarily believe that death controls us," I amend carefully. "But you can't argue that it wins in the long run. Every time. Because we all die, Dare. So death wins, not love."

He snorts. "Tell that to Perseus and Andromeda. They're immortal in the sky."

I snort right back. "They're also not real."

Dare stares at me, willing me to see his point of view and I'm suddenly confused about how we started out talking about love and are now talking about death. Leave it to me to work that into conversation.

"I'm sorry," I offer. "I guess it's a hazard of living where I do. Death is always present."

"Death is big," Dare acknowledges. "But there are things bigger than that. If there aren't, then this is all for nothing. Life is worth nothing. Putting yourself out there, and taking chances and all that. All of that stuff is bollocks if it can just disappear in the end."

I shrug and look away. "I'm sorry. I just believe in the right here and right now. That's what we know and that's what we can count on. And I don't like to think about the end."

Dare looks back at the sky, but he's still pensive. "You seem rather pessimistic today, Calla-Lily."

I swallow hard, because I do sound like a shrew. A jaded, ugly, bitter person.

"My mom died a few weeks ago," I tell him and the words scrape my heart. "It's still hard to talk about."

He pauses and nods, as though everything makes sense now, as though he's *sorry* because everyone always is. "Ah. I see. I'm sorry. I know how that feels. My mom is gone too."

I shake my head and look away because my eyes are watering and it's embarrassing. Because God. Am I ever going to be able to think about it without crying?

"It's ok. You didn't know," I answer. "And you're right. I'm probably jaded. Being surrounded by death all the time... well, I guess it's made me ugly."

Dare studies me, hard, his eyes glittering in the light of the driftwood fire which reflects purple flames into his black bottomless depths.

"You're not ugly," he tells me, his voice oh-so-beautiful. "Not by a long, long shot."

His words make me lose my train of thought. Because of the way he's looking at me right now... *like I'm beautiful,* like he knows me, when I'm really just Calla and he doesn't.

"I'm sorry I'm so emotional tonight," I tell him. "I'm not usually like this. It's just... there's a lot going on."

203

"I see that," he answers quietly. "Is there anything I can do?"

You can call me Calla-Lily again. Because it seems intimate and familiar, and it makes me feel good. But I shake my head. "I wish. But no."

He smiles. "Ok. Can I walk you back up to the house at least?"

My heart leaps for a second, but the idea of facing Finn right now isn't one I enjoy. So I shake my head.

"I'm not really ready to go back yet," I tell him regretfully. Because it's the truth.

He shrugs. "Okay. I'll wait."

My heart thunders in my ears as I pretend that I'm not thrilled with that.

"Have you heard the myth of the Gemini?" he asks. "Castor and Pollux were twins, and when Castor died, Pollux was so devastated that he asked Zeus if he could share his immortality with his brother. Zeus turned them into stars, and now they live forever as a constellation. We can't see it right now, so you'll have to trust me."

"Are you telling me this because I'm a twin?" I ask, my eyebrow lifted. He shrugs.

"Not really. I can tell just by looking at you and your brother that you'd do anything for each other. I'd expect nothing less out of you than to become a star for him."

He smiles and I shake my head because he has *no idea* what I might've done for my brother, and actually, as each day passes, I have no idea what I might have done for him. I might have dreamed it all up, imagined it, and now it's not relevant.

We fall into silence and sit in the sand, so close that I can feel the warmth emanating from his body, so close that whenever he moves, his shoulder brushes mine. I shouldn't get so much pleasure from that, from the accidental touches, from his warmth.

But I do.

We sit in such a way for an hour.

In silence.

Staring at the ocean and the sky and the stars.

No one has ever felt comfortable like this to me before, with silence that isn't awkward. No one but Finn. Until now.

"Did you know that the Italian serial killer Leonarda Cianciulli was famous for turning her victims into tea cakes and serving them to guests?" I ask absently, still staring out at the water.

Dare doesn't miss a beat. "No. Because that's an odd thing to know."

I feel the laughter bubbling up in me, threatening to erupt.

"I agree. It is." It's something my brother shared with me yesterday.

Dare smiles. "I'll be sure to work that in at the next party I attend."

I can't help but smile now. "I'm sure it'll go over well."

He chuckles. "Well, it's a conversation starter, for sure."

I don't move because I sort of want to stay here forever, even though the dampness of the sand has leached into my jeans and now my butt is wet.

But even though I don't want this to end, the darkness is so black now that it swallows us up. It's getting late.

I sigh.

"I've got to go back."

"Okay," Dare answers, his voice low in the night, and if I didn't know better, I'd think I detected regret in it. *Maybe he wants to stay here longer, too.*

He helps me to my feet, and then keeps his hand on my elbow as we walk over the driftwood and through the tidal pools and up the trail. It's that thing that real men do, the guiding a woman across the room thing. It's gentlemanly and chivalrous and my ovaries might explode from it because it's intimate and familiar and sexy.

When we get to the house, he removes his hand and I immediately feel the absence of his warmth.

He looks down at me, a thousand things in his eyes that I can't define but want to.

"Good night, Calla. I hope you feel better now."

"I do," I murmur.

And as I pad up the stairs, I realize that I actually do.

For the first time in weeks.

I dream about him again, and he's so familiar and warm, his dark eyes sparkling as he looks into mine. *"You're better than I deserve,"* he tells me, and that startles me, because I think it's quite the opposite. I tell him so and he smiles knowingly, as though I'm wrong and I'll realize it. When I wake up, I still feel warm.

As the weeks go by, I feel better and better, even if my brother seems to feel worse.

Each day he sinks deeper, and I grow more and more helpless because I don't know how to reach him.

"Come with Dare and I to see the Iredale," I plead with him one rainy morning. Finn looks out the window, finally lifting his nose from his journal.

"No thanks," he says woodenly. "I'm not into being a third wheel."

"You aren't," I tell him, but he won't listen and I go with Dare alone.

"The Iredale ran aground in 1906," I explain to him as we walk down the beach, to where the remains of the old wreck rise out of the mist. Its weathered bones look at once ghostly and impressive, skeletal and freaky. "No one died, thank goodness. They waited for weeks for the weather to clear enough to tow her back out to sea, but she got so entrenched in the sand, that they couldn't. She's been in this spot ever since."

We're standing in front of her now, her masts and ribs poking out from the sand and arching toward the sky. Dare reaches out and runs a hand along one of her ribs, calm and reverent.

I swallow hard.

"It's a rite of passage around here," I tell him. "To skip school and come out here with your friends."

Except I never had any friends, other than Finn.

"So you and Finn came here a lot?" Dare asks, as though he read my mind, and his question isn't condescending, he's just curious.

I nod. "Yeah. We like to stop and get coffee and come sit. It's a good way to kill the time."

"So show me," Dare says quietly, taking my hand and pulling me inside the sparse shell. We sit on the damp sand, and stare through the corpse of the ship toward the ocean, where the waves rise and fall and the seagulls fly in loops.

"This must've been a good place to grow up," Dare muses as he takes in the horizon.

I nod. "Yeah. I can't complain. Fresh air, open water... I guess it could only have been better if I didn't live in a funeral home."

I laugh at that, but Dare looks at me sharply.

"Was it really hard?" he asks, half concerned, half curious.

I pause. Because was it? Was it the fact that I lived in a funeral home that made my life hard, or the fact that my brother was crazy and so we were ostracized?

208

I shrug. "I don't know. I think it was everything combined."

Dare nods, accepting that, because sometimes that's how life is. A puzzle made up of a million pieces, and when one piece doesn't exactly fit, it throws the rest of them off.

"Have you ever thought of moving away?" he asks after a few minutes. "I mean, especially now, I think maybe getting a break from...death might be healthy."

I swallow hard because obviously, over the years, that's been a recurring fantasy of mine. To live somewhere else, far from a funeral home. But there's Finn, and so of course I would have never left here before. And now there's college and my brother wants to go alone.

"I'm going away to college in the Fall," I remind him, not mentioning anything else.

"Ah, that's right," he says, leaning back in the sand, his back pressed against a splintered rib. "Do you feel up to it? After everything, I mean."

After your mom died, he means.

"I have to be up to it," I tell him. "Life doesn't stop because someone dies. That's something that living in a funeral home has taught me." And having my mother die and the world kept turning.

He nods again. "Yeah, I guess that's true. But sometimes, we wish it could. I mean, I know I did. It didn't seem fair that my mom was just gone, and everyone kept acting like nothing had changed. The stores kept their doors open and selling trivial things, airplanes kept flying, boats kept sailing… it was like I was the only one who cared that the world lost an amazing person." His vulnerability is showing, and it touches me deep down, in a place I didn't know I had.

I turn to him, willing to share something, too. It's only fair. *You show me yours, and I'll show you mine.*

"I was mad at old people for a while," I admit sheepishly. "I know it's stupid, but whenever I would see an elderly person out and about with their walker and oxygen tank, I was furious that Death didn't decide to take them instead of my mom."

Dare smiles, a grin that lights up the beach.

"I see the reasoning behind that," he tells me. "It's not stupid. Your mom was too young. And they say anger is one of the stages of grief."

"But not anger at random old people," I point out with a barky laugh.

Dare laughs with me and it feels really good, because he's not laughing *at* me, he's laughing *with* me, and there's a difference.

"This feels good," I admit finally, playing with the sand in front of me. Dare glances at me.

"I think you need to get off that mountain more," he decides. "For real. Being secluded in a funeral home? That's not healthy, Calla."

I suddenly feel defensive. "I'm not secluded," I point out. "I have Finn and my dad. And now you're there, too."

Dare blinks. "Yeah, I guess I am."

"And we're not in the funeral home right now," I also point out. We take a pause and gaze out at the vast, endless ocean because the huge grayness of it is inspiring at the same time that it makes me feel small.

"You're right," Dare concedes. "We're not." He pulls his finger through the sand, drawing a line, then intersecting it with another. "We should do this more often."

Those last words impale me and I freeze.

Is he saying what I think he's saying?

"You want to come to the beach more often?" I ask hesitantly. Dare smiles.

"No, I'm saying we should get out more often. Together."

That's what I thought he was saying.

My heart pounds and I nod. "Sure. That'd be fine. Do you care if Finn comes sometimes, too?" Because I feel too guilty to leave him behind all the time.

Dare nods. "Of course not. I want to spend time with you, however you want to give it to me."

Dare grins at me, that freaking *Dare Me* grin, and I know I'm a goner. I'm falling for him, more every day, and there's nothing I can do about it. In fact, there's nothing I *want* to do about it. Because it's amazing.

The Iredale is only a shell of a ship, so the wind whips at us and Dare shoves his hair out of his face. As he does, his ring shimmers with the muted light of the sun. A sudden feeling of déjà vu overwhelms me, as though I've watched his ring glint in the sun before, and we've been here in this ship, together.

We've been here before in this exact place and time.

It's not possible
It's not possible
But it is.
It has to be.
Because I feel it.

That's all I can think as I stare at him, as I watch his ring shimmering in the light, as I watch him shake his hair in the wind.

Dare drops his hand and the feeling fades, yet the remains of it linger like the wispy fingers of a memory or a dream.

I stare at him uncertainly, because the feeling was so overpowering, and because I know what he's going to say next. I know it.

Are you ok?

I wait hesitantly to see.

Dare draws back and stares at me. "Are you ok?"

I nod, because Oh my God, I was right. I try to breathe, and try to remind myself that *God, it's just déjà vu, Calla.* It happens. But it's been happening a lot, to me and to Finn.

And it felt so real. I shake my head, to shake the oddness away. I can't slip away from reality, I can't be like Finn. *God.*

Dare's hand covers my own, and we stare out at the ocean for several minutes more.

His hand is warm and strong, and I relish it, and I push away all disturbing thoughts because honestly nothing matters right now but this.

I relish the way Dare rests his hand against my back as we walk down the beach toward his bike. And I relish the way I fold against him as we ride back home. I relish it all because it's amazing. No matter what else is going on, *this* is amazing.

I feel like I'm floating as I slide off the bike and stand in front of him.

We pause, like neither of us wants to call an end to this day.

Finally, Dare smiles, a slow grin, a real grin that crinkles the corners of his dark *Dare Me* eyes. He reaches up and tucks an errant strand of hair behind my ear, and I swear to God I have to force myself to not lean into that hand.

"I'll see you soon, Calla-Lily," he promises huskily. I nod, and watch him turn and walk away.

God, he looks good walking away.

He pauses, and turns, and I think he must've read my thoughts.

"Calla?"

"Yes?"

"Do you believe in fate?'

I smile, because what a silly question. "I don't know."

"Well, I do."

I'm filled with warmth and I float up to my room.

Chapter Twenty

When I wake the following morning, the first thing I notice is piano music.

Since I know there isn't a funeral today, this is very odd. My mother was the only one who knew how to play in our family.

I crawl out of bed and pad down the stairs, inching into the chapel, not sure what I expect to see. But nothing I expect prepares me for what it is.

Dare sits at the piano in the front, the sunshine pouring in from the windows above and reflecting off of his dark hair, like he's been chosen by God Himself. His eyes closed in concentration, he plays as if the music flows through him like blood or air, like he has to play to live.

I lean against the door, watching his hands span the keys, urging the music from them, with all the grace of an accomplished pianist. I don't recognize the song, but it's beautiful and haunting and sad.

It's just right for this place.

And even though Dare is wearing dark jeans and a snug black shirt and that trendy silver ring on his middle finger, he's right for this place too.

Because he's playing the piano as it should be played.

With reverence.

Here in this chapel, it's only right to revere our surroundings, the quiet peacefulness of a room used to honor the dead.

I close my eyes for a minute, unable to stop myself from imagining what it would be like if his hands worshipped my body in the same way as they worship the keys. My dreams have been like foreplay, because every night, he touches me. He claims my body as his own, and every night, I enjoy it. Right now, I recall those dreams, and my cheeks flush as I picture his fingers trailing over my hip, up my abdomen, pausing at my breasts. My lips tingle from wanting his kiss. My breath hitches, my tongue darts out, licking at my lips, my face slightly feverish.

It's only now that I realize the music has stopped.

I open my eyes and find Dare turned toward me, watching me. There is amusement in his eyes, like he knows exactly what I'd been daydreaming.

If ever there was a time to wish the floor would open up and swallow me, it is now.

"Hi," he offers. "I hope I didn't wake you. Your dad said I could come in and grab some orange juice. I saw the piano and…well, I intruded. I'm sorry."

His accent makes everything ok. And the fact that he plays the piano. More than ok, in fact, it might make him the sexiest man alive.

"You're not an intrusion," I tell him. Or if he is, he's a welcome one. "You play beautifully."

He shrugs. "It was one of my step-father's rules. Everyone in his family had to learn to play because that's what refined people do." He looks bored with the sentiment and closes the lid to the keys.

I raise an eyebrow. "Are you? Refined, I mean."

He smiles. "I'm a bit of a rogue, I'm afraid."

I'm not. Afraid, that is.

"Your dad said to tell you that he had to run into town," he offers as he gets up and lithely moves toward me. I can't help but draw a parallel... between Dare and a graceful jungle cat. Long, lithe, slender, strong. He and I are connected by an invisible band, and he flexes that band as he strides down the aisle of the chapel before he stops in front of me like a panther.

Am I his prey?

God, I hope so.

In the light, his eyes are golden, and I find I can't look away.

"Thanks," I tell him. "I bet my brother went with him." I don't mention that my brother slept in my bed last night, because that would seem weird. Like always, I have to hide certain things for appearances' sake.

"I don't know about that," Dare answers. "I haven't seen Finn today."

"He must've," I murmur. In fact, my father probably took Finn in to his Group. I'm free to focus on what is standing in front of me.

Dare DuBray.

His smile gleams.

"I have another question to ask you," he tells me, with a certain smug look settling on his lips. I raise an eyebrow.

"What, already? You just asked one days ago."

He chuckles. "Yep. But not here. I want to ask it somewhere else."

I wait.

And wait.

"And that is…where?" I finally ask.

He smiles. "Out on the water."

I pause. "On the water? Like, on our boat?"

He nods. "Is that ok?"

Of course it is.

"It's just a little boat," I warn him. "Nothing fancy."

"That's perfect," he answers. "Because I'm nothing fancy, either."

Au contraire. But of course I don't say that. And it's a good thing I slept in my clothes because this way, we can go straight there without pause. But of course I don't say that either.

Instead, I simply lead the way outdoors and to the beach, not hesitating in the rain.

"We can still go," I tell him. "It's just a little rain, the waves aren't bad."

"I'm not worried," he grins. "I'm used to rain."

"That's right," I answer as I motion for him to climb aboard. "I forgot."

He steps across and I untie the boat from the dock, before I toss the rope to him. I leap before the boat can float away, and land unceremoniously beside him.

He lounges against the hull as I steer through the bay, and suddenly, the rain stops as suddenly as it started. The clouds part, the sun shines down upon us and I lift my face to the warmth.

I live for times like these, when my grief pauses long enough for me to enjoy something.

And I have to admit, I've been enjoying more and more moments since Dare came to my mountain.

"You make me feel guilty," I tell him quietly, opening my eyes. He's sprawled out, his legs propped up on a seat. He glances at me, his forehead furrowed.

"Why in the world is that, Calla-lily?"

The name makes me smile.

"Because you make me forget that I'm sad," I say simply.

Softness wavers in Dare's eyes for a minute before they turn back into obsidian. "That shouldn't make you feel guilty," he tells me. "In fact, that makes *me* happy. I don't like the idea of you being sad. Come sit by me."

He opens his arms and I sit on the seat next to him, leaning against his hard chest and into his beating heart. His arms close around me and for the first time in my life, I'm lounging in a guy's embrace. And not just any guy. Dare DuBray, who I'm guessing could have any girl he wants.

And right now, in this moment, he wants me.

It's unfathomable.

It's the perfect temperature as we drift in the sun, as the warmth saturates my shirt and soaks into my skin. I drag one hand over the side, letting it float on the surface of the water as I listen to Dare's heart.

It's strong and loud against my ear.

Thump. Thump. Thump.

The rhythmic sound reminds me of the day he was punching the shed.

I pause, then freeze, my fingers on his chest.

What day was that?

I focus and focus, trying to recall the memory through foggy haze, but all I get is an image of Dare punching at the woodshed like a machete, or a machine.

"What's wrong?" he asks, staring down at me.

"I…" I don't know what to say.

"Sometimes, I have memories that don't seem real," I finally admit, not caring how it makes me look.

He stares at me for the longest time, his gaze so deep and penetrating. "How do you know they aren't real?" he finally answers.

I cackle a hyena-like laugh. "Because they can't be. If you could see my memories, you'd understand why."

"I'm in your memories, right?" Dare asks, and each word is sharp.

"Yeah," I answer. "Usually."

He starts to answer, but I interrupt him, because he has taken off his shirt and his skin is getting a bit red.

"You're going to get skin cancer," I stare at him.

"I'm not," he answers. I don't argue because I like his bare chest, and the way the muscles ripple across his shoulders as he moves. I pause on my way to the helm, long enough to run my fingers over the letters of his tattoo. His skin is hot beneath my fingertips, and the friction makes me grit my teeth.

"I'm going to show you someplace new," I tell him, guiding the boat out of the bay and toward a small rock pier down the beach. It only takes ten minutes to get there, and I urge the boat aground so that we can step out onto land.

I hold my hand out to Dare and he takes it, climbing down next to me. We walk all the way out to the tip of the land finger, where the fingernail would be.

Dare sits, and I sit next to him, our feet splayed out in front of us on the rocks.

We're surrounded by nothing but the air and water, we're utterly alone out here, with no one to overhear or watch us like we're fish in a bowl.

The salty breeze blows Dare's hair around his face and I turn to him.

"I'm ready to use another question," I tell him. He grins.

"So soon? It's only been days since the last one."

I ignore that. "Why are you such a gentleman?"

Meaning, *why are you so resolute to keep your distance until I figure my shit out?*

He shifts his weight and crosses his feet at the ankles. "So you've noticed."

His tone is wry. I roll my eyes.

"Seriously. Why are you trying to force me into doing something for my own good that I don't want to do? All for the sake of being a gentleman? Maybe being a gentleman is overrated and archaic."

He scoffs at that, shielding his eyes from the sun with long fingers of one hand. I stare at his silver ring glinting in the light.

"It's not, trust me." The way he says that is so knowing, so strange.

I raise an eyebrow and he sighs.

"My step-father, while refined and rich, was not a gentleman behind closed doors. From the time I was very small, I decided that I would always be the opposite of him. I used to read my mother's journals, because that's all I had left of her, and she always spoke of wanting me to be a gentleman when I grew up. She spoke of those traits with such...reverence that

I knew that's what I wanted to be." He pauses. "Are you going to make fun of me now?"

He stares at me, his jaw so sculpted, his eyes so guarded. I find all I want to do is reach out and stroke the coarseness of his stubble with my hand. "No," I tell him. "Not at all. Why did you have to read your mother's journals?"

"Because she died when I was small."

God, he has made that hidden part of me ache, the maternal place, the place that wants to protect him from everything, even if that means from me.

"What did your step-father do?"

My question is quiet in its simplicity and Dare sighs again.

"You're really burning through your questions today."

I nod, but I don't back down.

"My stepfather was unfortunately, very much like his mother. A very calculating, controlling person. He had to have everything his way exactly and those people who didn't comply were punished severely."

I swallow hard at the closed look on Dare's beautiful face.

"How severely?"

He turns to look at me, his black eyes staring into my soul.

"Severely."

My heart twinges at the vulnerable pain in Dare's eyes. He thinks he's concealing it, but he's not. "And being the rogue that you are, I'm guessing you were punished a lot."

He nods and looks out at the sea and I pick up his hand, spinning his ring round and round.

"And no one interfered? Not your grandmother?"

He looks at me now, stricken. "She wouldn't interfere. She never approved of me. She thinks I deserved everything I got and then some."

The feel of this conversation is dark and ominous and scary. I examine his face, the planes and angles, and grip his hand harder. "Well, now that your mom is gone, you're done with your step-father's family. Thank goodness. You're here in America and they can't hurt you anymore."

He sighs, a ragged sound, his slender fingers weaving around my own. "Can't they?"

I start to answer and he interrupts. "You've burned through most of your questions, Cal. It seems to me like you've only got a couple left."

I nod, because he's right. "I've only got one more to ask today, and then I'll save my last one for later."

Nerves cause my heart to pound, adrenaline to rush, rush, rush through my veins as I look at him, the Adonis sitting next to me. *Do it. Do it.* Everything about him touches me... his voice, his story, his vulnerability that he tries so hard to hide. All of it. I want him. All of him.

"You've been such a gentleman," I start, before I lose my nerve. "And it's sexy as hell, I'll admit.

You're sexy. And beautiful. And I want to be close to you, Dare. I want it more than I've ever wanted anything."

Dare swallows. I see his throat move, I see him grip his leg with long fingers.

"And?" he asks hesitantly. "What is your question?"

He swallows again.

"Be with me," I urge him. "Today. Right now. Out here where it's only the two of us. Please."

Dare closes his eyes, and his face is bathed by the sun.

"That's not a question," he states softly. But his hands are gripping his legs so tightly his knuckles are turning white.

I move over, close, close, closer. Until my thigh is pressed against his, and I unclasp his fingers from his thighs. Leaning over our intertwined hands, I kiss his neck, beginning at the base, slowly and softly working my way up to his ear.

"Will you be with me? *Today?*" I whisper in his ear. With my last raspy word, I release his hand and slide mine along his inner thigh. I feel him harden beneath my fingers, pulsing through his jeans.

He closes his eyes and I tighten my fingers, increasing my grip.

"Don't," he whispers. His voice husky and so sexy.

"That's not an answer," I tell him, stroking him through the denim. A surge of feminine power shoots through me, lifting me up, propelling me onward, until my own hormones explode and cloud my thoughts.

"I want you, Dare," I tell him hotly, all logic and reason abandoning me. And then I kiss him, pressing my body into his, plunging my tongue into his hot mouth. His hands come up and lift me until I'm straddling him and I feel his hardness, his rigidity, pressing between my legs.

He's hard for me.

I swallow hard, absorbing his moan, sucking it down.

"You don't know what you want," he rasps into my neck.

"I do," I insist quietly, rocking in his lap, grinding my hips into his, creating an exquisite, amazing friction. "I've wanted you all along."

Dare pulls away, his dark eyes heavy-lidded with want for me. Warmth floods me, wetting my panties and I cling to him.

"Are you sure?"

"Yes." My answer is simple.

With a growl, Dare scoops me up, and carries me down the peninsula, to a place where the ground is soft. He lays me down, on his knees above me, gloriously back-lit.

"I shouldn't," he wavers.

"You have to," I tell him, grabbing him and pulling him down on top of me.

His weight is delicious and perfect and he molds into me, making it seem like we're one person as we writhe together, trying desperately to get closer.

His tongue finds mine, as his fingers explore my body, every inch, every hidden place. I arch against him, palmed in his hand, as he finds where I want him the most.

"Please," I say softly, my breath escaping me. Dare smiles against my lips, knowing the effect on me, knowing and loving it.

He leans forward and rests his forehead against mine, and we're so very close that I can feel his breath mingling with mine as his hands work absolute magic. Pleasure laps against me, like the water against the shore and I lose all cognizant thought, and instinct takes over.

I tug at his jeans, unbuttoning them and pushing them away, and suddenly, he's naked and in my hand, long and thick and bare.

I can't breathe.

I can't think.

I can only move.

I slide my hand along him, softly, gently, then harder, harder.

He bucks into me, his eyes shuttering closed.

"I've waited for this," he murmurs into my neck, as he wedges his rigidity into my thighs, closer, closer. "For so long."

"Please," I say again, my hand cupped around his neck, pulling his mouth to mine, so I can taste him, inhale him. He pulls off my sundress, and stares at me in the sunlight, as the light exposes every plane of my body to his searching eyes.

"You're beautiful," he whispers, his eyes glittering in the sun. "You're so much better than I deserve."

Wordlessly, he pulls back for a moment, and I protest, but then I hear the crinkle of a wrapper and he's back, and he's sliding into me and I can't think anymore.

Motions become blurs, blurs become colors, and all I can do is feel.

His hands, his mouth, his skin. The way he slides in and out of me, the friction causing me to crest in waves, his fingers bringing me to it faster.

"I...you...*God*," I manage to say, because the words I want won't come.

Dare smiles slightly and slides back into me, moaning my name.

"I want you to know me," he says, his voice a husky chant. "I want you to know me."

I'm *knowing* him now like I've wanted to for weeks. Intimate and close and I can't believe this is finally happening, I can't believe it's so amazing, I can't focus, I can't focus, I can't focus.

The lights, the sun, the sea, Dare's scent, his fingers, his hands.

I grip his back, where his words say LIVE FREE and I've never felt freer in my entire life.

And then my world explodes in a kaleidoscope of colors and lights.

I'm limp as I cling to him, as he finally arches against me and groans and says my name in a ragged whisper before collapsing against me, his head against my chest, his beautiful hands holding me close.

I can't even answer. My legs are shaky, my mind is spinning. But as I come back to myself, as my thoughts form logically together again, as the sun hangs heavy in the sky, with the oranges and reds on the water, something comes to me. Something Dare said in the heat of the moment, exact words that I've heard before in my dreams.

You're better than I deserve.

Chapter Twenty-One

My swollen lips part and I stare at him, at the face I love, at the lips that just spoke words from my dream.

It's impossible.

Yet it's not.

"You...there's something..." my voice trails off and he looks at me questioningly, a smile lingering on his lips, the after effects of something beautiful.

Something that's now tarnished by ugliness.

By confusion.

"You said I'm better than you deserve," I say shakily, not wanting to speak the truth, because the truth sounds crazy. "Why would you say that?"

He shrugs. "Because you're soft and honest and beautiful. You're better than I deserve."

"But why?" I demand persistently, refusing his answer. "You must have a reason."

He shakes his head, still staring, still questioning.

"It doesn't make sense," I tell him.

"Life doesn't make sense sometimes, Cal," is his only reply. He takes his hand away now, the warmth gone from me, and my fingers turn instantly cool with the breeze.

It's his turn to examine me, to study me in the breeze.

"Do you feel ok?" he asks hesitantly. "Are you... do you... you seem different."

I shake my head. "I'm just the same. I just... those words stood out to me somehow, like I've heard them before, *like you've said them before.*"

If I didn't know better, I'd say he turns pale. He shakes his head slowly, with such a strange expression on his face.

"Do you know why?" he asks strangely, an odd glint in his eye, his beautiful lips pulled tight.

"No. Do you?"

He gives me a droll look. "Why would I know your mind?" he asks vaguely, but his face tells a different story as an expression that puts my nerves on edge floods his face.

"How cryptic," I murmur.

He shakes his head. "I'm not trying to be. It's just... I thought... never mind. You've got enough to worry about right now without adding more to it."

"Everyone has secrets," I say blankly, my heart numb. He nods.

"Yeah. I guess."

My blood is ice, my heart is heavy, my very being filled with terror and foreboding, when just a scant moment ago, I was filled with exquisite belonging. It's been shattered now, by the sheer expression on Dare's face.

"What are yours?" I ask calmly. "Your secrets, I mean. What are they, Dare? You're hiding something and I know it. Just tell me."

He looks sad as he looks away from me, and that terrifies me even more. My heart picks up a little as I wait, pounding in my chest, echoing in my temples.

He's hiding something.

"I can't tell you. Not right now. It's not a good time." His voice is expressionless, solemn.

"Will there ever be a good time?" I ask. He shrugs.

"I don't know. I hope so."

I don't like that answer.

"We just... I... I trusted you," I tell him limply. "And I know you're keeping a secret and I know it affects me. I can't...I can't."

My heart is racing and I suddenly feel weak, and I crawl off the slippery rocks and walk quietly back to the boat without another word. Lately, I feel more and more like I'm the crazy one, like I'm losing my mind, like the whole world is composed of secrets and I don't have the slightest clue how to figure them out.

Dare follows me and lifts my hand to help me into the boat.

The quiet between us is loaded and charged and I don't know why. I don't know why I feel like I'm standing on a precipice and if I make one move, I'll fall.

When we're halfway across the bay, Dare sits straight up.

"Let's go to your little cove," he suggests softly.

He sits on the hull, his shirtless chest gleaming in the dying light, his eyes vulnerable and hopeful and I can't say no.

Instead, I just wordlessly steer toward the cove and wedge the boat on the sand. I don't know why, I just don't want to stay here. I have to move. I have to think. I have to try and stay sane, because it feels like I'm fraying.

I don't know why.

All I know is... I suddenly feel lost.

Dare holds my hand as we walk through the water, to the enclosed little inlet that I so love. Without a word, I dig out the little bag holding the lighter and I make a little driftwood bonfire.

With the violet light surrounding us, we sit facing each other over a tide pool. The moon rises over the edge of the water and this place seems ethereal and peaceful and infinite.

"Do you trust me?" Dare asks seriously, his eyes ever-so-dark. He brushes a tendril of my hair behind my ear. "I mean, really trust me?"

I'm puzzled by that, by his uncertainty.

I'm scared by the hidden meaning of his words.

I reach up and trace the lines of his face, the cleft in his chin, the strong jaw, his forehead.

"Why wouldn't I?" I ask finally. "Is there some reason I shouldn't?"

"That's not an answer," he replies.

"Then yes," I tell him quickly. "I trust you."

Don't I?

He stares into my eyes, his hands on my knees. "Would you still trust me if I told you that I want to tell you everything. That I want to spill all of my secrets, everything that you've been wondering about... but I can't?"

There is genuine angst in his voice, and his face is pained and I can't figure it out.

"Are you a mass murderer?" I ask, trying to lighten the mood, but it doesn't work. His face doesn't change.

"No. But there are things... that I wish I could say, but can't."

I drop my hand, stricken by the look in his eye.

"Like what?" I ask bluntly. "Just tell me right now. Tell me *all the things,* Dare."

He ignores that.

"You have so many moments when you think you have memories, right? Memories that seem impossible?"

I nod my head, because I'm suddenly terrified to speak.

"Maybe I'm the same way," he says quietly, his voice husky and low. "Maybe I have the same memories, and maybe that's because they're real, only you've forgotten them."

This stuns me, freezes me, catapults me from this moment and I sit up in the sun.

"What?" I ask stiltedly.

Dare sits up next to me, and his beautiful face is troubled.

"There are things about me that you don't know. And if I don't tell you about them, if I don't tell you about them right now, terrible things might happen, and I'll be the reason why."

"Then tell me," I whisper, and the words pain my heart and my heart pains my chest. "Tell me."

He reaches over to me and his ring shines in the light and the silver touches my face and everythingeverythingeverything swirls.

The world tilts and spills.

Fragmentsfragmentsfragments

Piece together and come apart,

Like my mind,

Like Finn's.

I grasp at him, trying to right myself and all that matters all that matters all that matters is his warmth. He grounds me, he holds me, he keeps me safe.

My fingers reach for him, then I kiss him.

His lips are warm and firm and there's so much familiarity here... so much want and we can deal with the craziness later, after after after. Right now, I just need him. To ground me, to keep me sane. To be with me.

His hands trace my collarbone, running down my arms, setting my nerve endings on fire. They burst into flame, burning away anything else but the desire to be with him, right here and right now.

"You think you don't deserve me," I whisper against his neck. "But that's not true. I'm the one... I don't deserve *you.*"

I kiss him again, and he groans in my mouth, the sound of it driving me to the brink because I know he wants me too.

"You want me," I tell him urgently, pulling at him. "I know you do."

"I've always wanted you," he tells me roughly. "Always."

"It's just you and me now," I tell him. "You and me. That's all that matters."

Make me feel something besides pain.

I kiss him again and his hands splay around my hips, positioning me so that I'm lodged against his hardness. I suck in a breath and look up into his eyes, eyes that hold a thousand secrets, but eyes that I love.

I love him.

"No matter what," I whisper. He pauses from kissing my neck and looks at me questioningly as he lifts his hand to brush my hair back. The light glints from his ring, again and I'm frozen.

Because fragments come flying into my mind. Memory fragments. Images of that same exact expression, of his ring glinting in the moonlight as he tells me something. It's a confession and he's alarmed, upset, anxious.

It's the night of the accident. *Before* the accident. I see his lips moving, but I can't hear the words. It's like he's in a wind tunnel, the words are static, and I've seen this exact scene before in a dream.

I strain to hear the words from my memory.

"What's wrong?" Dare asks me now, lowering his head once more, sliding his warm lips across my neck as he leans me back.

At this exact inopportune moment, as Dare's touch lights my skin ablaze, the fragments finally fit into place. The puzzle pieces fit together. *At last.*

The memory forms and I suck in an appalled breath as I yank away from him.

"I remember," I whisper. Dare pauses in apprehension, his onyx eyes glittering, his hands frozen on my arms. "I've known you...for so long...you...you were here for me all along. *You came here for me.*"

His eyes close like a curtain and I know that I'm right.

His breath is shaky and his hands tremble as he touches me, as he refuses to pull away even now.

"You have one question left, Calla," he reminds me, his voice somber. "Ask it."

So with fear in my heart and ice in my veins...I do.

"*What is real?*" I finally ask, choosing my words carefully. "I don't know anymore. My memory has holes, and the memories I do have seem impossible."

"They aren't impossible," Dare tells me. "Trust me."

"Can you explain?" I ask him. "Please, please. I can't take much more of this. I just need the truth."

"Where do you want me to start?" Dare is resigned, and he's sad.

"Start with the night my mom died," I suggest.

Something wavers in Dare's gaze, but he gathers himself.

"Do you remember it? Do you remember how bloody I was?"

I'm already shaking my head from side to side, slowly, in shock. Not because I don't remember, but because I don't want to.

"There was a lot of blood," I recall, thinking about the way it'd streaked down Dare's temple and dripped onto his shirt. It'd stained the t-shirt crimson, spreading in a terrifying pool across his chest. "I didn't know if it was yours or... hers."

"It was neither," he says now, his face as grave as death. "It was Finn's."

But that's impossible, because I'd only imagined that Finn died. It was my mother.

"You held me up," my lips tremble. "When I was falling down. You held me while I waited for... Finn."

I'd waited for Finn to call.

I'd waited and waited and waited.

The sirens wailed in the night, and I'd paced the floor.

Dare nods. "I've always held you up, Cal."

"When my father came in, and said... when he told me about the accident, everything else faded away," I recall, staring out at the ocean. *God, why does the ocean make me feel so small?* "Nothing else mattered. Nothing but him. You faded away, Dare."

The truth is stark.

The truth is hurtful.

I lay it out there, like flesh flayed open, like pink muscle, like blood.

Dare closes his eyes, his gleaming black eyes.

"I know," he says softly. "You didn't remember me. For months."

We know that. We both know that. It's why we're here, standing on the edge of the ocean, trying to retrieve my mind. It's been out to sea for too long, absent from me, floundering.

I snatch at it now with frantic fingers, trying to draw all of my memories back. They're stubborn though, my memories. They won't all come.

But one does.

My eyes burn as I fix my gaze on Dare.

"You confessed something to me. It scared me."

239

Dare's lids are heavy and hooded, probably from the weight of guilt.

He nods. One curt, short movement.

"Do you remember what I told you?"

He's silent, his gaze tied to mine, burning me.

I flip through my memories, fast, fast, faster... but I come up empty-handed. I only emerge with a feeling.

Fear.

Dare sees it in my eyes and looks away.

"I tried to tell you, Cal," he says, almost pleading. "You just didn't understand."

His voice trails off and my heart seems to stop beating.

"I didn't understand what?" I ask stiltedly. *Just tell me.*

He lifts his head now.

"It isn't hard to understand," he says simply. "If you remember all that I told you. Can you try?"

I stare at him numbly. "I've tried already. I... it's not there, Dare."

Dare's head drops the tiniest bit, almost imperceptibly, but I see it. He's discouraged, disappointed.

He shakes his head. "It *is* there. Trust yourself, Calla. Your memories are real. Finn was dead, and then he wasn't."

"My mom died instead. I thought I was crazy," I murmur. "Because if it was real, then I somehow exchanged my mother for Finn."

Dare sighs, a ragged and broken sound. He tries to touch my hand, but I yank it away. He doesn't get to touch me. Not anymore.

"You don't understand," he says quietly. "But you're not crazy."

I stare at him. "No, I don't understand." *And you have no idea what this feels like.*

"You will," he replies tiredly. "I swear to God you will."

A lump lodges itself in my throat as the sea breeze rustles my hair. I take a deep gulp of it, filling my lungs with the clean scent.

"Did you ever love me at all?" I ask, the words choking me, because no matter what, it's the most important thing to me right now.

Pain flashes across Dare's face, real pain, and I brace myself.

Don't.

Don't.

Don't.

Don't hurt me.

"Of course I did," he says quickly and firmly. "And I do still. Right now."

He stares at me imploringly and I so want to believe him. I want to hear his words and clutch them to my heart and keep them there in a gilded cage.

But then he speaks again. "You're not safe, Calla. You have to come with me now. There's something you need to know."

"I don't know where I belong anymore," I whimper and Dare grabs me.

"You belong with me," he tells me, his lips moving against my hair. *"You don't hate me, Calla. You can't. I didn't lie to you. I tried to tell you."*

His voice is afraid, terrified actually, and it touches a soft place in me, a hidden place, the place where I protect my love for him. The place where my heart used to be before it was so broken, and the emotions, the feelings... they trigger a memory. What he told me to do that night.

"You told me to run," I say suddenly, and Dare is sadder now than ever.

"I wish you would've," he answers. "Because now it's too late. We have to ride this out, and if you don't stay with me, you'll be lost."

"You're my own personal anti-Christ," I whisper into his shirt. His hands stroke my hair frantically, trailing down my back and clutching me to him."

"I'm not," he rasps. "Things are complicated, and I don't want you to think I'm a monster. I've failed you, but I'll fix it. I swear I'll fix it."

"How?" I whisper, and don't think I want to know. "How have you failed me? What have you done?"

My hand is anchored by Dare's.

His fingers shake, and it scares me.

"I've done a terrible thing," he confesses, and each word is staccato. "I don't expect your forgiveness. But I have to fix it. And to do that, I need your help. You have to help me, Calla. Help me save you."

Save me, and I'll save you.

That's in Finn's journal. Those are Finn's words, not Dare's.

Right?

I feel… I feel… I feel.

I feel a wave of déjà vu. I feel a wave of emotion, of sensation, of things I should know but don't, like there are holes in my brain and details have fallen out and scattered in the wind and blown away.

"What have you done?" I ask him through fractured thoughts. "What do I need saving from? Because I don't think I can be saved. I'm broken, I think."

"You're wrong," he insists, and his eyes beg me. "I can save you."

I shake my head and the movement is painful.

"You love me," he tells me, his stare cutting me into pieces. "You just haven't realized it yet."

"I know," I whisper, throwing those pieces away. "But…"

But

But.

But I have to protect myself from him.

From Dare.

243

I feel it now, stronger than I've ever felt anything.

It's a heavy foreboding, centering my chest and spreading through every blood vessel in my body. It's real and it's tangible and it's a warning.

It's intuition.

I draw my knees to my chest and look away, taking a deep shaky breath.

"I know I sound crazy," I admit. "I know it. But I can't help what I feel. I have to protect myself from you. I know that much is true. My heart is telling me to be afraid of you."

And it is. It's telling me there's a reason.

I feel it in my bones, in my hollow reed bones.

Dare closes his eyes, and it is minutes before he opens them, and when he does, they're so empty, so lost.

"Fine," he says simply. "Protect yourself from me. Hell, *I'll* protect you from me. But come with me to Whitley. That's where you'll find the answers. There are answers to questions you haven't even thought of yet."

"At Whitley? Is that where you're from?"

I stare at Dare, at the body I love, the eyes that I can fall into, the heart that has held me up... and hidden so many secrets.

He nods like I should know that already, and it's like the movement is painful for him. He doesn't want to go to there, to Whitley, but he's willing to go for me. I see that.

"Your dad wants you to go," he adds. "Can you do it for him?"

Why would my dad want me to go to England?

Nothing makes sense.

That's the story of my life.

The ominous feeling cripples me, almost sending me to my knees. I don't know. I only know... if I don't find answers, I might lose my sanity and end up just like Finn, back where I started.

The answers are at Whitley.

I exhale, realizing that I'd been holding my breath.

"Ok. I'll go. But only if Finn comes too."

Dare agrees immediately.

"Of course. Obviously. He needs my help, too."

Obviously.

Chapter Twenty-Two

"We live a little ways from Hastings. It's close to Sussex," Dare tells me, after we land at Heathrow and drive through the country. He speaks of England as though I know anything at all about it. I nod like I do, because so much of what we say is a pretense now. We go through the motions.

Thirty minutes later, our car is still gliding over the winding ribbons of road, but I finally see a rooftop in the distance, spires and towers poking through trees.

Dare stirs, opening his eyes, and I know we're almost there. Finn is still sleeping, so I nudge him awake, and he rubs at his eyes.

I crane my neck to see. When I do, I'm stunned beyond words, enough that the breath hitches on my lips.

This can't be my family's home.

It's huge, it's lavish, it's creepy.

It's ancient, it's stone, it's beautiful.

A tall stone wall stretches in either direction as far as I can see, encircling the property like an ominous security blanket. It's so tall, so heavy, and for one brief moment, I wonder if it's meant to keep people out... or to keep them in.

It's a foolish notion, I know.

As we pull off the road, large wrought iron gates open in front of our car as if by magic, as if they were pushed by unseen hands. Puffs of mist and fog swirl from the ground and through the tree branches, half concealing whatever lies behind the gate.

Even though the grounds are lush and green, there's something heavy here, something dark. It's more than the near constant rain, more than the clouds.

Something that I can't quite put my finger on.

I'm filled with a strange dread as the car rolls through the gates, as we continue toward the hidden thing. And while the 'hidden thing' is just a house, it feels like so much more, like something ominous and almost threatening.

I catch glimpses of it through the branches as we drive, and each glimpse gives me pause.

A steep, gabled roof.

Columns and spires and moss.

Rain drips from the trees, onto the car, onto the driveway, and everything gleams with a muted light.

It's wet here, and gray, and the word I keep thinking in my head is *gothic.*

Gothic.

Despite all the beauty and the extravagance here, it still looks a bit terrifying.

I count the beats as we make our way to the house, and I've counted to fifteen before the limousine finally comes to a stop on top of a giant circular driveway made of cobblestone.

The house in front of us is made from stone, and it sprawls out as far as I can see. The windows are dark, in all sizes, in all shapes.

Rolling, manicured lawns, an enormous mansion, lush gardens. Stormy clouds roll behind the massive setting of the house, and one thing is clear. Ominous or not, this estate is lavish, to say the least.

"Is our family rich?" I ask dumbly.

Dare glances at me. "Not in the ways that matter."

He pauses, and there is a rope between us, pulling us together, but at the same time, coiling around us, holding us apart.

"Calla, don't let your guard down," he tells me quickly. "This place... it isn't what it seems. You have to..."

Jones opens the door, and Dare stops speaking abruptly.

I have to what?

"Welcome to Whitley," Jones tells me with a slight bow. We climb out and suddenly, I'm nervous.

I'm in a foreign country, getting ready to meet a family consisting of strangers, and I know nothing about them.

It's daunting.

Dare squeezes my hand briefly, and I let him. Because here, I'm alone.

Here, Dare and Finn are the only familiar things.

Here, they're the only ones who know me.

Of course, maybe they always were.

Jones leads the way with our bags, and before we even reach the front doors, they open, and a small wrinkled woman stands in the doorway. She's slightly bent, barely a wisp of a woman, with an olive complexion and her hair completely wrapped in a bright scarf twisted at the top. She looks like she might be a hundred years old.

"Sabine!" Dare greets the elderly woman. The little woman's arm close around him, and her head barely reaches his chest.

"Welcome home, boy," she says in a deep gravely voice. "I've missed you."

Dare pulls away and glances at me, and I can see on his face that Sabine is important. At least to him. "This is Sabine. Sabine, this is Calla Price."

Sabine stares at me, curiously, sadly.

"You're the spitting image of your mother," she tells me.

"I know," I tell her, and my heart twinges because my mother is gone. "It's nice to meet you."

I offer her my hand, but she grasps it instead of shaking it. Stooping over, she examines it, her face mere inches from my palm. She grips me tight, unwilling to let me go, and I feel my pulse bounding wildly against her fingers.

Startled, I wait.

I don't know what else to do.

The little woman is surprisingly strong, her grip holding me steady as she searches for something in my hand. She traces the veins and the ridges, her breath hot on my skin. Her face is so close to my palm that I can feel each time she exhales.

Finn coughs, and abruptly, Sabine drops my hand and straightens.

Her eyes meet mine and I see a thousand lifetimes in hers. They're dark as obsidian, and unlike most elderly people, hers aren't cloudy with age. She stares into me, and I feel like she's literally sifting through my thoughts and looking into my soul.

It's unsettling, and a chill runs up my spine, putting me on edge.

She glances at Dare, and nods ever so slightly.

If I didn't know better, I would almost think he cringed.

What the hell?

But I don't have time to ponder, because Sabine starts walking, leading us into the house.

"Come. Eleanor is waiting for you," Sabine tells us solemnly over her shoulder as she uses much of her strength to open the heavy front doors.

Dare sighs. "I think we'd better freshen up first. It's been a long flight, Sabby."

The nanny looks sympathetic, but is unrelenting. "I'm sorry, Dare. She insists on seeing all three of you."

Dare sighs again, but we obediently follow Sabine through lavish hallways. Over marble floors and lush rugs, through mahogany paneled halls and extravagant window dressings, beneath sparkling crystal chandeliers. My eyes are wide as we take it all in. I've never seen such a house in all my life, not even on TV.

But even as it is opulent, it's silent.

It's still.

It's like living in a mausoleum.

We come to a stop in front of massive wooden doors, ornately carved. Sabine knocks on them twice, and a woman's voice calls out from within.

"Enter."

How eerily formal.

Sabine opens the doors, and we are immediately enveloped by an overwhelmingly large study, painted in rich colors and patinas, encircled with wooden shelves filled by hundreds and hundreds of leather-bound books.

A woman sits at the heavy cherry desk, facing us with her back to the windows.

Her face is stern, her hair is faded, but I can see that it used to be red. It's pulled into a severe chignon, not one strand out of place. Her cashmere sweater is buttoned all the way to the top, decorated by one single strand of pearls. Her unadorned hands are folded in front of her and she's waiting.

Waiting for us.

How long has she been waiting? Months? Years?

For a reason that I can't explain, I feel suffocated. The room seems to close in on me, and I'm frozen. Dare has to literally pull me, then pull me harder, just to make me move.

I feel like I can't breathe, like if I approach her, something bad will happen.

Something terrible.

It's a ridiculous thought, and Dare glances at me out of the corner of his eye.

We come to a stop in front of the desk.

"Eleanor," he says tightly.

There is no love lost here. I can see it. I can sense it. I feel it in the air, in the formality, in the cold.

"Adair," the woman nods. There are no hugs, no smiles. Even though it's been at least a year since she's seen him, this woman doesn't even stand up.

"This is your grandmother, Eleanor Savage," Dare tells me, and his words are so carefully calm. Eleanor stares at me, her gaze examining me from head to toe. My cheeks flush from it.

"You must be Calla."

I nod.

"You may call me Eleanor." She glances at the door. "Wait outside, Sabine."

Without a word, Sabine backs out, closing the door. Eleanor returns her attention to us.

"I'm sorry for your loss," she tells me stiffly, but her voice lacks any sign of emotion, of sympathy or sadness, even though it was her daughter who was lost.

She looks at me again. "While you are here, Whitley will be your home. You will not intrude in rooms that don't concern you. You may have the run of the grounds, you may use the stables. You won't mingle with unsavory characters, you may have use of the car. Jones will drive you wherever you need to go. You may settle in, get accustomed to life in the country, and soon, we'll speak about your inheritance. Since you've turned eighteen, you have responsibilities to this family."

She pauses, then looks at me and then at Finn.

"You've suffered a loss, but life goes on. You will learn to go on, as well."

She looks away from us, directing her attention to a paper on her desk. "Sabine!" she calls, without looking up.

Apparently, we've been dismissed.

Sabine re-enters and we quickly follow her, jumping at the chance to leave this distasteful woman.

"Well, she's pleasant," I mutter.

Dare's lip tilts.

"She's not my favorite."

Understatement.

We share a moment, a warm moment, but I shove it away.

I can't.

I can't.

Sabine stops in front of double wooden doors.

"This was your mother's suite," Sabine tells me. "It's yours now. Finn's is across the hall. Dare's room is across the house." After she says that, she waits, as if she's expecting a reaction from me. When she doesn't get one, she continues. "Dinner will be at seven in the dining room. Be prompt. You should rest now."

She turns and walks away, shuffling down the hall on tiny feet. Finn ducks into his room, and Dare stares at me, tall and slender.

"Do you want me to stay with you?"

"No." My answer is immediate and harsh.

He's startled and he pulls away a bit, staring down at me.

"I just... I need to be alone," I add.

I'm not strong enough to resist you yet.

Disappointment gleams in his eyes, but to his credit, he doesn't press me. He swallows his hurt and nods.

"Ok. I'm wiped out, so I'm going to take a nap before dinner. I suggest you do the same. You must be tired."

I nod because he's right, I'm utterly exhausted. He's gone, and I'm left alone in the long quiet hallway.

I take a step toward my bedroom, then another, but for the life of me, I can't seem to turn the doorknob.   Something settles around me, dread, I think, and I just can't do it.

The look on Eleanor's face emerges in my head, the way she was examining me, and I can't breathe. Something crushes me, that dark thing that I felt in the driveway.   It feels like it's here, pushing on me, lapping at me.

I know it doesn't make any sense.

Something pulls me.

It pulls me right into my mother's old rooms.

And there, I sit, surrounded by her memories.

Chapter Twenty-Three

My mother's rooms are as lavish as the rest of the house. There are no childhood posters taped to the walls here, no teenage heart-throbs, no pink phones or plush pillows.

The suite is carefully decorated, with heavy off-white furniture and sage green walls. The bed is massive, covered in thick blankets, all sage green, all soothing.

But it's not the room of a child, or a teenager, or even a young woman.

It lacks youthful energy.

But I still feel her here.

Somehow.

Sinking onto the bed, I find that I'm surrounded by windows.

All along one wall, they stretch from floor to ceiling. They let in the dying evening light, and I feel exposed. Getting to my feet, I pull the drapes closed.

I feel a little safer now, but not much.

My suitcases are stacked inside the door, and so I set about unpacking. I put my sweaters away, my toiletries in the fancy bathroom, and while I'm standing on the marble tiles, I envision my mother here.

She loved a good bath, and this bathtub is fit for a queen.

I imagine her soaking here, reading a good book, and my eyes well up.

She's gone.

I know that.

I pull open the closet doors, and for a moment, a very brief moment, I swear I catch a whiff of her perfume.

She's worn the same scent for as long as I've known her.

There are shelves in this walk-in closet, and on one, I see a bottle of Chanel.

Her scent.

I clutch it to me, and inhale it, and it brings a firestorm of memories down on my head. Of my mother laughing, of her baking cookies, of her grinning at me over the top of her book.

With burning eyes, I put the bottle back.

This isn't helping anything.

I hang my shirts and my sweaters.

There's a knock on the door, and Sabine comes in with a tray. A teapot and a cup.

"I brought you some tea," she tells me quietly, setting it on a table. "It'll perk you up. Traveling is hard on a person."

Losing their entire life is hard on a person.

But of course I don't say that.

I just smile and say thank you.

She pours me a cup and hands it to me.

"This will help you rest. It's calming."

I sip at it, and Sabine turns around, surveying my empty bags.

"I see you've already unpacked. These rooms haven't been changed since your mother left."

I hold my cup in my lap, warming my fingers because the chill from the English evening has left them cold.

"Why *did* my mother leave?" I ask, because she's never said. She's never said *anything* about her childhood home.

Sabine pauses, and when she looks at me, she's looking into my soul again, rooting around with wrinkled fingers.

"She left because she had to," Sabine says simply. "Whitley couldn't hold her."

It's an answer that's not an answer.

I should've expected no less.

Sabine sits next to me, patting my leg.

"I'll fatten you up a bit here," she tells me. "You're too skinny, like your mama. You'll rest and you'll... see things for what they are."

"And how is that?" I ask tiredly, and suddenly I'm so very exhausted.

Sabine looks at my face and clucks.

"Child, you need to rest. You're fading away in front of my eyes. Come now. Lie down."

She settles me onto the bed, pulling a blanket up to my chin.

"Dinner is at seven," she reminds me before she leaves. "Sleep until then."

I try.

I really do.

I close my eyes.

I relax my arms and my legs and my muscles.

But sleep won't come.

Eventually, I give up, and I open the drapes and look outside.

The evening is quiet, the sky is dark. *It gets dark so early here.*

The trees rustle in the breeze, and the wind is wet. It's cold. It's chilling. I can feel it even through the windows and I rub at my arms.

That's when I get goose-bumps.

They lift the hair on my neck,

And the stars seem to mock me.

Turning my back on them, I cross the room and pull a book from a shelf.

Jane Eyre.

Fitting, given Whitley and the moors and the rain.

I open the cover and find a penned inscription.

To Calla. May you always have the courage to live free, and the strength to do what is right.

The ink is fading, and I run my fingertips across it.

A message to me? It's almost like my mother knew I would be here, and she left this very book for me on these very shelves in this very room.

I slip into a seat with it, pulling open the pages, my eyes trying to devour the words my mother once read.

But I've only gotten to the part where Jane proclaims that she hates long walks on cold afternoons when I hear something.

I feel something.

I feel a growl in my bones.

It's low and threatening, and it vibrates my ribs.

I startle upright, looking around, but of course, I'm still alone.

But the growl happens again, low and long.

My breath hitches and the book hits the floor, the pages fluttering on the rug.

A sudden panic overtakes me, rapid and hot.

I have to get out.

I don't know why.

It's a feeling I have in my heart, something that drives me from my mother's rooms out into the hall, because something is chasing me.

I feel it on my heels.

I feel it breathing down my neck.

Without looking back, I rush back down the corridor, through the house and out the front doors.

I've got to breathe.

I've got to breathe.

I've got to breathe.

Sucking in air, I walk aimlessly around the house, over the cobblestone and down a pathway. I draw in long even breaths, trying to still my shaking hands, trying to gather myself together, trying to assure myself that I'm being silly.

There's no reason to be afraid.

I'm being ridiculous.

This house might be strange and foreign, but it's still a home. It just isn't *my* home. It's fine. I'll get used to it.

I look behind me, and there's nothing there.

There is no growl, there is no vibration in my ribs, there is nothing but for the dim twilight and the stars aching to burst from behind the clouds.

The house looms over me and I circle back, only to find myself in front of a large garage with gabled edges.

There are at least seven garage doors, all closed but one.

To my surprise, someone walks out of that door.

A boy.

A man.

His pants are dark gray and he's wearing a hoodie, and he moves with grace. He slides among the shadows with ease, as though he belongs here, as though Whitley is his home too, even though I don't know him, even though I feel like I do. I feel it I feel it I feel it.

"Hello," I call out to him.

He stops moving, freezing in his tracks, but he doesn't turn his head.

Something about that puts me on edge and I tense, because what if he's not supposed to be here?

"Hello?" I repeat uneasily, and chills run up my spine, goose-bumps forming on my arms once again.

I back away, first one step, then another.

I blink,

And he's gone.

I stare at the empty space, and shake my head, blinking hard.

He's still gone.

He must've slipped between the buildings, but why?

I'm too nervous to find out, and so I turn to walk back to the house. As I do, two enormous shadows bound out of the trees and race toward me, panting and skidding to a halt in front of me.

I'm frozen as I stare at two of the biggest dogs I've ever seen.

"It's okay," I tell them, as they examine me with dark eyes. "I'm supposed to be here. I'm not an intruder."

They stare at me.

I stare back.

Then one steps forward and nudges my hand, sliding his massive head beneath my palm like he knows me, like he's not going to attack me.

"Castor!" Sabine yells from behind me. "Pollux!"

The dogs stand at attention, and when she yells Come, they do.

She looks at me. "I'm sorry if they got you muddy," she tells me. "They're the estate dogs. And as you can see, they aren't always graceful."

I follow her gaze and she's staring at muddy paw-prints on my legs, and when did that happen?

"They're fine," I tell her, because they didn't hurt me. In fact, even though they're enormous, they have such sweet faces. Sabine acts like she knows what I'm thinking.

"They wouldn't hurt anybody," she tells me. "It's their size that is intimidating." She pauses. "They'd protect you with their lives, though."

Me?

Before I can ask, she returns to the house and the dogs go with her. Down the path a ways, one of them pauses and turns to look at me, but then he continues on his way and I try to put my uneasiness to rest.

Why am I uneasy?

They're just dogs.

And the guy I saw was just a gardener or something.

Nothing to be unnerved about.

Yet I'm still unsettled as I wash my face, so when I'm finished, I poke my head out into the hall. There's nothing there.

With a sigh, I lock my bedroom door and I'm chilled from the wet English air. Glancing at the clock, I find it's only six thirty. I can rest for a few minutes more, and I'm thankful for that.

Because clearly, jet lag has made me its bitch.

Chapter Twenty-Four

As I step into the grand foyer of Whitley, my feet have barely hit the floor when I feel the overwhelming sense of being stifled, of the coldness that permeates a person's bones here. To put the feeling in perspective, my home in Oregon is a funeral home. Whitley is far, far worse.

Finn picks my hand, aware of my faltering steps. "You ok?" he whispers, his blue eyes searching mine. I nod.

Of course I'm lying. I'm not ok. Why would I be?

I stand in the foyer windows, staring across the moors. England has such haunting moors, such rolling, wet fields, such places that are conducive to melancholy. It makes me think of sadness, of Charlotte Bronte, of Jane Eyre.

I don't know why I identify so much with Jane. She's plain, and I know that I'm not. I have hair like fire, eyes like bright emeralds. I'm not being conceited in admitting that, because after all, physical attributes are things that we cannot help. I am pretty, but I didn't earn it. I was simply born this way, a product of a beautiful mother. Internal traits though, they're important and praiseworthy. Jane Eyre is fierce in

265

spirit, and I like to believe that I am, too. Fierceness is much more commendable than my pretty face.

To be honest, I almost wish that I weren't pretty. It makes me self-conscious. People tend to stare, and when they do, I always feel like they're staring at me because they think I'm crazy.

Crazy

Crazy

Crazy.

Just like my brother.

It's like a whisper, echoing through the rooms of Whitley, across the grounds, through the air. Everyone watches us, my brother and me, to see which one of us will crack.

"I'm going for a walk," I tell Finn. His head snaps up.

"Alone? You'll get lost."

"No, I won't. I'm just going to explore."

"I'll come too."

"No. Go get something to eat. I just need a few minutes to breathe, Finn."

He nods now because he understands that.

I slip outside, out the door, away from the doom of the house.

The breeze is slightly chilly as I make my way deep into the grounds. I've come to believe that it never truly warms up here. The rain makes the lawns lush, though. Green and full and colorful. It's viridem. And green means life.

The cobbled path turns to pebbles as I get further away from the house, and after a minute, I come to a literal fork in the road. The path splits into two. One leads toward a wooded area, and the other leads to a beautiful stone building on the edge of the horizon, shrouded in mist and weeping trees.

It's small and mysterious, beautiful and ancient. And of course I have to get a closer look. Without a second thought, I head down that path.

The closer I get, the more my curiosity grows.

I can smell the moss as I approach, that musty, dank smell that comes with a closed room or a wet space. And with that dark scent comes a very oppressive feeling. I feel it weighing on my shoulders as I open the heavy door, as I stare at the word SAVAGE inscribed in the wood, as I take my first tentative step into a room that hasn't seen human life in what looks like years.

But it *has* seen death.

I'm standing in a mausoleum.

Growing up in a funeral home, I'm well versed in death. I know what it looks like, what it smells like, even what it tastes like in the air.

I'm surrounded by it here.

The floor is stone, but since it is deprived of light, soft green moss grows in places, and is soft under my feet. The walls are thick blocks of stone, and have various alcoves, filled with the remains of Savage family members. They go back for generations, and it makes me wonder how long the Savages have lived at Whitley.

Nearest me, are Richard Savage I, my grandfather, and Richard Savage II, my uncle. *When did he die?* And next to him is Olivia.

Olivia.

I run my fingers along her name, tracing the letters cut in the stone, absorbing the coolness, the hardness.

What do I know about her, other than she must have been Dare's mother?

Why is she significant in my memory?

Did Dare have her eyes, or her hair? Was she the only spot of brightness in his world? Does he miss her more than life itself?

I don't know.

Trailing my fingers along the wall, I circle the room, eyeing my ancestors, marveling at the silence here.

It's so loud that my ears ring with it.

The open door creates a sliver of light on the dark floor, and it's while I'm focusing on the brightness that I first hear the whisper.

Calla.

I whip my head around, only to find nothing behind me.

Chills run down my spine, and goose-bumps form on my arms as I eye the empty room. The only people here are dead.

But... the whisper was crystal clear in the silence.

I'm hearing voices.

That fact terrifies me, but not as much as the familiarity in that whisper.

"Hello?" I call out, desperate for someone to be here, for someone real to have spoken. But no one answers.

Of course not.

I'm alone.

I lay my hand on the wall and try to draw in a deep breath. I can't be crazy. It's one of my worst fears, second only to losing my brother.

A movement catches my eye and I focus on it.

Carnation petals and stargazers, white and red, blow across the floor. Funeral flowers.

Startled, I turn toward them, bending to touch them. I run one between my fingers, its texture velvety smooth. It hadn't been here a moment ago. None of them had, yet here they are, strewn across the floor.

They lead to a crypt in the wall.

Adair Phillip DuBray.

My heart pounds and pounds as I race to the plaque, as I trace the fresh letters with my fingertips. His middle name is the same as my father's.

And this wasn't here before.

What the hell?

I gulp, drawing in air, observing the fresh flowers in the vase beside his name.

There is no moss here, because this had been freshly carved, recently opened, and very recently sealed. But there's no way Dare can be here, because I just saw him last night. He's fine, he's fine, he's fine.

As my hands palm his name, as I reassure myself, pictures fill my head, images and smells.

The sea, a cliff, a car.

Blood, shrieking metal, the water.

Dare.

He's bloody,

He's bloody,

He's bloody.

Everything is on fire,

The flames lick at the stone walls,

Trying to find any possible way out.

The smoke chokes me and I cough,

gasping for air.

I blink and everything is gone.

My hands are on a blank wall, and Dare's name is gone.

The flowers are gone.

I'm alone.

The floor is bare.

I can't breathe.

I can't breathe.

I can't breathe.

I'm crazy.

It's the only explanation.

I scramble for the door and burst out into the sunlight, away from the mausoleum, away from the death. I fly toward the house, tripping on the stones.

"Calla?"

My name is called and I'm afraid to look, afraid no one will be there, afraid that I'm still imagining things. Is this what Finn felt like every day? Am I starting down that slippery path? It's a rabbit hole and I'm the rabbit and I'm crazy.

But it's Dare, standing tall and strong on the path, and I fly into his arms, without worrying about pushing him away.

His arms close around me and he smells so good, so familiar, and I close my eyes.

"You're fine," I tell him, I tell myself. "You're ok."

"Yes, I'm fine," he says in confusion, his hands stroking my back, holding me close. "Did you think something happened to me?"

I see his name, carved in the mausoleum stone, and I shudder, pushing the vision away, far out of my mind.

"No. I...no."

He holds me for several minutes more, then looks down at me, tucking an errant strand of my hair behind my ear.

"Are you ok? You've been gone for hours."

Hours? How can that be? The sky swirls, and I steady myself against his chest.

I hear his heart and it's beating fast, because he's afraid.

271

He's afraid for me because he recognizes the signs, he's seen them before, he's seen them in my brother.

"It's ok, Cal," he murmurs, but I can hear the concern in his voice. "It's ok."

But I can tell from his voice that it's not.

Craziness is genetic.

I'm the rabbit.

And I'm crazy.

"Is your father's name Phillip?" I ask him tentatively, and he glances down at me.

"Yes."

"Mine is too."

"I know," he says. "But things aren't always what they seem, Cal. Remember?"

That seems so silly. My father's name is Phillip and his father's name is Phillip and it is what it is. Dare's arm is around my shoulders as we walk back to the house, and I can feel him glance at me from time to time.

"Stop," I tell him finally as we walk through the gardens. "I'm fine."

"Ok," he agrees. "Of course you are."

But he knows better, and he knows that I'm not.

Sabine is kneeling by the library doors, digging through the rich English soil, and she looks at us over her shoulder. When she sees my face, her eyes narrow and she climbs to her feet.

"Are you all right, Miss Price?" she asks in her gravelly voice. I want to lie, I want to tell her that I'm fine, but I know she can tell the difference. In fact, as she stares at me with those dark eyes, I feel like she can see into my soul.

I don't bother to lie.

I just shake my head.

She nods.

"Come with me."

She leads us both to the back of the house, to her room. It's small and dark, draped in colorful fabrics, in mystic symbols and pieces of gaudy jewelry, shrouded in mirrors and dream-catchers and stars.

I'm stunned and I pause, gazing at all of the pageantry.

She glimpses my expression and shrugs. "I'm Roma," she says, by way of explanation. At my blank expression, she sighs. "Romani. Gypsy. I'm not ashamed of it."

She holds her head up high, her chin out, and I can see that she's far from ashamed. She's proud.

"You shouldn't be," I assure her weakly. "It's your heritage. It's fascinating."

She's satisfied by that, by the idea that I'm not looking down at her for who she is.

Her dark eyes tell a story, and to me, they tell me that she knows more than I do. That she might even know more about *me* than I do.

It's crazy, I know.

But apparently, I'm crazy now.

Sabine guides me to a velvet chair and pushes me gently into it. She glances at Dare.

"Leave us," she tells him softly. "I've got her now. She'll be fine."

He's hesitant and he looks at me, and I nod.

I'll be fine.

I think.

He slips away, and I don't want him to go, but he has to. Because he's part of this, I can feel it, and I can't trust him. My heart says so.

Sabine rustles about and as she does, I look around. On the table next to me, tarot cards are splayed out, formed in an odd formation, as though I'd interrupted a fortune telling.

I gulp because something hangs in the air here.

Something mystical.

After a minute, Sabine shoves a cup into my hands.

"Drink. It's lemon balm and chamomile. It'll settle your stomach and calm you down."

I don't bother to ask how she knew I was upset. It must've been written all over my face.

I sip at the brew and after a second, she glances at me.

"Better?"

I nod. "Thank you."

She smiles and her teeth are scary. I look away, and she roots through a cabinet. She extracts her prize and hands me a box.

"Take this at night. It'll help you sleep." I glance at her questioningly. She adds, "By night you are free, child."

I don't know what that means, but I take the box, which is unmarked, and she nods.

I glance at her table again. "Are you a fortune-teller, Sabine?" It feels odd to say those words in a serious manner, but the old woman doesn't miss a beat.

"I read the cards," she nods. "Someday, I'll read yours."

I don't know if I want to know what they'll say.

"Have you read Dare's?" I ask impulsively, and I don't know why. Sabine glances at me, her black eyes knowing.

"That boy doesn't need his fortune told. He writes his own."

I have no idea what that means, but I nod like I do.

"You'll be ok now," she tells me, her expression wise and I find myself believing her. She's got a calming nature, something that settles the air around her. I hadn't noticed that before.

"My mother never mentioned you," I murmur. "I find that odd, since she must've loved you."

Sabine looks away. "Your mother doesn't have happy memories from here," she says quietly. "But I know her heart."

"Ok," I say uncertainly. "Sabine, why did my mother leave here? Why does my father have the same name as Dare's?"

Sabine is so knowing as she sinks back into her chair.

"Your father as you know him isn't your father," she says simply, and I gasp, my hands shaking as they grip the chair.

"What do you mean?"

"Phillip has raised you as his own. But you are the child of Richard Savage."

My breath

My breath

My breath.

"My uncle?"

I can't

I can't

I can't.

Sabine nods, and she's unhesitant, as though this is just another face of life, as though it weren't unnatural.

"Yes. It was necessary. Your mother did as she was told."

"Necessary for what?"

I'm still appalled, and sickened, and Sabine hands me a basin and I vomit into it.

"Your mother and uncle came together, and you were conceived," Sabine tells me. "Your mother fled to France with her lover, and she conceived again. She gave birth to twins… you and Finn. But you don't share the same father."

"Phillip," I utter. "Phillip is Finn's father? And Phillip is Dare's father?"

Sabine nods, pleased that I have grasped it. "Yes. They are half-brothers."

"And Finn, my twin, is only my half-brother?"

She nods again. "It happens very rarely in life, child. But you are rare."

I'm afraid to ask, but I do it anyway.

"Why?"

Sabine pours more tea and hands it to me, and I can't help but drink it because it calms me it calms me it calms me, and I'm on the verge of hysteria.

"Because you are a descendent of Judas, and of Abel. Your blood is as powerful and old as is possible. Your brother is a descendent of *both* Cain and Abel. If he is sacrificed, the cycle will finally be broken."

"What cycle?" I ask and my lips are numb they're numb.

"Cain killed his brother," she answers. "Abel made a sacrifice to God, and Cain was jealous so he killed him. God is owed another sacrifice from this family, a true sacrifice, one born of grief and torment, to pay for the sins of your fathers."

"I don't understand," I whisper. "I don't understand."

"Of course you don't," she nods. "Dare understands, though, because Dare is of Salome.

Salome harnessed the curse of Judas into a ring. The ring you gave back to Dare. You are all cursed, and only you can stop it by making the right choice, by not betraying what is right. The Rom believe curses are real, Calla. And surely by now, so do you."

"I..."

My lips can't move.

"It's one for one for one, Calla," Sabine adds. "That's the way it's always been. Make the right choice, and this will all end."

Maybe her tea has valium in it, because I find myself agreeing. I find myself deciding that she is right.

But as I walk into my room, I decide I must've imagined the whole thing. Salome? Cain and Abel? Judas? Ancient biblical curses and Dare's grave?

These things are impossible. Rom beliefs aren't real.

I'm confused, like normal. I haven't been sleeping well.

Obviously.

That's the explanation.

I raise my hand to tuck my hair behind my ear, and that's when I freeze.

My fingers smell like carnations and stargazers, the flowers that were on Dare's grave.

It was real.

Chapter Twenty-Five

"We're related," I tell Dare, and my voice is urgent and my hand is on his chest. "We can't...we can't...we can't be together."

Dare's face is pained and he knew.

"You knew," I whisper, and the pain in my heart pangs loud loud louder, and he looks at me, and his gaze is so sorrowful and real.

"Things change," he tells me, and I snort with disgust because we were together and it was incest and I still love him more than anything but Finn. I still love him I still love him I still love him.

"God, I want to die," I groan, and I push him away and he shakes me hard hard harder.

"Don't you ever say that again," he snaps. "Don't you ever. We've been through worse and we will weather this storm, Calla. We're not truly related. It's just complicated."

I look at him and my eyes feel like they will explode with pain and with sadness.

"I don't want to live if I can't be with you," and my words are painfully raw with honesty. "I truly don't."

"It won't be this way," Dare insists, and he is hiding something from me.

Something

Something

Something.

"What is it?" I ask, and I'm hopeful for just a moment.

"I want to tell you everything, but it's something you have to figure out for yourself," he tells me. "You have to see it, or you won't believe it. It's complex, it's complicated, it's real."

His fingers lace with mine and the touch doesn't feel wrong, it feels right.

He pulls me to him, and he kisses me, and his lips are warm and his breath is hot and his body is hard against mine.

"This isn't wrong," he tells me, and his lips move against my cheek. "Does it feel wrong to you, Calla-Lily?"

No

God

No.

It feels as right as anything.

His hands splay against my back and he whispers. "Don't ever say that you want to die, Calla. It's not your fate to sacrifice yourself. It's not."

"How do you know what fate has planned?" I ask him, and I pull away so that I can see into his face and he is so serious so serious so serious.

"Because I just do."

"That isn't an answer," I tell him.

"But it is," he says, and then his hands fall away and he walks into the house.

I'm alone, and the answers chirp from the trees, across the moors and I have to get them. I have to get the answers, because my sanity is slip slip slipping and if I don't figure it out soon, I'll be lost.

I know that.

I know that.

So I find my brother, and I insist that we seek out the truth. Finn loves me so he comes and he's doubtful, but he's here.

I stand at the mouth of the woods, and the trees bend and hiss and sway, and words form on my lips.

"One for one for one."

"What does that mean?" Finn asks me, because he's standing at my elbow.

He won't leave me, not now that he thinks I'm as crazy as he is.

"We have to keep each other sane," that's what he said yesterday after I told him what happened in the mausoleum and in Sabine's room.

I look at him now.

"I don't know what it means," I tell him honestly. "I just hear it in my head, over and over."

Finn looks at me, and he's scared and his pale hand grasps mine.

"That's bad, Cal," he tells me, and he doesn't have to say the words because I already know. Of course I know.

I step into the mossy forest, and I'm surrounded by the cool ferns and shadows, and I don't know why, but I know I'm supposed to be here.

"Don't," Finn urges me to come back, and he won't follow. "I don't like the way it feels in there."

"I don't either," I tell him, but I keep going, one foot after the other, because I'm being pulled by an invisible tether or a cord.

Finn stays and his face is worried, but he's unable to follow, and I don't judge him for that. The feeling in the woods is oppressive, and dark, and terrifying.

There's something here.

Something here for me.

Ahead of me, a shadow moves, it lurches, it glides.

I follow it, unable to remain still. It flits in and out of trees, and so do I.

And then finally, finally,

It's gone, and I'm alone.

I feel the stillness, and I taste it with my tongue, and I'm alone.

I stare about, I whirl in a circle, and there are charred wooden pieces arranged in a circle, a bonfire.

I see something amid the ashes, something brown, something tattered, something old.

I bend and touch it, and it burns my finger.

The embers are still hot.

I rock back on my heels and prod at it with a stick until it falls away, out of the embers and to safety.

It's a book and it falls open and the first page stares up at me, with my brother's scrawling handwriting.

The Journal of Finn Price.

My eyebrows crimp and knit, and I take a breath, because why was Finn out here?

I wait while the breeze cools the pages, and even though they are charred, there are still some left that I can read.

NOCTE LIBER SUM NOCTE LIBER SUM
BY NIGHT I AM FREE.
ALEA IACTA EST. THE DIE HAS BEEN CAST.
The die has been cast.
The die has been cast.
Serva me, servabo te.
Save me, and I'll save you.
Save me.
Save me.
Save me.

My breath comes in pants and I can't I can't I can't.

Because Sabine said these words to me, these same exact words, in different times and places.

She said the same things to my brother?

What do they mean?

The pages are fragile and the edges come off in my fingers, black and charred, but I can still make out more of the words.

I'M DROWNING. DROWNING, DROWNING.
IMMERSUM, IMMERSUM, IMMERSUM.
CALLA WILL SAVE ME OR I WILL DIE I WILL
DIE I WILL DIE.
SERVA ME, SERVABO TE.
SAVE ME AND I'LL SAVE YOU.
SAVE ME.
SAVE ME,
SAVE ME, CALLA.
AND I'LL SAVE YOU.

There are stick figures and symbols, and some of the faces are scratched out, and I don't remember his journal being so morbid or nonsensical when I found it so long ago. If it had been, I would've taken it straight to our parents because this, this, this is crazy.

I stare at a picture, and it's of two boys and a girl. One of the boys is scratched completely out, but I can still see his eyes and his eyes are black and I know the boy is Dare. Finn scratched out Dare.

ONE FOR ONE FOR ONE.
THE DIE HAS BEEN CAST, IT'S BEEN CAST.
ONE FOR ONE FOR ONE,
AND IT WON'T BE ME.

IT WON'T BE CALLA.
ONE
FOR
ONE
FOR
ONE.

I'm frozen as an ominous feeling builds in my belly, spreading to my chest where it threatens to stop my heart. Dark fingers seem to grab my shoulders and shake hard, harder, harder until my teeth chatter.

DEATH IS THE BEGINNING.
The beginning.
The beginning.
I need to start.

I drop the journal and take off running, back through the trees. The branches whip at my face and I slip around in the dew, but it doesn't matter.

I know why Finn wouldn't come with me.

He knew I'd find his journal, and he knew I'd stop him from whatever stupid thing he's going to try and do. I can tell from his writing... he believes what Sabine told me. A sacrifice must be made, and he's not going to let it be me.

DEATH IS THE BEGINNING. I NEED TO START.

A sacrifice.
A sacrifice.
The sacrifice is me.
We pay for the sins of our fathers.
I am the sin.
I am the sacrifice.

The words race through my head, over and over, as I burst from the trees, and I see him. I see Finn, and he's running with the hooded boy, with Death.

I chase after them into Whitley, as I bound up the stairs, as I race to Finn's room. It's empty…except for Pollux and Castor. Finn had closed them up in the room, and there's only one reason. So that they couldn't follow him.

"Go," I tell them firmly. "Go find Finn."

They run from my room, their great bodies so loud as they thump down the halls. I follow as fast as I can, and I slam into Dare as he rounds a corner.

"What the devil…?" he asks, and he's confused and I shove past him.

"My brother is in trouble," I yell over my shoulder. He doesn't ask questions, but I hear him behind me, I hear him running, I hear his breath. But I can't pay attention to that. All I can do is follow the dogs. I chase them from the house, I chase them through the gardens, and I watch the tips of their black tails disappear through the gates of Whitley.

"Calla, wait," Dare grabs my arm. "We've got to get the car."

"There's not time," I mutter, and Dare yanks me to the side.

"Then the scooters. We'll never keep up."

The old scooters are next to the gate and I don't know why they aren't put away, but I'm grateful as I grab one and the battery is charged and I go full throttle down the road. Dare is with me on the other one, and we go and go, until the dogs race up a cliff.

Our scooters make winding sounds and lag behind because the climb is too steep and so I cast mine aside and run, my breathing labored, because somethingsomethingsomething is going to happen. I can feel it, I can feel it.

My brother.

My brother.

It's a chant in my head and I can't focus, and then I clear the crest at the top and there's Finn.

He's standing on the edge and the dogs have skidded to a stop and we all watch my brother.

"Don't do it," I plead with him because his face is serious and pale. "I don't know what this is about, but please don't do this, Finn. I need you."

"I need to save you," he says simply, and his voice is emotionless and there is no fear in his eyes. Absolutely no fear. "It has to be me. I've always known. Dare told me long ago."

His black Converses teeter on the edge and he lifts his hands.

"I love you, Calla," he tells me. "I'd die for you. It's got to be me, because it can't be you."

Life is in slow motion, and he limply falls back, like he's falling into bed, but instead, he falls off the side of the cliff.

I race to the edge, and I watch and there's no sound when he hits the water. No sound at all. How can that be?

Dare grabs my shoulders and I scream and scream and scream, and then two black flashes sail over the edge next to me.

Castor and Pollux.

They dive right through the air with purpose and I remember what Sabine said.

"He'd die to protect you."

Maybe they'd die to protect Finn, too.

The dogs hit the water and I do hear them, and I turn, racing to the bottom, desperate to reach my brother and when my feet hit the wet sand, I run and the dogs are limping in from the surf, dragging my brother's limp form between them.

The dogs are bloody and they're dragging their bodies on splintered legs and they're broken broken broken, and a wave of familiarity rushes over me and through me and I've seen this before,

I've seen this before,

I've seen this before.

I've been here before, but that's not possible and I can't think about it because all I can think about right now is my brother.

I yank him away from the dogs and I breathe into his cold mouth, and he's limp and he's cold and he's wet.

I drag him onto my lap and we're halfway into the water, and I hear Dare on the phone and he's talking to someone.

"There's been an accident," he's saying, and I've heard those words before, from his mouth from his lips from his voice.

"Was it?" I look up at him, and my eyes are burning burning burning. "Was it an accident?"

Because Finn's words his words his words. *I've always known. Dare told me long ago.*

Dare closes his eyes, and Finn's eyes are closed, and he's limp and he's cold and he's dead.

He's dead.

Death is the beginning and he needs to start.

"I can't do this without you," I whisper in his wet ear. "Please God, please God, please God. Finn. Please."

Silver glints and it's his St. Michael's medallion and he was wearing it and he wasn't protected he wasn't protected.

"Fuck you, St. Michael," I scream and Dare's hand is on my shoulder and I yank away because somehowsomehowsomehow, this is Dare's fault. I feel it. I feel it. The pictures that Finn drew in his journal... Dare's face was scratched out. Finn knew something I didn't.

"What did you do?" I screech at Dare, and I refuse to let go of my brother. I clutch at his buttoned up shirt, and I clutch at his cold skin.

Help comes, but they're too late, and they try to pry me away from my brother and I hate them I hate them I hate them.

I hold my brother's hand as they lift him into the ambulance, but there's a sheet over his face and they know he's dead and no one has the guts to make me move. No one.

I ride with him to the hospital, and I hold his hand the whole way.

"What did you do?" I ask Finn, into his ear. He doesn't answer and the sheet is over his face. His hand doesn't move and he's dead and he's dead.

"Miss, you have to let go," one of the paramedics tells me. She's sympathetic, but firm, and they don't know what to do with me.

"Never," I tell them. And that's metaphorical, and they know that. My hand falls away and they take my brother.

I sink to the floor and I stay there until Dare comes to get me, until he carries me to the car and straps me in and my head is on the window.

"What did you do?" I ask him, my eyes closed.

"Nothing," he says simply. "That's what I did."

He reaches over and his hand is warm. "Because it can't be you, Calla. I can't let it be you."

Nothing makes sense and when I get home, Sabine ushers me to my room and she forces me to drink tea, and I do it because I need the oblivion it brings.

I need to be in darkness.

I need to be with Finn.

I can't exist in a world without him. He's my light. He's my light.

Chapter Twenty-Six

I'm wooden for days. I barely speak, I only eat what they force me to eat. I don't want to exist, not without Finn.

Jones takes me to church, because I need to pray, even if it's to a God who took Finn away. It's the only thing I can do.

With a plain brick Gothic Revival exterior, the church looms against the cloudy sky, sort of severe and imposing.

I'm hesitant as I peer out the glass.

"It's the Church of St. Thomas of Canterbury," Jones tells me. "This is where Savages go."

I know he means the family, but the irony isn't lost on me because people seem savage to me right now, all people, particularly people who follow a God who takes away my brother.

"I'll wait, miss," Jones tells me, settling into the seat. I nod, and with my shoulders back, I walk straight to the doors.

Once inside, the demeanor of the church changes, from severe gothic, to lavishly decorated, firmly in line with Catholic tradition.

It feels reverent in here, holy and serene. And even if I'm not a religious person, I enjoy it.

The statues of saints and angels hanging on the walls are gilded and full of detail, including the crucifix of Christ at the front.

His face is pained, His hands and feet are bleeding.

I look away, because even still, it's hard for me to imagine such a sacrifice, but at the same time, I can feel it. Because my brother is gone, and that's the biggest sacrifice in the world.

"Are you here for confession, child?"

A low voice comes from behind and I turn to find a priest watching me. His eyes are kind above his white collar, and even though he doesn't know me, this man, this priest, is kind simply to be kind.

I swallow.

"I'm not Catholic," I tell him, trying to keep my words soft in this grand place. He smiles.

"I'll try not to hold that against you," he confides, and he holds his hand out. I take it, and it's warm.

"I'm Father Thomas," he introduces himself. "And this is my parish. Welcome."

Even his hands are kind as he grasps mine, and I find myself instantly at ease for the first time in weeks.

"Thank you," I murmur.

"Would you like a tour?" he suggests, and I nod.

"I'd love one."

He doesn't ask why I'm here or what I want, he just leads me around, pointing out this artifact and that, this architecture detail or that stained glass window.

He chats with me for a long time, and makes me feel like I'm the only person in the world, and that he has no place else to be.

Finally, when he's finished, he turns to me. "Would you like to sit?"

I do.

So he sits with me, and we're quiet for a long time.

"My mother used to come here, I'm told," I finally confide. "And I just wanted to feel like I'm near her."

The priest studies me. "And do you?"

My shoulders slump. "Not really."

"I've been here for a long time," he says kindly. "I knew your mother. Laura Savage?"

I'm surprised and he laughs.

"Child, you could be her mirror image," he chuckles. "It wasn't hard to figure out."

"You knew her?" I breathe, and somehow, I do feel closer to her, simply because he was.

He nods and looks toward Mary. "Laura is a beautiful soul," he says gently. "And I can see her in your eyes."

I swallow because of pain and the priest blinks.

"I'm so sorry. She's with the Lord now, though. She's at peace. Your brother is too."

My breath leaves me. "Did you know my brother?"

Father Thomas shakes his head. "No. But I gave him the Last Rites at the hospital. And I'll be coming to the family mausoleum this week for his funeral."

My eyes burn and fill, and I twist and turn Finn's medallion in my fingers.

"I cursed St. Michael," I admit to him. "On the beach. Do you think that's why we couldn't save Finn?"

He's surprised and his eyes widen. "Of course not, child. God and St. Michael knew your pain. You have to believe that. Everything happens for a reason."

He stares at the medallion and it's around my neck and I don't know why I'm wearing it. I guess because it's Finn's.

"My mother gave it to my brother a long time ago," I tell the priest. "But it didn't work. It was supposed to protect him...."

Father Thomas nods. "It was Finn's time. Keep wearing the medallion. You'll feel close to your brother and St. Michael will protect you, Calla. You just have to trust."

Trust.

That's actually a bit laughable in my current circumstances.

"Let's pray together, shall we?" he suggests, and I don't argue because it can't hurt.

Our voices are soft and uniform as they meld together in the sunlight,

In front of Christ on the Crucifix,

and the two Marys.

St. Michael the Archangel, defend us in battle. Be our defense against the wickedness and snares of the Devil. May God rebuke him, we humbly pray, and do thou, O Prince of the heavenly hosts, by the power of God, thrust into hell Satan, and all the evil spirits, who prowl about the world seeking the ruin of souls. Amen.

"Do you believe in evil?" I whisper when we're finished, and for some reason, my goose-bumps are back. I feel someone watching me, but when I open my eyes, Christ Himself stares at me. From his perch on the wall, his eyes are soft and forgiving while the blood drips from his feet.

"Of course," the priest nods. "There is good in the world, and there is evil. They balance each other out, Calla."

Do they?

"Because energy can't be destroyed?" I whisper. Because it goes from thing to thing to thing?'

The priest shakes his head. "I don't know about energy. I only know that there is good and evil. And we must find our own balance in it. You will find yours."

Will I?

The priest examines me for a moment. "Twins are such an interesting thing," he tells me. "Did you know that some believe that Cain and Abel were twins?"

I shake my head.

"There are scholars who believe that," the priest nods. "They feel like they were the first example of the darkness and light capable in people."

"Cain killed his own brother," I manage to say. "That's pretty dark."

"And Finn died thinking he was saving you," Father Thomas says. "*That* is light."

I don't ask him how he knows that. I just thank him and stand up and he blesses me.

"Come back to see me," he instructs. "I've enjoyed our chat. If you're not Catholic, I can't hear your confession, but I am a good listener."

He is. I have to agree.

I make my way out of the church, out of the pristine glistening silence, and when I step into the sun, I know I'm being watched.

Every hair on my head feels it, and prickles.

I turn, and a boy is standing on the edge of the yard, just outside of the fence. He's watching me, his hands in his pockets, but I can't see his face. His hood is pulled up yet again.

With my breath in my throat, I hurry down the sidewalk to the car, practically diving inside and slamming the door behind me.

"Has that guy been standing there long?" I ask Jones breathlessly.

"What guy, miss?" he asks in confusion, hurrying to look out the window.

I look too, only to find that he's gone.

297

Chapter Twenty-Seven

Finn's bedroom is still and quiet. Since Castor and Pollux are dead, not even the dogs keep me company. Yet somehow, I still feel Finn in here, as though if I spoke to him, he'd answer.

"Finn?"

I feel ridiculous, but God, I miss my brother. It's only been a few days without him, but it feels like eternity.

There's no answer, of course, and I press my forehead to the glass, watching the cars come and go. Finn is laid out in a room downstairs, for visitation. His funeral will be tomorrow and I can't bear it.

I lay with my face on his pillow and I close my eyes and I rest.

"You don't belong here, do you?"

The voice is quiet, yet cool.

Startled, I open my eyes and stare up at the boy in the hoodie. With a gasp, I sit straight up in bed, because the voice was feminine.

His head is tilted just enough that I can't see his face.

I peer toward him and his face is dark.

"Who are you?" I ask, and my words sound hollow. He cocks his head but doesn't answer, although there's a low growl in his throat.

"What do you want?"

He's calm, his head is down. But his arm comes up,

And he points at me.

He wants me.

"Me?"

"Of course." I know him I know him I know him.

But I can't place from where.

"I can help you, you know."

"You can?"

He nods.

"Let's get out of here. I'll show you where horrid things hide."

His smile is one of camaraderie, and any port in a storm.

When we're in the driveway, he turns to me.

"Maybe you should've brought a wrap. You might get cold."

But he puts the top down on his car anyway, and we speed through the night, away from Whitley.

"Where are we going?" I finally ask, relieved to be so far away.

He glances at me.

"Someplace you should see. If you think you want to be with Dare, you should know all about him."

"Do you know Dare?"

"Of course," he says. "He's my brother."

I'm surprised, but not, because I knew that I knew that I knew that. I just don't remember how. There's something in his voice now, something rigid, and I startle, because maybe I shouldn't have chosen this port.

He turns down a dark road, a quiet lane, and then we pull to a stop in front of an old, crumbling building.

"Come on," he calls over his shoulder, traipsing up the steps. The sign by the door says Oakdale Sanitarium and I freeze.

"What is this place?" I whisper as he opens the door.

"You'll have to see it to believe it," he murmurs.

In front of us, a long hallway yawns farther than I can see, the walls crumbling with age, the lights dim when he flips a switch.

There's no one here, but I can hear moans, screams, whimpers.

"I don't understand," I feel like whimpering myself. He rolls his eyes.

"Do you really think someone like Dare is without baggage? Grow up, little girl."

He pushes open the doors as we pass, and they're all empty, every single one.

But I feel presences here,

Ugliness.

When we're almost at the end of the hall, he turns to me, his gaze ugly now and I should've known.

In my head, I see Dare and he's so small.

He sits on a bed in this place, and his arms and his legs are bound.

The screams around us are deafening.

Dare's eyes are wide and dark,

Haunted,

Haunted,

Haunted.

"Mum?" he asks, his eyes searching the wall behind us, and his tiny voice is hopeful.

A nurse hustles past us, and gives him a shot in the arm. "Hush, boy," she tells him. "You know your mum is dead. She chose you instead of your brother, and then she went crazy. It's your fault."

Dare's eyes cloud over before he closes them. "I know she's dead because of me."

"And you're here because of that," the nurse agrees. "You're a little monster. If it weren't for you, your mum would be alive."

The hooded boy turns to me and his eyes are pained and he has Dare's eyes.

I can't breathe.

I can't breathe.

"The nurse is wrong," he tells me in a strange tone. "If it weren't for *you,* I'd be alive and Dare would never have been here. You can change it, Calla. You can change it. Do it. Do it."

He reaches out his hand to me,

And I reach to take it,

Then I open my eyes.

And *we never left Finn's bedroom.*

We. Never. Left.

And I'm alone.

What is happening to me?

I do need help.

I need Dare.

Because he was so hurt, and I don't know why, but I know I'm hurting him now, more and more each day as I keep pushing him away.

He didn't deserve that.

He doesn't deserve *this.*

I'm reeling,

I'm reeling.

The room presses down on me, swirling and bending and stifling. I lunge for the door, and find Dare on the veranda, a drink in his hand as he stares absently into the night.

"Dare... I..."

Tears streak my cheeks and he grabs me.

"You're not a monster," I whisper. "You're not. It's not your fault your mother chose you."

Without looking back, he leads me away,

Away from the veranda,

Into the gardens.

"I saw the sanatorium," I whisper, and I turn into his tuxedo jacket, hiding my face. "I know you were there when you were small. I know they tied you to your bed and called you a monster. Am I crazy?"

"You're not crazy," his words are gentle, and it's a soft tone I haven't heard from him in awhile. My walls come crumbling down, and I cry.

The next few minutes are a blur.

I reach for him,

he pulls me close.

His breath is sweet,

his shirt is starchy and smells of rain,

musk,

and man.

His hands are everywhere,

Firm,

Strong,

And perfect.

His lips are full,

Yet

Soft.

His tongue finds mine,

Moist,

Minty.

His heart beats hard,

The sound harsh in the dark,

And I cling to his chest,

Whispering his name.

"Dare, I…"

"Let's leave," he suggests. "Let's leave it all behind. Let's spin the wheel and the chips will fall. Things will change but they can't get worse. Let's go, Calla. Come with me."

So I do.

He takes my hand and I follow him,

Because I'd follow him to the ends of the earth.

I know that now, and I tell him.

He turns to me, his eyes so stormy and dark.

He scoops me up, and he's striding through the hallways of Whitley.

His room is dark and masculine, the bed looming against the wall. We tumble into it, and his hand is behind my head as I fall into the pillow.

Our clothing is stripped away and our skin is hot and flushed and alive.

I'm alive.

Dare lives free.

We breathe that freedom in, and he strokes his fingers against me, into me, deep inside and I gasp and sigh and quiver.

"I... yes." I murmur into his ear.

Consequences can be damned.

I don't care who he is.

I don't care what he's done.

He's here.

He makes me feel.

I want him.

He wants me.

So he takes me.

There is no pain.

He's inside and fills me, and his hands...

work magic.

His lips…
breathe life into me,
Filling me,
Creating me.
I call his name.
He calls mine.
I'm intoxicated by the sound, by the cadence, by the beat.
His heart matches, in firm rhythm.
We're so very alive,
And together.
Our arms and legs tangle.
Our eyes meet and hold.
His stare into mine as he slides inside,
Then out.
I clutch his shoulders,
To hold him close.
He shudders,
The moonlight spills from the window,
Onto my skin,
And his.
His eyes, framed by thick black lashes, close.
He sleeps.
But he wakes in the night and we're together again, and again and again.
Each time it's new,
Each time is reverent and raw and amazing.

In the morning, as he is bathed in sunlight, Dare finally looks away. Shame in his eyes, guilt in his heart.

"Sometimes, I wish I could just go away, and everyone would be better for it, and we'd never have to go through this again."

"Don't say that," I breathe. "You're the only thing keeping me sane.

"You don't know what you're saying," he tells me, and his voice is rather hard. "I'm the one keeping you insane. We're in a loop, you and I. And it's never going to get better because neither of us will give in."

"What loop?" I ask, confused, but Dare looks away.

"It doesn't matter. All that matters is that I don't deserve you. Can you see why?"

His voice is almost fragile.

You're better than I deserve.

He's said it before, over and over, and I never knew what he meant.

I'm not better than he deserves, not by a long shot, not ever.

He sits straight up in bed.

"Go check Finn's room," he tells me and his voice is tired. I look at him because Finn is dead and he knows it.

"He's not," Dare tells me, as if he can read my thoughts. "He's not dead. You have to trust me. Go."

He limply watches me leave the room, and I race to Finn's, and when I do, Finn is there.

He's sleeping peacefully in his bed and Pollux is at his feet.

And he's breathing.

I can't. I can't.

The room swirls again and again, and I hold my hands out.

I'm falling,

Falling,

Falling, and I don't know where I'll land.

The world is a stage and we all act falsely upon it.

The die has been cast,

Has been cast,

Has been cast.

I feel it,

The truth.

It's coming,

And it's dark,

And I won't like it.

I feel it.

I feel it.

We all have our parts to play, and I'll play mine well.

But what is it?

I concentrate,

And think,

And more will come.

We're all a bit mad, aren't we?

Yes.

Chapter Twenty-Eight

Sabine picks me up from the floor and she leads me to her room, her dark mystic room, where the walls are covered in darkness.

She sits me down and takes my hands and stares into my eyes.

"Finn is alive," I say slowly, and the words the words the words.

She nods.

"But he was dead."

She nods again.

"The hooded boy I kept seeing... all my life... it's been Dare's brother all along, and his brother is dead."

Sabine nods.

I'm numb, I'm confused, and I'm so so tired of being this way. I tell her and she looks away, then back into my eyes.

"I'll get you some tea."

"I don't want your tea."

My voice is rigid and sharp. "I feel like I'm a pawn, and I'm being played."

"Always trust your instincts, girl," she tells me throatily.

And

Suddenly

Suddenly,

I feel the danger.

It laps around me, igniting in the air and crackling in my hair and Sabine's eyes are as cold as death and she's the danger.

My instincts are on fire, crackling, popping, snapping, and my eyes scan the room, quick, quick, quicker. My gaze comes to rest on something

Something

Something.

A photo, sticking out of a drawer. Just the corner, just the edge, but I'm drawn to it.

It's important.

I know it.

I lunge to it, I grab it, I pull it out and peer at it.

And it's Olivia.

And her eyes

Her eyes

Her eyes.

Black as night, black as coal,

Black as Sabine's.

Black as Dare's.

Jagged pieces of ice form in my heart and pump through my veins,

Ripping them

Ripping them.

"You," I breathe. "You're doing this. Somehow. How are you...."

My voice trails off because the look on Sabine's face... I've seen it before.

"She was yours," I realize aloud. "Olivia was yours."

Sabine nods. "She was my daughter. My only child. I trained her, raised her as Roma, taught her the old ways. That girl was everything to me. Everything. And you took her. You and your brother and Adair."

I don't know what to say because the realization is overwhelming.

Sabine has been related to Dare all along?

The familiar feeling continues to grow and grow, and spread, and *this room.*

This room.

It swirls and twirls and it's familiar. From before, from a time I don't remember.

"There was fire here," I say aloud, looking around, trying to retrieve the memories. "In all the corners. And Dare. And your voice."

We invoke you.

We invoke you.

Restore my daughter, and I offer you

These lives,

Always

Yours.

Allow them to change the patterns,

Change the events.

I invoke you.

I invoke you.

Restore my daughter.
I invoke you.
End the cycle.
Take them as the sacrifice.

Her voice, like always, was a raspy whisper and I remember it now. I remember holding Dare's hand, but he let go, and he stepped back, and Finn was there with me.

One for one for one.

There was fire, and we burned.

Finn and me.

Sabine burned us to death,

For something

Something

Something.

Something that didn't work,

And we've spent the rest of this time

Cycling through.

Over

And

Over.

"You killed my daughter," Sabine says simply. "All of you."

She touches my hand, her own like a claw, and the events the events the events of that night flood me.

It was dark.

It was so long ago.

Dare's mom was taking us for a midnight swim. We were so small and she was crazy. Schizoaffective disorder and she hadn't taken her medicine and no one knew. We were going to dance on the beach, she said. But the car rolled off the cliffs

And

We

Fell.

The water filled up the car, and the windows the windows held us in. And then suddenly, Olivia broke us free, and we drifted to the surface, but she didn't because she drowned.

"My daughter drowned saving you," Sabine says, and there's something akin to hatred in her eyes.

"Dare is your grandson," I say stiltedly. "Olivia was Richard's wife. But Dare wasn't Richard's."

I remember that. I remember hearing the whispers and not knowing what they meant. *Olivia was unfaithful. Olivia was unfaithful. Dare had a lot in life and I didn't know what it was. Dare can't leave the grounds because he's an embarrassment. Dare is a bastard. What's a bastard, mom? Nothing you should worry about, my darling.*

"Of course he wasn't," Sabine hisses. "Olivia was in love with Phillip, who was Salome's. Olivia is Salome, Calla. And Dare is Salome. We're all of her blood, and Phillip has always loved her, he was her brother, her twin. No one knows that of course. History has changed and says that he was her uncle. Either way, our bloodline is pure.

314

"It is pure so that we could offer a pure sacrifice, to end the cycle. It wasn't supposed to be Olivia. It was supposed to be Finn. Olivia's death was in vain, because she's not from Cain and Abel, like Finn. But Olivia died saving you and Dare and Finn instead. Finn was supposed to die. The universe gives back what you put into it, girl."

"Olivia had SAD," I say slowly. Sabine's smile is eerie, and it stretches from ear to ear.

"Yes, she did. And now you and Finn pass that very thing back and forth, after you killed her. Do you find that to be a coincidence?"

Her voice her voice her voice is knowing and I know she's right. It's not a coincidence.

"We didn't kill her," I say weakly. "Not on purpose."

"Either way, it happened. The Universe always has its way, child. You were supposed to have a heart condition. You were born with it. But you gave it to Dare, and now it seems to be gone. But it's not. Things never are. Fate is what it is, and it will always have its way. Dare knows that."

"Has Dare known all along?" I ask and my words are pieces of wood just like my heart.

Her smile stretches wider.

"Of course he has," she says and she is heartless, her heart is black, her heart is gone. "He was trying to save his mother, after all."

The fire

The fire. Dare led me to the fire, and he let go, and he left me with Finn to die.

Only we didn't.

"You tried to kill us," I say aloud. "So long ago. It didn't work."

She looks away now, disgruntled. "It should've worked," she snaps. "It should've been easy. But nothing in this life ever is, I suppose. You've fought and fought against us, but you can't fight forever."

"Us?" I want to melt into a puddle and stay there, because I know who she means.

"Dare and I, of course."

That's what I thought, and it kills me kills me kills me.

"It has to be Finn," she explains with her heartless tongue. "And Dare knew that. To sacrifice, to set things right, it has to be Finn. Olivia tried. She offered up one son, but that offering was rejected. It wasn't her fault."

All I can think of is one thing.

Dare is with Sabine.

Dare is with Sabine.

"How have you done this?" I ask her. "How are you making us crazy? How are you doing it? Is it your tea?"

She laughs and it's like a cackle. "Of course not, child. I have my old Rom ways, and I adhere to them. Everything will come to pass as it should. Time is fluid and it can change. You can change it. You can change it to the right thing if we just wait long enough."

"And Dare?"

Sabine shrugs. "He doesn't matter. The only thing that matters is the end."

My veins turn to ice and I don't understand. All I know is that all along, my memories have been real, even when they haven't seemed possible. The deva ju, the craziness.

"One for one for one," Sabine tells me. "You are of Judas, and you must betray your brother in order to set things right. There are sacrifices to be made, girl. You must be strong enough to do it."

My mother's words in the book she left come back to me come back to me come back.

May you always have the courage to live free, and the strength to do what is right.

My breath hitches and hitches and hitches, because it seems that my mother was saying to sacrifice Finn, to choose to live free with Dare. But that can't be right. She told me that I couldn't be with Dare.

But then things changed,

Again

And again. And who knows anymore?

"You're the crazy one," I tell Sabine as I study the look in her eyes, the unsettling, unbalanced gleam. She doesn't deny it.

The door bursts open and Dare is here, thank God, and he grabs me.

"We've got to go, Calla."

I look at him, and his eyes are wide and full of pain and guilt, and I pull away.

"It's true?" I ask softly.

"You came to get us? You were going to kill us for Sabine? You were going to kill Finn?"

His dark eyelashes are inky against his cheeks as he closes his eyes and he sighs, so loud. "I was so small when I agreed. She was my mother, and I just wanted her back. Sabine told me that if I participated, my mother would come back. I didn't know all of this would happen. I didn't know."

"But you knew that Finn or I would die," I press, and his fingers are cold against my own.

He opens his eyes and stares into mine, and I want to dive into his, to swim in them, to float.

"When you're a child, you don't understand mortality," he offers simply. "Not really. And once we started, I couldn't stop. It was a bullet out of a gun, and I couldn't put it back. I'd already agreed, and a Roma's word is a bond."

He's part Roma, and I know that now.

"When I realized, as I got older, what it all really meant, I'd already fallen for you. I can't let it be you. I'll do anything to stop it."

"But we're cursed," I say quietly, and it feels like the only answer. "You're Finn's brother, and I'm

Finn's sister, and I'm a child of incest. Everything has been orchestrated because of some grand belief in Roma magic."

"It's not just a belief," Dare sighs. "I wish it were, but it's not. Cal... you change things. You've changed them over and over your whole life, without even knowing it. You loved your brother so much that you've literally changed time to bring him back. It's because you're descended from Abel. God made him the Judge of Souls and so are you. You know what is right. You know."

Sabine watches us and she's serious and silent.

"I don't believe you," I say and it sounds like a whimper.

"You don't understand anything yet, do you?" Sabine is snide. "Time is fluid and malleable, and you yourself wield the power to change it. It's a tapestry and we're the pieces."

I'm confused and I'm stunned, and Dare is silent and strong and he stares at me.

"This is real," he tells me. "All along, you've known it, but you were afraid you were crazy."

"The déjà vu, the memories..." I whisper.

"Real," he nods, and he's sad and his eyes are stormy. "The déjà vu was real. Everyone gets it because everyone has the extent to change things with their dreams, but not like you. You're stronger than most because of your blood."

"This is impossible," I say, but I know I'm wrong. It's possible. I feel it in my bones in my bones in my bones.

I hesitate, but something Sabine said comes back to me. "It has to be me or Finn in order to bring things to a close."

Dare's silence is his agreement.

"And you chose Finn," my words are slow. "You chose Finn, you let him die. Over and over and over."

"Finn chose to die over and over and over," Dare insists. "He chose things to be the sacrifice, but you kept changing things back. You're like Castor and Pollux. You love each other to a fault, and the universe will make everyone pay for it. You have to let the cycle end."

Dare's face is tortured, pained, and it looks like my heart, it's shattered, it's broken.

"But my brother...." I whisper. "You were willing to let Finn die. You love Finn."

"I do," he agrees. "But it couldn't be you," he says simply and he reaches for me, but I shirk away.

"And somehow, I changed it, I kept bringing him back because I love him, I love him more than life, and every time, you somehow managed to undo it and kill him again."

"I didn't," Dare protests. "Finn did. Because he knows that Fate is real. Kismet is real. That is his fate."

Sabine's eyes are knowing and dark.

320

"You must let it happen, girl," she says. "When you change it, you just prolong the torment."

"I don't care," I say coldly. "I don't care if you are tormented forever and the entire universe burns. Nothing matters but Finn."

Dare is stunned, but he understands, finally finally finally.

Finn is my other half. I can't live without him.

"Everyone must pay a price in this family," Sabine says, driving her point home. "The universe demands it, to set things right. One for one for one. Olivia already paid her price. Now you must pay yours."

I'm numb

I'm alone

I'm afraid

I'm determined.

It won't be Finn.

I love Dare and I love life, but my brother is life. He's everything. He's always been everything.

Dare falls back and watches as I touch Sabine's fingers. His dark dark eyes are the last thing I see as the room spins and spins and it makes me so dizzy that I close my eyes.

When I open them, I'm alone.

I'm walking across Whitley, across foggy moors, breathing in the wet morning air, and something is pulling me pulling me pulling me to the mausoleums.

I open the door and the musty smell and the dark, and Dare's name.

On the wall.

Adair Phillip DuBray.

There are flowers there and I'm not alone.

A hooded woman stands, weeping, her head against the stone.

She turns to me, and her eyes are black and she's sobbing.

"You did this," she tells me. "You killed him. It should've been me. It should've been me."

Sabine comes in and takes Olivia's shoulders and guides her to the door. She looks over her shoulder at me, though and Sabine smiles and it stretches from ear to ear. And I sob.

I sob at Dare's grave because even though he knew, even though he was willing to risk Finn, he was a pawn, just like me and I love him I love him.

The mausoleum grows dark and I cry until I can't cry anymore, until there are no tears left, until I'm limp.

Then I sleep and the oblivion takes me into its arms and I'm spinning spinning and when I open my eyes, my memories have been taken again by oblivion, and something has changed and everything has changed.

I'm staring at Sabine.

In her mystical room, and I've been here before, I've been here before.

She sits me down and takes my hands and stares into my eyes.

"Finn is alive," I'm saying slowly, and the words the words the words.

I've said them before,

I've been here before.

I cling to that knowledge as the old woman nods.

"But he was dead."

She nods again, and my next words spill out without my consent, like I'm playing a part in a play.

"The hooded boy I kept seeing... all my life... it's been Dare's brother all along."

The words

The words.

I've been here.

I remember. I remember.

I remember what happened in Sabine's room, and her part in everything, how she's pulled the strings and controlled Dare, and all she cares about is fulfilling some strange Roma prophecy and Finn is supposed to die because I'm supposed to betray him and let it happen.

Dare bursts through the door like I knew he would, and he's alive.

He's alive.

"We've got to go, Calla," he says and I go with him this time. There is guilt in his eyes and in his heart, but I don't care. I go with him anyway. Because he's a pawn and I'm a pawn, and we'll be pawns together.

He pulls me to the door and Sabine clings to me and her eyes her eyes they burn me.

"You can't get away," she tells us as she falls behind. "The die has been cast. Know this, child. Your brother was meant to die long ago. You were brought into the world on purpose, as a descendent of Judas. You were meant to offer your brother, to betray him. But you haven't. Over and over, you've betrayed the universe instead and saved your brother. Death wants your brother, and you can't stop it."

Dare pulls me along, through the halls, and through the dark and his hand is warm and I'm so scared.

"We're lost," I tell him, because it seems to be true.

"No, we aren't," he argues. "I'd die for you, Cal. I'll do it."

But God, my heart pounds at the thought of that.

"I can't be without you again," I tell him, and it's true. And it's also true that I can't be without Finn. And Sabine says one of us must die, and that Finn is supposed to be dead already.

"The die has been cast," I add, and that sounds so bleak.

Because it is.

Chapter Twenty-Nine

"I don't understand how this is happening," I say as we race through Whitley, through the halls, through the rooms.

"No one does," Dare says as we burst into Finn's room. "Romani ways are mysterious. Your mother knew, though. Even though you kept changing things, she knew in the beginning, and she did try to change things by running to America. But it didn't work. Fate had a plan."

"I really change things?" I ask, and Finn wakes up and I hold his hand.

"At night, your mind is free," Dare explains. "That's what I've figured out so far. "You and Finn. Your minds wander in sleep, and for whatever reason, you can change things without even trying, or without knowing how. Something happened to you that night so long ago in Sabine's room. She tried to sacrifice you, but something went wrong. It must have something to do with Cain and Abel's blood."

I think about this. How Finn has died several times, and each time I went to sleep wanting him back. And each time, when I woke he was there.

"We're stuck in a loop," Dare says and the words sound crazy, but crazy is my life and it's the only thing that makes sense. "We're in a loop, reliving different scenarios until the right one happens. The one where the cycle ends, and Finn is accepted as the sacrifice, because Cain's sacrifice was rejected so long ago. Sabine can't affect the changes," he finishes. "Only you, or Finn. I don't know why."

Finn stares at us and he acts like he knows.

"You knew?" I whisper.

"I did," he answers. "But then I thought I was crazy, because all of the déjà vu and things happened over and over, and my memories didn't seem real."

"Maybe we're all crazy," I say, and Dare shakes his head.

"No. They think we are, because it doesn't seem plausible. But we're not. Sabine knows the truth, but she's been using their perceptions against us. They're making people think that we're sick, that we are insane. But we're not."

"What do we do?" I ask and the future seems bleak. "The past is a prison."

And we'll never break free.

"We have to stick together," Dare says, and he's resolute. "We'll get this sorted. We'll figure out what to do. Sabine needs us. We just have to control our dreams. That's how we spin out of the moment and into another."

"But how can we control dreams?" Finn asks doubtfully.

It's an excellent question.

"We'll have to figure it out," Dare says, and he's tired. "My mother died, and I don't agree with Sabine that it was a mistake. I think things happen for a reason and if we try and change it, *that* is the mistake."

I agree.

Dreams aren't real. They're only real if we make them that way.

"I need to talk to you," I tell Dare, and he knows what I need to say. He's hesitant but he walks with me through the gardens, away from the house, away from people who can hear us.

"You betrayed me," I tell him and my whisper is broken with sadness.

"I tried to tell you," he says sadly, and I know I know I know when it was. The night my mother was killed, one of the many times I re-lived that moment. "You tried to tell me, but we spun. It changed."

Dare nods and his eyes glisten and my heart breaks.

"I love you, Calla. I couldn't bear to lose you. I thought it was hopeless. Sabine let me believe that it had to be you or Finn, and she convinced me that Finn was already lost. He was supposed to die when he was small."

He was, I know that's true. "But I can't live without him," I manage to utter, and my words are hot, my eyes are hot.

Dare nods. "I know that now. I know."

My heart freezes in pain, frozen at the mere thought.

"I'll die without Finn, Dare."

"I know. I'll sacrifice myself. Perhaps that will work."

"No," I almost scream, because the panic the panic the panic. "No. I can't lose you, and they say it has to be Finn. So your sacrifice would be for nothing, just like your mother's. There has to be another way. I'll change it in my dreams. We'll do something."

"I don't think that will work," he says doubtfully. "It's going to take a sacrifice from Cain's blood to finally make this stop. You're not of Cain. You're of Abel."

"Please promise me," I beg, clutching at his shirt. "It won't be you. It won't be Finn. We won't give up."

He's wordless as we enter the secret garden,

Our place.

The angels stare at us with empty eyes, and I sag into Dare.

He's so warm,

So strong, so strong,

So real.

"Is this really happening?" I ask him. "Because sometimes, I can't tell the difference."

He tilts my head back with his thumb, lifting my face to the sky. His eyes claim me, stroke me, ignite me.

I fold into his palms,

And he holds me up.

"I'm real," he says into my hair. "You're real."

We're standing in the moonlight,

There's no reason to be afraid.

Right?

Dare kisses me and his lips are sunlight. He touches me and his fingers are the moon. It's night somewhere, and by night we are free.

We come together like the stars,

Beneath the shelter of the gazebo.

Away from sight,

Away from everything.

Just us.

Our skin is hot,

Our mouths are needy.

We are alone.

But for the godforsaken angels.

"The angels scare me," I whisper to Dare, and I clutch him close.

He holds me tight.

"I know," he says. "Why is that?"

"I don't know," I answer, and it's the truth. "Maybe it's their eyes. They see me."

"I see you," he reminds me, and his eyes are black.

Black, black,

Black as night.

"Will you always?" I murmur, and his neck tastes like salt. My fingers find his LIVE FREE.

"Yes," he promises.

"Repromissionem," I tell him. "It's Latin."

"I know."

That night, I sleep in my room and Finn sleeps with me.

"Have I died in your memories?" he asks me suddenly, just when I'm slipping into sleep. I'm hesitant, but I nod.

"Yeah."

"More than once?"

"Yeah. How about me... in your memories, I mean?"

He shakes his head. "No. You lost your mind a few times, but you never died. You were sick once, and Dare was sick once. Something was wrong with your heart, but then I gave it to Dare in my dream. Then he was sick... but then it changed again. I don't know how, but I saved you once. I'll save you again."

Save me, and I'll save you.

"You lost your mind in my memories, too," I tell him, and I think we must've passed the madness back and forth, taking it from each other, over and over. Because we never want each other to suffer. We're twins. We're closer than the very closest thing on earth.

"Calla," Finn starts to say and I want to interrupt him because I think I know what he's going to say. "What you said earlier, about not changing things... you were right."

My heart sinks.

"And you changed things for me. I was supposed to die already."

"You fell, in kindergarten. From the climbing rope at school," I tell him. "How is that something that should be meant to be?"

He shrugs. "It just is. And I think changing it and changing it and changing it is just banging your head against a rock."

"You're not going to die, Finn," I instruct him, and he laughs without humor.

"I'm not sure it's up to us," he answers. "Not in the end. I'm meant to save you, Calla. I feel it in my bones."

I don't know if he's right. All I know is that I can't live without him. I fall asleep holding his hand. In the morning, Dare is sitting in the room, waiting for us to wake up.

My eyes are groggy as I stare at him, and the things from yesterday come back to me, and I sit straight up.

"Did anything change while we slept?" I ask him quickly, and he doesn't know.

"All I know is that we're going to Oregon," he tells us. "I called your father and we're leaving on the next flight."

Finn and I pack because going home seems reasonable, because Whitley is filled with secrets and danger and because Sabine is here.

When we leave, when we drive away, I look over my shoulder and I swear I see the curtains move from a small room upstairs. Someone is watching us go, and the hair raises on my neck, because Sabine isn't trying very hard to keep us from going… it's almost as if she wants us to.

Dare drives, and I'm beside him and he grasps my hand.

"It'll be ok," he promises me. "Just stay awake. Stay awake for now, until we figure out what to do. Don't dream." Finn agrees from the backseat and we drive away away away away from Whitley. We drive to the airport, and we fly home, and when we get home, it's night and we drive to the funeral home through the rain.

If we can just get there, it will be ok. I feel it in my heart, in my bones, in my soul. The tires crunch on the road, and the lightning lights up the sky, and cliffs are jagged and real. I'm so exhausted and my eyelids are heavy, but if I close them if I close them if I close them… I do. They're too heavy to resist and the hooded boy is outside my window.

He's next to the car window and he moves with us and his lips are moving and I hear his whisper.

"Go

to

sleep."

His fingers are on the glass and I touch them because I can't help it, and I feel my energy slip slip slipping away, and I can't resist it and I drift away in sleep.

I think I'm only asleep for moments, but it might be years. I don't know anymore.

But

When

I

Wake,

the road is humming beneath us and we are at a fork, and instead of turning left, Dare turns right, and the tires shriek in the rain.

There's a fork in the road and even though I see it, I can't avoid it.

One road goes left, one goes right, and neither of them ends well.

I feel it in my bones,

In my bones,

In my hollow reed bones.

"Why are we going this way?" I ask him curiously, and I'm scared, because it's like a magnet magnet magnet is pulling me, and I know it's pulling him too.

333

"I don't know," he answers honestly, and he seems as perplexed as me. "I just feel like we have to."

Because it's fate.

I'm unsettled and terrified, but we drive and we climb, and the road twists and turns and the cliffs, and I know where we are.

We've been here before.

"You died here," I tell Finn and my words are anxious and Dare nods.

"So did your mother," he says uncertainly.

"This place...this place...this place," I whisper, and I'm drawn here and it's a magnet.

Dare is pale, he's white, like a ghost and he's silent, because there are no words. This moment is important, it's relevant, and we can all feel it.

We're pulled to it.

And we can't turn away.

Finn takes off his medallion and he hands it to me because the car crackles with danger.

"Wear this," he instructs and his voice is firm. "Don't argue." I try to give it back and he won't take it, so I slip it over my head.

St. Michael, protect us.

The road curves and Dare sucks in his breath and I look.

His brother lowers his hood in the middle of the road, and stares at us with black eyes. Olivia Savage stands with him, her face paler than paler than pale.

334

"Dare... she's not real," I tell him. But we know that anything is possible. She's a daughter of death, of Salome.

"This has to end," Dare says and I don't know who he's speaking to. "Calla, get out of the car. Finn, you too."

"No," Finn says flatly, and I try to say no, but Dare is pushing me, shoving me, making me get out of the car. His mother takes a step, and the door is open and I can't stay in the seat because Dare is stronger.

"I love you, Calla," he tells me and his eyes are hauntingly black. "I'm going to end this. It's going to be me."

"Dare!" I shriek, and Finn looks at me, and I scream his name, too. "Finnnnnn!"

But Olivia steps one least step, and I know now what Dare meant so long ago when he told me he'd done a terrible thing. It was always going to lead to this, and I think he's known all along.

"Dare, no!" I shriek and he doesn't listen. He's intent on ending it and I think I know how.

"Do it," his mother whispers and I watch her lips move and I know I know I know what must be done. I know...and so does Dare.

All I can do is try to leap back into the car as Dare slams his foot onto the accelerator. Dare looks at me in alarm, and he can't stop, he can't put this bullet back into the gun. He grabs at me, trying to save me, trying to save me.

St. Michael protect us in battle.

We plow through Olivia and it's like she's mist. She fades away as we pass.

Be our defense against the wickedness and snares of the devil.

I clutch the medallion and we sail over the cliff and the tires don't touch the road and we're airborne.

I hear Finn in the back and he loves me, and the squeal of tires and the sound of metal and the water rush rush rushing.

May God rebuke him, we humbly pray, and do though, O Prince of the heavenly hosts, by the power of God, thrust into hell Satan.

My chest is ablaze, it's got a heavy heavy weight and I can't take the pain.

I'm falling,

Falling,

Falling,

And the water is cold,

The sand is damp.

And I'm broken,

I'm broken,

I'm broken.

Dare is with me, and there's blood all over his shirt.

"Are you ok?" he asks quickly, and his hands are on mine. "God, Calla, are you ok? Open your eyes, open your eyes."

"Calla, be ok," a voice urges and I can't tell if it's Dare or Finn.

I can't tell

I can't tell

I can't tell.

"Be ok," it instructs again and I try but the heavy heavy weight on my chest is too much and I can't breathe and I can't breathe. But I have to protect my brother, and if I live, Finn cannot. I release my grip and my lungs are empty and I stop.

I stop.

I stop breathing.

"You're dying," Dare whispers into my neck. "If you don't wake up, you'll be lost."

The water slides down my cheek into my neck and a hand holds mine and blackness is here and I slip into oblivion.

Oblivion is real.

That much I know.

It's warm and comforting like a blanket.

It hugs me, and I'm gone.

And all the evil spirits, who prowl about the world seeking the ruin of souls.

Amen.

Chapter Thirty

The world slows to a stop.

It's dark.

There is no ocean.

There are no waves.

There is no sun or rain or moon.

I stay this way for so long, suspended, alone, unafraid.

And then,

A breath.

From my lips.

Suddenly, without warning.

I gasp, and there is only my breathing, and beeps, and fingers wrapped around my hand, and I'm in a bed. I'm not in the ocean or on the cliffs.

"Come back to me, Calla," Dare whispers, and angst laces his words, and his words impale my heart. "Please God, come back to me. Time is running out. Don't do this, please, God, don't do this. They're going to take you off the machine, and if you don't breathe on your own, you'll die. Please God. Please."

He begs someone, whether it is God or me, I don't know.

"We've already lost everything else," he whispers. "Please, God. Come back to me. Come home to me. Come home."

I try to open my eyes, but it's too hard.

My eyelids are heavy.

The darkness is black.

Dare keeps talking, his words slow and soothing and I might float away on them. It would be so easy.

Death waits for me,

Only it's not death.

It's Olivia Savage.

I can see her face now, and she waits in the light behind Dare's shoulder.

She nods.

It's time.

But it can't be. Because Dare is here, and still holding my hand. He talks to me, he tells me everything that's happened, and when he gets tired of talking, he hums.

The same wordless, tuneless song I've been hearing all along.

Death moves closer, one step nearer.

I try to cry out, but nothing comes.

I try again to open my eyes, but I can't. And I can't move my fingers.

It's all too much.

Too much.

I think about getting frantic,

And I almost do.

But to keep calm,

I replay the facts in my head.

My name is Calla Price.

I'm eighteen years old, and I'm half of a whole.

My other half, my twin brother, my Finn, is crazy.

Finn is dead.

My mother is dead.

Dare's mother is dead.

I've spent every summer at Whitley my entire life.

I've loved Dare since I was small.

I've been floating in a sea of insanity, and I can't wake up.

I can't wake up.

Dare is my lifeline.

He's still here.

I focus every ounce of strength I have, trying to force my hand into gripping his, the hands that I love so much, the hand that has held mine for so long.

But I'm helpless.

I'm weak.

Olivia, takes another step, but I can't scream.

It's when she touches Dare that I bolster my strength.

She puts his hand on Dare's shoulder,

And I can't take that.

Don't touch Dare, I want to scream. *You died, but you're not taking* him! *He's innocentHe'sInnocentHe'sInnocent!*

But her fingers drum on Dare's skin,

340

And everything in me boils,
And screams.
And somehow,
Some way,
I harness my energy,
And my finger twitches.
Dare's humming stops.

"Calla?" he asks quickly, hope so potent in his voice. "Wake up. If you don't wake up, you'll die."

I move my finger again, and it's all the strength I have left.

I can't move again, but I think it was enough.
Dare's gone,
Gone from my side,
Yelling for someone,
For anyone.
Other voices fill my room,
Circling my bed,
And Dare's voice is drowned.
He's gone,
but others have replaced him.
I'm poked,
I'm prodded,
My lids are lifted and lights are shined into my eyes.

"It's a miracle," someone announces. "It took. She's not rejecting it anymore."

I can't stay awake.
My strength is gone.

I fall asleep wishing Dare would come back.

I don't know how long I sleep.

I only know that I dream,

And now, when I dream,

They're lucid.

I'm no longer insane.

I don't know why.

Olivia sits in front of me, her smile gentle and soft.

"My boy wasn't meant for you, but you took him anyway. I thought you'd be each other's downfall, but maybe you saved each other."

I swallow hard because I did take him.

"You have to know that's the way of things," I offer. "Boys can't stay with their mothers forever. It wasn't my fault you died."

"I killed myself," she says simply. "I'm a child of Salome, and I thought my blood was bad. I didn't mean to, but I couldn't take any more pain. I made sure you were all three safe, then I just let go. I drifted away and the darkness came, and it was soft and warm. And I let go."

I understand pain.

I nod.

"If you're choosing to be dead, then can my brother live?"

Hope surges through me, but the look on Olivia's face shuts it down. And my chest hurts and hurts and hurts as she shakes her head.

"He chose," she answers, and her words her words her words. "He chose to die to keep you safe."

And I think about the blackness and how I stopped breathing, and how I suddenly was alive. Finn did that.

Save me, and I'll save you.

A lump a lump a lump forms in my throat and I can't swallow it.

"I can't live without my Finn," I say limply. But Olivia is firm.

"You have to. He's gone, but you're not. He chose you, Calla. He chose to protect you." In my head, I remember him handing me his medallion and I cry because she's right. Finn chose for me to live.

Olivia gets up and her form is so slight, so small. She's dark like Dare and her eyes gleam like the night.

Black, black eyes that examine my soul.

She cocks her head, in the same way that Dare does.

"History can't keep repeating itself. Mr. Savage killed himself to protect his children. He chose himself rather than them because sons shouldn't have to pay for the sins of their fathers. But his son Richard was evil and it should've been him. Laura sacrificed Finn because that's the way it had to be. Let it be now, Calla. It is as it should be. You're descended from Judas, and it's in your blood, but don't betray this."

"Wait," I suck in my breath. "What about Dare?"

He was by my bed,

He's been here the whole time,
humming to me.
"Is Dare safe?" I ask her breathlessly.

"A sacrifice has been made," she answers. "It's been accepted. Don't change it."

Her voice is small because the sacrifice was Finn.

"Our story is so sad," I tell her, because it is. The saddest thing I've ever heard, because it makes everything seem hopeless, as though our own actions don't matter, because we pay for the sins of those who came before us. Olivia shakes her head knowingly.

"It's not. The saddest thing is if everything was in vain and if history keeps repeating. Don't let that be, girl. Save my son. Save yourself. Don't sink into the oblivion. You've got to open your eyes. Open your eyes.

Open your eyes.

Open your eyes."

I startle awake, the insistence of her voice shocking me into lucidity.

My eyes open.

The light is so bright it's blinding.

The humming stops.

Chapter Thirty-One

The room swirls white and medicinal, filled with beeps and blank walls and cold skin. Goosebumps chase each other in confusion up my arm, and I gulp hard.

I'm in a hospital.

I'm cold.

I'm afraid.

But.

Dare is.

Dare is.

Those are the words in my head, and the words sound like Finn's voice. And at first I think it's an interruption in the sentence, but then I realize. It's not *Dare is...* it's a statement. *Dare is.*

Dare exists.

Dare is alive.

I exhale, and I think about where I am.

I wiggle my fingers and they're heavy, and there's pain, and I can breathe.

Slowly

Slowly

Slowly,

I open my eyes.

I'm alone, and even though the echo of Finn's whispers linger here, I know that he's not.

My body feels heavy and I can't lift my arms, and a nurse comes in and when she sees my eyes open, she's startled, then she rushes to my side.

"Ms. Price! You're awake. How are you feeling?"

I don't know. My thoughts are murky and my chest hurts so much. I try to lift a hand to rub at it, at my chest, but I can't. There are too many tubes, too many wires.

"Don't," the nurse tells me as she watches my attempt. "You've been through a lot. You've got to rest to recover."

"Where is Dare?" I ask and my voice is hoarse and my throat is sore, like I haven't spoken in a hundred years.

"He's in another room," she tells me. "He's fine. He's going to make it."

Joy leaps at me, lapping at my face, and then I picture my brother and everything falls around me.

"Finn?" I ask, and even I can hear the fear in my voice.

"I think it's best if the doctor explains everything that happened," she tells me. "I'll be right back with her."

I close my eyes because I'm exhausted and afraid, and it isn't long before the doctor comes and when she speaks with her raspy voice, I know immediately who it is and I try to leap from the bed.

Sabine stands there, calm as can be in a white lab jacket, and she places a hand on my arm to restrain me.

"Ms. Price," she says, her dark eyes staring into mine. "You've been through quite an ordeal. I'm Dr. Andros."

"I know who you are," I hiss at her and she stays calm, because she knows who she is, too.

"You were in a car accident. Mr. DuBray drove off the road. You suffered extreme trauma to your chest and your heart. Your brother suffered massive injuries that unfortunately, he wasn't able to recover from. He remained alive on life support until a transplant could be made. Your brother's heart saved your life."

My hand fingers my chest and there is a fresh scar from my collarbone to my belly, swollen and warm.

"My brother is dead."

My words are deflated.

Sabine nods.

"I have his heart."

"You do."

Save me, and I'll save you.

I'm supposed to save you, Calla.

The words chant in my head and the voice is Finn's and the world tips and swirls.

I saved him so long ago, and now he saved me.

And now he's gone forever.

My loss is profound and unexplainable and the void is enormous. A chasm that I don't think I'll ever come back from.

The heart that beats in my chest is not mine. It's my brother's. My dear, sweet, perfect brother. My Finn.

Good night, sweet Finn.

"I need to see Dare," I tell Sabine, because she and I both know who she is, who she really is.

She shakes her head and she's firm, and her eyes are vicious because her daughter is gone and never coming back, and Dare and I are both here instead.

Somethingsomethingsomething is off though, something is off and I look out the window and there is a peaceful pond, and benches, and someone is feeding the ducks. Someone who is wearing a hospital bracelet, just like mine.

"Where are we?" I ask Sabine and she smiles and it's grotesque.

"Oakdale Sanitorium," she grins.

No. A mental hospital?

That can't be.

"But it is," Sabine answers, and I don't know if she read my thoughts or if I said them aloud.

"You're disturbed, poor girl," she says. "And so is Adair. Growing up the way you did, it's no wonder. Your mother was with her own brother, Dare's step-father molested him and abused him... obviously you're both from bad blood."

348

"We're not crazy," I shout, but I'm not sure and I struggle and she smiles. There's a sharp pain in my arm and she leaves and everything goes beyond black to oblivion and I'm in a sleep so so deep that I can't dream.

Days pass and finally, finally, Dare comes to see me, when he's strong enough.

He's paler, but he's the same. His dark dark eyes penetrate me and he grasps my hand.

"We're not crazy. We've fixed it before, we'll fix it again," he tells me. There's promise in his voice but I'm so tired. "You have Finn's heart, so he's not really gone."

"Is this even real?" I ask him, groggy from the medicine they pump into my veins. "Maybe we've been crazy all along."

Dare smiles and his smile is real and it's bright and it penetrates my fog.

"You don't believe that."

"I don't know what to believe."

"Believe in *me*," he instructs, and I do.

Because Dare is mine and he lives free.

"I want to live free, too," I tell him.

"And you will," he promises.

Days pass with nurses coming in and out, to make sure I take my pills, the colorful pills that will keep my body from rejecting Finn's heart. I'll have to take them forever and their waxy residue gets stuck on my tongue. But I take them, because I have to keep Finn's heart alive. It's the only part of him I have left, and he's my brother and I love him I love him I love him.

Oakdale and its grounds look so much like Whitley. The halls, the rooms, and one day, one gray day, I find Finn's journal.

It's hidden in one of my bags and I know it's his because it says.

The Journal of Finn Price.

The end is the beginning, one of the pages says. I don't know about that, but I know the middle was jumbled up and changed and changed and changed.

But it can all be changed back.

I have to believe that.

Destroy the ring, it says. *You have to you have to you have to.*

And I have to believe that I can save my brother in the end, because *serva me, servabo te. Save me and I'll save you, Finn.*

Destroy the ring.

How does one go about destroying a ring?

Dare and I sneak away into the forest, and burn the journal before anyone can see, before anyone even realizes we're gone. They can't see his words, they can't see our story.

If they do, we'll never get out of here.

We'll never be free.

And we have to.

We have to live free.

"I can't live without Finn," I tell Dare on the way back in.

He holds my hand and looks at me, and smiles a sad sad smile.

"I know."

We walk and walk, and Dare turns to me.

"I love you more than life, and I've been doing some research. Salome married her brother, and she became a necromancer. She wanted to live forever, but Phillip didn't. Phillip has been trying for centuries to end the curse, while Salome wants it to continue. They've been at odds, and that has been born into twins in your family for generations. That has to be it."

I'm dubious, but intrigued.

"Are we related?" I ask, and it's a question I've been afraid to ask, afraid to know the answer.

Dare stares at me with his black black eyes. "I don't know. But you can undo *anything*. Perhaps the answer is not to destroy the ring, but to change things so that it was never created in the first place. If you can do that... you can prevent everything from happening. You won't have to change it. Surely that will end the cycle."

"But what if it ends us?" I ask and I'm afraid. "If I prevent events from happening, maybe we'll never be born."

Dare shakes his head. "I don't believe that. I believe in Fate, and we're fated, Calla. We're fated. I feel it."

"But I won't remember," I tell him. "When I change things and I wake up, I never remember. What if I forget you?"

"Then I'll find you, Calla-Lily. I'll always find you."

Hope leaps into my heart and his eyes are so sincere, so true.

"Do you promise?" I ask, and he smiles at me, and I'm afraid to hope.

"I do," Dare says as he puts the ring in his pocket. "We'll get this sorted."

"What a British thing to say," I say.

"That's the meanest thing you've said all day."

As we laugh, I feel like we've been here before, in this time and place and with these same words. But I'm getting used to that feeling. Because by night we are free, and things change, because we change them, and déjà vu is real, and we're stuck in it.

Because of that, we'll change things again, because time is fluid and malleable and it never stays the same. We'll save my brother. I feel it I feel it I feel in my bones, in my hollow reed bones.

"Nocte liber sum," I whisper to Dare.

He nods. "Keep dreaming, Calla Lily. And one day, we'll be free."

I squeeze his hand because I know.

After lights out, after the nurses have made the last rounds and given us all our medicine, I sneak from my room and into Dare's.

"You can do this," Dare whispers into my hair. "Think back to the beginning. Imagine it, imagine what happened. Let Salome die without creating the ring, without creating the curse. Let Phillip be her uncle, not her brother. Let them die without re-living over and over. Keep your mother from being with her brother, keep us from being related. You can do it. You can."

His words empower me, and I believe him. I *can* do it, and I imagine what he says and I snuggle into his chest because his arms are home, and I close my eyes, knowing that I'll dream.

And when I dream, I change things.

I sleep

And sleep

And sleep.

And when I open my eyes, it's a beautiful Oregon morning, and my brother wants to go to group therapy.

I stretch and yawn and grouse, but he's right. We should go. I roll out of my bed, get dressed.

"Drive safe!" my father calls out needlessly when we leave. Because of the way my mom died, among twisted metal and smoking rubber, my father doesn't even like to *see* us in a car, but he knows it's a necessity of life.

Even still, he doesn't want to watch it.

It's ok. We all have little tricks we play on our minds to make life bearable.

I drop into the passenger seat of our car, the one my brother and I share, and stare at Finn.

"How'd you sleep?"

Because he doesn't usually.

He's an insufferable insomniac. His mind is naturally more active at night than the average person's. He can't figure out how to shut it down. And when he does sleep, he has vivid nightmares so he gets up and crawls into my bed.

Because I'm the one he comes to when he's afraid.

It's a twin thing. Although, the kids that used to tease us for being weird would love to know that little tid-bit, I'm sure. *Calla and Finn sleep in the same bed sometimes, isn't that sick??* They'd never understand how we draw comfort just from being near each other. Not that it matters what they think, not anymore. We'll probably never see any of those assholes again.

"I slept like shit. You?"

"Same," I murmur. Because it's true. I'm not an insomniac, but I do have nightmares. Vivid ones, of my mother screaming, and broken glass, and of her cellphone in her hand. In every dream, I can hear my own voice, calling out her name, and in every dream, she never answers.

You could say I'm a bit tortured by that.

Finn and I fall into silence, so I press my forehead to the glass and stare out the window as he drives, staring at the scenery that I've been surrounded with since I was born.

Despite my internal torment, I have to admit that our mountain is beautiful.

We're surrounded by all things green and alive, by pine trees and bracken and lush forest greenery. The vibrant green stretches across the vast lawns, through the flowered gardens, and lasts right up until you get to the cliffs, where it finally and abruptly turns reddish and clay.

I guess that's pretty good symbolism, actually. Green means alive and red means dangerous. Red is jagged cliffs, warning lights, splattered blood. But green... green is trees and apples and clover.

"How do you say green in Latin?" I ask absentmindedly.

"Viridem," he answers. "Why?"

"No reason." I glance into the side-mirror at the house, which fades into the distance behind us.

Huge and Victorian, it stands proudly on the top of this mountain, perched on the edge of the cliffs with its spires poking through the clouds. It's beautiful and graceful, at the same time as it is gothic and dark. It's a funeral home, after all, at the end of a road on a mountain. It's a horror movie waiting to happen.

Last Funeral Home on the Left.

Dad will need a miracle to rent the tiny Carriage House out, and I feel a slight pang of guilt. Maybe he really does need the money, and I've been pressuring him to give it to Finn or me.

I turn my gaze away from the house, away from my guilt, and out to the ocean. Vast and gray, the water punishes the rocks on the shore, pounding into them over and over. Mist rises from the water, forming fog along the beach. It's beautiful and eerie, haunting and peaceful.

We arrive at the hospital early, so we decide to get coffee and breakfast in the cafeteria while we wait.

I grab my cup and head to the back, slumping into a booth, while Finn buries his nose in a Latin book.

I close my eyes to rest for a minute longer because the perpetual rain in Astoria makes me sleepy.

The sounds of the hospital fade into a buzzing backdrop, and I ignore the shrill, multi-pitched yells that drift down the hallways. Because honestly, I don't want to know what they're screaming about.

I stay suspended in my sleepy dark world for God knows how long, until I feel someone staring at me.

When I say feel, I *literally feel it,* just like someone is reaching out and touching my face with their fingers.

Opening my eyes, I suck my breath in when I find dark eyes connected to mine, eyes so dark they're almost black, and the energy in them is enough to freeze me in place.

A boy is attached to the dark gaze.

A man.

He's probably no more than twenty or twenty-one, but everything about him screams *man*. There's no *boy* in him. That part of him is very clearly gone. I see it in his eyes, in the way he holds himself, in the perceptive way he takes in his surroundings, then stares at me with singular focus, like we're somehow connected by a tether. He's got a million contradictions in his eyes...aloofness, warmth, mystery, charm, and something else I can't define.

He's muscular, tall, and wearing a tattered black sweatshirt that says *Irony is lost on you* in orange letters. His dark jeans are belted with black leather, and his fingers are long and bare.

Dark hair tumbles into his face and a hand with long fingers impatiently brushes it back, all the while his eyes are still connected with mine. His jaw is strong and masculine, with the barest hint of stubble.

His gaze is still connected to mine, like a livewire, or a lightning bolt. I can feel the charge of it racing along my skin, like a million tiny fingers, flushing my cheeks. My lungs flutter and I swallow hard.

And then, he smiles at me.

At me.

His eyes are frozen on me as he waits in line, so dark, so fathomless. This energy between us... I don't know what it is. Attraction? Chemistry? All I know is, it steals my breath and speeds up my heart. I feel like I've seen him before, but that's so stupid. I would remember something like that.

Someone like him.

I watch as he pays for his coffee and sweet roll, and as his every step leads him to my back booth. There are ten other tables, all vacant, but he chooses mine.

His black boots stop next to me, and I skim up his denim-clad legs, over his hips, up to his startlingly handsome face. He has a slight stubble gracing his jawline and it makes him seem even more mature, even more of a man. As if he needs the help.

I can't help but notice the way his shirt hugs his solid chest, the way his waist narrows as it slips into his jeans, the way he seems lean and lithe and powerful. Gah. I yank my eyes up to meet his. I find amusement there.

"Is this seat taken?"

Sweet Lord. He's got a British accent. There's nothing sexier in the entire world, which makes that old tired pick-up line forgivable. I smile up at him, my heart racing.

"No."

He doesn't move. "Can I take it, then? I'll share my breakfast with you."

He slightly gestures with his gooey, pecan-crusted roll.

"Sure," I answer casually, expertly hiding the fact that my heart is racing fast enough to explode. "And I'll take a bite. I'm starving."

"Perfect," he grins, as he slides into the booth across from me, next to Finn, ever so casually, as though he sits with strange girls in hospitals all of the time. I can't help but notice that his eyes are so dark they're almost black. He cuts his roll into two and offers me half, and I chew the bites.

Finn barely even glances up from his book because he's so absorbed, but this strange boy doesn't seem to mind.

"Come here often?" he quips, as he sprawls out in the booth. I have to chuckle, because now he's just going down the list of cliché lines, and they all sound amazing coming from his British lips.

"Fairly," I nod. "You?"

"They have the best coffee around," he answers, if that even *is* an answer. "But let's not tell anyone, or they'll start naming the coffee things we can't pronounce, and the lines will get unbearable."

I shake my head, and I can't help but smile. "Fine. It'll be our secret."

He stares at me, his dark eyes shining. "Good. I like secrets. Everyone's got 'em."

I almost suck in my breath, because something is so overtly fascinating about him. The way he pronounces everything, and the way his dark eyes gleam, the way he seems so familiar and I swear to God I know him. But that's impossible.

"What are yours?" I ask, without thinking. "Your secrets, I mean."

He grins. "Wouldn't *you* like to know?"

Yes.

"My name's Calla," I offer quickly. He smiles at that.

"Calla like the funeral lily?"

"The very same." I sigh. "And I live in a funeral home. So see? The irony isn't lost on me."

He looks confused for a second, then I see the realization dawn on him as he glances down at his shirt.

"You noticed my shirt," he points out softly, his arm stretched across the back of the cracked booth. He doesn't even dwell on the fact that I'd just told him I live in a house with dead people. Usually people instantly clam up when they find out, because they instantly assume that I must be weird, or morbid. But he doesn't.

I nod curtly. "It stands out." *Because* you *stand out.*

The corner of his mouth twitches, like he's going to smile, but then he doesn't.

"I'm Adair DuBray," he tells me, like he's bestowing a gift or an honor. "But everyone calls me Dare."

I've never seen a name so fitting. So French, so sophisticated, yet his accent is British. He's an enigma. An enigma whose eyes gleam like they're constantly saying *Dare me.* I swallow.

"It's nice to meet you," I tell him, and that's the truth. "Why are you here in the hospital? Surely it's not for the coffee."

"You know what game I like to play?" Dare asks, completely changing the subject. I feel my mouth drop open a bit, but I manage to answer.

"No, what?"

"Twenty Questions. That way, I know that at the end of the game, there won't be any more. Questions, that is."

I have to smile, even though his answer should've annoyed me. "So you don't like talking about yourself."

He grins. "It's my least favorite subject."

But it must be such an interesting one.

"So, you're telling me I can ask you twenty things, and twenty things only?"

Dare nods. "Now you're getting it."

"Fine. I'll use my first question to ask what you're doing here." I lift my chin and stare him in the eye.

His mouth twitches again. "Visiting. Isn't that what people usually do in hospitals?"

I flush. I can't help it. Obviously. And obviously, I'm out of my league here. This guy could have me for breakfast if he wanted, and from the gleam in his eye, I'm not so sure he doesn't.

I take a sip of my coffee, careful not to slosh it on my shirt. With the way my heart is racing, anything is possible.

"Yes, I guess so. Who are you visiting?"

Dare raises an eyebrow. "I'm visiting a grief group. My grandmother died recently, and my mother wants me to attend group therapy."

"That's what we're doing too," I tell him, surprised and excited by his answer. Surely we're not attending the same group.

"You're going to a grief group? Is yours in the Sunshine Room, perchance?"

My heart slams, because it is.

"Is that your first question? Because turn-about is fair play." I suck at being flirty, but I give it my all.

Dare smiles broadly, genuinely amused.

"Sure. I'll use a question."

"Yes, we're going to a grief group in the Sunshine Room. Our mother died recently."

"I'm so sorry," Dare says, and his voice is soft and I can tell that he is... sorry. He nods like he understands, and somehow, I feel like he does.

He takes a drink of his coffee. "What are the odds that you and I would be going to the same grief group? I think it must be kismet."

"Kismet?" I raise an eyebrow.

"That's fate, Calla," he tells me. I roll my eyes.

"I know that. I may be going to a state school, but I'm not stupid."

He grins, a grin so white and charming that my panties almost fall off.

"Good to know. So you're a college girl, Calla?"

I don't want to talk about that. I want to talk about why you think this is kismet. But I nod.

"Yeah. I'm leaving for Berkeley in the fall."

"Good choice," he takes another sip. "But maybe kismet got it wrong, after all. If you're leaving and all. Because apparently, I'll be staying for a while. That is, after I find an apartment. A good one is hard to find around here."

He's so confident, so open. It doesn't even feel odd that a total stranger is telling me these things, out of the blue, so randomly. I feel like I know him already, actually.

I stare at him. "An apartment?"

He stares back. "Yeah. The thing you rent, it has a shower and a bedroom, usually?"

I flush. "I know that. It's just that this might be kismet after all. I might know of something. I mean, my father is going to rent out our carriage house. I think."

And if *I* can't have it, it should definitely go to someone like Dare. The mere thought gives me a heart spasm.

"Hmm. Now that *is* interesting," Dare tells me. "Kismet prevails, it seems. And a carriage house next to a funeral home, at that. It must take balls of steel to live there."

I quickly pull out a little piece of paper and scribble my dad's cell phone on it. "Yeah. If you're interested, I mean, if you've got the balls, you can call and talk to him about it."

I push the paper across the table, staring him in the eye, framing it up as a challenge. Dare can't possibly know how I'm trying to will my heart to slow down before it explodes, but maybe he does, because a smile stretches slowly and knowingly across his lips.

"Oh, I've got balls," he confirms, his eyes gleaming again.

Dare me.

I swallow hard.

"I'm ready to ask my second question," I tell him. He raises an eyebrow.

"Already? Is it about my balls?"

I flush and shake my head.

"What did you mean before?" I ask him slowly, not lowering my gaze. "Why exactly do you think this is kismet?"

His eyes crinkle up a little bit as he smiles yet again. And yet again, his grin is thoroughly amused. A real smile, not a fake one like I'm accustomed to around my house.

"It's kismet because you seem like someone I might like to know. Is that odd?"

No, because I want to know you, too.

"Maybe," I say instead. "Is it odd that I feel like I already know you somehow?"

Because I do. There's something so familiar about his eyes, so dark, so bottomless.

Dare raises an eyebrow. "Maybe I have that kind of face."

I choke back a snort. *Hardly.*

He stares at me. "Regardless, kismet always prevails."

I shake my head and smile. A r*eal* smile. "The jury is still out on that one."

Dare takes a last drink of coffee, his gaze still frozen to mine, before he thunks his cup down on the table and stands up.

"Well, let me know what the jury decides. If we don't get going, we'll be late for our grief therapy."

And then he walks away.

I'm so dazed by his abrupt departure that it takes me a second to realize something because *kismet always prevails* and I'm *someone he might like to know.*

He took my dad's phone number with him.

"Cal? You ready?"

Finn's voice breaks my concentration, and with it, the moment. I glance up at my brother, almost in confusion, to find that he's standing up, waiting for me. It's time to go. I scramble to get up, feeling for all the world like I'm rattled, but don't know why. It's this moment, it's this place, it's...the same.

"Do you feel like you've been here before?" I ask Finn in bewilderment as we walk through the doors of the Sunshine Room. He glances at me and grimaces.

"Yeah. Every week since Mom died."

That's not what I meant and he knows it. The sense of déjà vu is strong, almost overwhelming, and I feel like I almost know what will happen next.

But I don't.

Because Dare DuBray is across the room and his smile is brilliant and new.

When our eyes connect and the sparks fly and the air sizzles between us, he holds up my father's phone number and winks.

Warmth rushes through me because
Kismet always prevails.
The jury has decided.
I feel it in my bones.

Author's Note

I know what you're wondering.

Was it real, or not real?

Was Calla crazy, or not?

Well, dear reader, let me ask you....

What do you think?

That's the beauty of stories. Sometimes, the ending resides in you. If you don't like an ending, choose another.

I've always been a person who believes things happen that we can't understand, that the energy we put into the world comes back to us. There are lots of different cultures, including the Romani, who believe the same.

Is it possible to be cursed, to re-live time, to change it? Do ghosts exist? Is there a reason for déjà vu?

I have no idea.

But I'm open-minded enough to think that anything is possible.

And because of that, *to me,* Calla's story was real. Her ending was real, and she saved Finn, and she'll live happily-ever-after with Dare. Because I love a good Happily-Ever-After story. Calla managed to change time and prevent the curse.

But if you don't like to think about mysticism, or supernatural elements, or things we can't explain,

Then you can choose to believe that Calla was crazy all along and none of this happened, and that she and Dare met and fell in love in a psych ward.

It's entirely up to you.

I hope you've enjoyed this story.

I know it was a twisted journey, where the end was the beginning and the beginning was the end. I know that, and I did it on purpose.

I wanted to try to take you down a path where your mind wasn't your own, just like Calla's.

It had to happen in order.

And it did.

Acknowledgements

This series has been mind-bending to write, and mind-bending to read. Due to personal issues and contractual obligations, the release date was pushed back, and I'm so thankful to you, my awesome amazing fans, for sticking with me and being so kind and patient. I hope Lux was worth the wait.

I'd like to thank Natasha Tomic, for her keen eye and general amazingness. I love her, and she knows that. I'm also going to marry her gorgeous accent. But she knows that, too.

Thank you so much to Talon Smith, Maria Blaylock and Jennie Wurtz. You ladies were awesome at giving me your input and advice, and not being afraid to tell me the truth.

To the members of the Nocte Support Group: Your support and enthusiasm over this past year has been extraordinary, and you'll never know how much I appreciate it.

To my family: Thank you for putting up with my craziness this year while I put myself in Calla's shoes and walked her dark path.

To my readers: You are all amazing--- each one of you. Thank you so much for reading my words, and being so kind and awesome.